WATERMELON
SNOW

A NOVEL

WILLIAM A. LIGGETT

Sandra Jonas Publishing
Boulder, CO

Sandra Jonas Publishing
PO Box 20892
Boulder, CO 80308
www.sandrajonaspublishing.com

Printed in the United States of America

Book and cover design: Sandra Jonas
Map on page iv: Allison Shanks

Publisher's Cataloguing-in-Publication Data

Names: Liggett, William A.
Title: Watermelon snow / William A. Liggett.
Description: Boulder, CO : Sandra Jonas Publishing House, 2017.
Identifiers: LCCN 2017937035 | ISBN 9780997487107
Subjects: LCSH: Climatic change—Fiction. | Blue Glacier
    (Jefferson County, Wash.)—Fiction. | Scientists—Fiction. |
    LCGFT: Science fiction.
Classification: LCC PS3612.L54 | DDC 813.6 — dc23
LC record available at http://lccn.loc.gov/2017937035

To my wife, Nancy

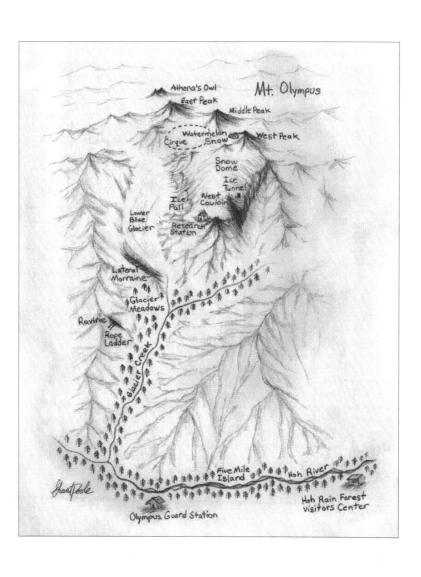

1

Blue Glacier, Olympic National Park
Western Washington State

Monday, September 15

The thick layers of ice groaned and let out a deafening crack. Professor Kate Landry jumped, unnerved by the sounds, each one more ominous than the one before. The blue light filtering through the frozen walls gave everything an eerie, otherworldly hue, adding to her unease.

Kate feared this would be her last opportunity to collect data in the tunnel, chiseled deep inside a living, flowing glacier. She and Frank, her PhD student, hurried to collect ice samples into sterile plastic containers to salvage what they could before retreating outside.

A week earlier, she had stared in horror at the telltale signs of the tunnel's fate—fissures in the roof and droplets of meltwater forming puddles on the floor, where small streams joined to drain from the tunnel. Particles of dirt pockmarked the once-solid ice at the entrance. How much time did they have left? Months? Days? Maybe hours? How long before the huge slab overlying the tunnel sloughed off or the roof collapsed, sealing the opening forever?

The samples they collected were worth the risk—the pollen and spores in the layers of ice confirmed that climate change was increasing at an alarming rate. Nature's clock was ticking—faster and faster. Before entering the tunnel that day, she had measured a record high air temperature for the second time in a week.

"Let's wrap this up and get out of here while we can." She approached Frank working at the end of the tunnel. The muffled sound of her voice made her feel claustrophobic, but she willed herself to stay calm.

As he swung his hammer at the chisel, Frank stopped in midair. "Hold on, Kate. Take a look at this." He aimed his headlamp into the cloudy ice in the wall in front of him.

"Got another layer?" She stood on her toes, straining to peer over his shoulder.

"Here." He ran his insulated glove over the blue ice.

"What the hell?" She squeezed in next to him to get a closer look, their parkas making it nearly impossible to stand side by side.

"What do you think it is?"

The powerful light of their combined headlamps penetrated the thick ice, revealing a large, shadowy mass—something she'd never encountered in her eight years of glaciology work.

Kate shook her head, making the beam of her headlamp dance across the ice. "How did we miss this?" She and her students had been through this tunnel inch by inch every year for five summers. "The melting ice must have exposed it." She trained her handheld flashlight at the dark mass from a different angle. "I'd say it's some kind of body."

Her pulse quickened. The image of a brown skeletal mummy flashed in her mind—the Ötzi Iceman that had melted from a glacier in the Alps. What if they'd found their own iceman? That would surely get people to notice their thawing glacier.

"Maybe a bear?"

Frank's question brought her back to considering more plausible ideas. Built like a linebacker, yet amazingly agile, Frank had led the junior members of the research crew for the past two summers. Over that time, he and Kate had come across the frozen remains of pica, marmot, and ptarmigan—the usual high-alpine wildlife of the Pacific Northwest. This thing in the ice appeared a lot bigger than any of those.

"Can't we radio Tom to postpone our flight this afternoon?" he asked. "If we stayed another day or two, I bet we could chip away enough ice to see what this is."

She hesitated, staring at the mysterious object. Should they take the chance? "We might be able to catch him if we—"

A series of loud, sharp cracks echoed through the tunnel, sending a tremor through her boots and up her legs. "Oh my God." The air closed in around her, thick and heavy.

Frank let out a long, low whistle. "Damn."

"Okay, that's it." She stepped away from him. "This place isn't safe. We need to leave. Now. Maybe we can check it out next June—if the tunnel's still here. And it could be after this winter's freeze."

He glanced at the entrance. "You're right. It's getting too dicey in here."

Kate hated making a last-minute discovery. It reminded her of Professor Howard, who would end his last lecture of the school year with a question he refused to answer until the fall. The dangling mystery of the shadow in the ice would haunt her for the next nine months. "This tunnel could cave any minute. And I don't want us to get stranded either. Remember the blizzard last September?"

"Sure do. Came out of nowhere."

"We should keep quiet about what we've found until we identify what it is. Let's not fuel curiosity at the university, and that includes the students who've already left." She touched his arm. "Are you okay with that?"

He nodded. "Not a word."

"Thanks for your support." Kate moved her flashlight in small increments over the dark object buried in the ice—the ice that had been the focus of her life, her research, her second home, for almost a decade.

She always dreamed of making a discovery on the glacier that would capture the world's attention. But now all she wanted to do was run to safety. "C'mon, Frank. Let's get the hell out of here."

2

Department of Atmospheric Sciences
University of Washington

Monday, April 6

Kate sat at a circular table with the department chair, Dr. John Rollins, in his corner office on the seventh floor of the Atmospheric Sciences-Geophysics Building at the University of Washington in Seattle. After she agonized for months over the state of the tunnel and the frozen mass in the glacier, Rollins unwittingly threatened to reveal her secret with his plans for her upcoming summer research. She rubbed the back of her neck, struggling with the urge to yell at her boss.

"But why the Blue Glacier Project?" she asked.

Rollins pushed his chair back. Once a successful field scientist, he had the paunch and rounded shoulders of an administrator sitting behind a desk too long. He reminded Kate of her father, especially his stubbornness, although the two men differed in one major way—Rollins appreciated her work.

"NASA wants to study the dynamics of research teams in isolated locations."

"So they aren't interested in glaciers." She sat back and crossed her arms.

"No, they need to prepare crews for long-duration space missions."

She leaned forward. "What does that have to do with us?"

"Your teams are productive—high morale, low conflict. NASA wants to learn how you do this in three short months."

"I don't like making lab rats of my crew."

He sighed and tented his fingers on his belly. "Kate, bottom line, I need you to do this for me—for our department. It's good publicity—a NASA project."

"Is this behavioral scientist they're sending physically capable of being on the glacier? I can't be held responsible for my team's safety and his."

"He assured me he's in good shape. Runs several times a week."

She'd still have to show him how to navigate the ice. But more than that, the mysterious thing in the tunnel was her team's discovery to document. This soft-science observer would get in the way and might take credit for it.

Rollins narrowed his eyes. "Whatever's bothering you, get a handle on it, Professor. If you want funding for your project this summer, Dr. Grant Poole is going to work with you."

"Okay." Her lips flattened into a tight line. "But there's no way in hell I'll let Dr. NASA interfere." She stood and walked toward the door.

"Don't worry," Rollins called to her as she stepped into the hallway. "Poole's role is solely to observe. You'll forget he's even there."

Though secretly pleased her research had caught the attention of NASA, Kate had enough on her mind without having to deal with an interloper. She punched the button in the elevator for the fourth floor. When the doors opened, she charged down the hall and approached Frank at his desk in the outer bay.

He looked up from the journal he was reading. "Your morning's not going so well?"

"You got that right. We need to talk." She continued into her office and plopped into her desk chair. "Come in and close the door."

Kate appreciated Frank's patience with her frustrated moods. She could always count on him. Since the first time he'd led a brilliant panel discussion on climate change and glaciers in her graduate class three years earlier, he had been her favorite. And she didn't know what she would have done without his help two summers before when one of her students had to be medevaced off the glacier.

"What's up, Professor?" He took a seat, his long, muscular legs angling out sideways into the room.

"We're going to have a visitor—no, worse, a spy! Courtesy of NASA. He's going to follow us around the glacier all summer."

"Are you serious? Oh man." Frank raked both hands through his mop of curly dark hair. "It's bad enough when we've had a visiting dignitary for a day."

"Exactly."

"So what does this mean for our team?"

"I don't know yet." She opened her laptop. "I've never met or even talked to this Dr. Poole. All I know is that he's a professor at UC Santa Cruz." She Googled his name, and several images and articles appeared.

"Hmm. Looks fairly young, maybe mid-thirties, your height or a little less, with a slim build. He's supposedly a runner. I would have guessed he's a California surfer dude with his longish light-brown hair." She turned her laptop so Frank could see the screen.

"The lady on his arm is cute, but he has wimp written all over him. He won't last all summer on the glacier—I give him a week."

He typed a few keystrokes. "Holy cow, he's got a full screen's worth of published articles on Google Scholar."

"Yeah, he's an academic, but there's no way to tell how he'll do on the mountain. We'll have to get to know him enough to see if he can be trusted with our secret and not grab credit for it. In any case, he'll be a huge distraction."

Frank leaned forward, his hazel eyes more intense than usual. "I've stayed in touch with the other students from last summer," he said, lowering his voice. "But I haven't said a word to anybody about what we found."

Kate had mulled over theories all winter and spring. At the top of her list was that they'd stumbled upon the frozen remains of some creature thousands of years old. The remains would most likely be accompanied by pollen from the plants growing at the time—powerful climate indicators. Such a discovery could ensure funding for her research for the rest of her life.

"Thanks for keeping it to yourself, Frank. We can't let a hint of this get out and risk someone else taking over. I've already been denied credit three times for research I participated in—I won't let it happen again. Science is so cutthroat, more than most people realize, especially now that funding has disappeared." She sat back in her chair. "With my tenure coming up next year, I could use something substantial—and I'll make sure you and the other team members also get the credit you deserve."

When she stopped by to pick up her final contract, Kate told her boss she would fly to the station with her students on June 7 and suggested Dr. Poole take the ski plane to the Blue Glacier the following week.

"I need six or seven days to get my team assigned and working," she said, "so Poole can witness an efficient team in operation from day one." She had calculated they'd need that amount of time to determine the shadow's identity and claim the find for her team, whatever it was.

"That's unacceptable," Rollins said. "Poole insisted that he start observing as soon as your team arrives."

"Well, that won't work for me. At the very least, we have to get our equipment unpacked and set up first. Tell him June 10." She gritted her teeth. "I want to reiterate that I'll be civil, but I still resent the intrusion." It seemed as though Rollins and Poole had conspired to disrupt her plans.

Kate shoved the contract into her briefcase and turned to leave.

"Professor Landry, we have something else to discuss. Please sit." He pointed at the two chairs in front of his desk.

Damn. What now?

"I received word this morning from the National Science Foundation that our proposal for next summer's research on the Blue Glacier has been rejected."

"What? They've always given us funding. Did they give you a reason?"

"I'm afraid Congress cut funds to all climate-related research. We can try for another source, maybe the Gates Foundation, but I'm not optimistic."

"So we're supposed to stick our heads in the sand, John? How can we adapt to global warming if we don't study it?"

"I know. I'm with you on this. Let's see what I can do. You'll just have to get the most out of this summer's data."

Kate only half listened. Her career, the future of climate research, and quite possibly the fate of the heating planet depended on whatever she and Frank had found trapped in her glacier—and on the tunnel leading to it.

3

Dr. Kate Landry's Apartment
Seattle

Friday, June 5

Kate stared at the neat piles of underwear, socks, sweaters, and rugged waterproof pants spread out on her dining room table. Her personal items didn't include much—she seldom wore makeup, and her short, straight hair would air-dry quickly. This ritual of packing for her three-month stint on the glacier came with more excitement and apprehension than it had in the past eight years—five of those as a professor leading student research teams to study the impact of global warming on her glacier.

Some of her anxiety stemmed from the telephone call to her father she had avoided but felt compelled to make, since cell phones were useless on the mountain. Chuck Landry, now sixty-five, still lived on the family ranch in western Wyoming, where she practically raised her three younger brothers after their mother died of breast cancer. Kate had been eight when they lost her, and her dad never remarried.

David, her youngest brother, stayed on the ranch to mend fences, shoe horses, and tend to the endless chores of a livestock operation. The other two brothers, the twins, had moved away years ago. One had a wife and two children in Idaho, and the other drank away most of the money he earned doing odd jobs in Montana.

The ranch no longer ran a large number of cattle but retained a herd of about fifty head, including two bulls. It was also home to a few horses, a half-dozen chickens, plus two cattle dogs. Ten years earlier, her father and brothers found oil on the property while drilling for water. Now two oil wells provided a modest income to help put food on the table and pay for expenses, supplementing what they earned from selling steers.

Kate sat at the small desk in her apartment and selected the familiar number from her cell phone directory.

"Hi, Dad."

No response.

"This is Kate."

"Yeah, I know who it is," the familiar, raspy voice replied. "But it would be easy to forget when I hear from you only once a year."

"I call you more often than that. Besides, the phone works both ways."

"Are you going to give me another lecture about why we should stop pumping oil?"

She sighed. "No. I called to see how you're doing."

"The same."

"How's David?"

"He's okay. Couldn't run things around here without him, while the rest of you are off gallivanting around the country."

"I've told you before, I'd come and help with the ranch from time to time if you'd plug those god-awful oil wells that pollute the whole place and contribute to global warming. I'm not going to breathe all that methane. Maybe you could install wind turbines instead."

"I thought I wasn't getting the lecture."

She dropped her head in her hand. "Listen, Dad, I'm about to go to the Blue Glacier again in a couple of days. This may be the last time because our funding got cut."

"It's about damn time the government stopped throwing away my taxes on trying to control the weather. You wouldn't have this problem if you'd majored in petroleum geology like I told you. You're wasting your time running around on ice that isn't any use to anybody."

"And you would know that glaciers don't matter because of your vast knowledge of them?"

"I know enough."

Kate paused to keep from yelling or hanging up. "Let's just agree to disagree and leave it there."

"Well, I can't give you any money. We're barely bringing in enough to keep this place afloat—especially with the low price of crude."

"I understand that, Dad. I didn't call for money. I just wanted to see how you're doing."

"I said we're fine."

"Well, I guess that's it then. I'll talk to you later."

"Bye." He hung up.

Kate slammed her fist on the desk. "God, I hate those calls!" she shouted.

Why did she bother? He would never see the value in what she did or understand how much it mattered—to her or to the planet. She sat staring blankly at the cell phone. He was such a stubborn son of a bitch. He used to be so gentle, so kind before Mom died.

She reached across the desk for her mother's picture. It was like looking in a mirror: Kate had her mom's angular face, strawberry-blonde hair, and blue eyes. She even had the same dusting of freckles across her nose. That photo was taken a year before she died, at age thirty-three, the same age as Kate now.

Her mom had an amazing glow about her. Kate remembered holding hands with her on the porch swing as they watched a harvest moon rise over the hill, the sharp smell of sagebrush filling the air. They'd have a contest to see who could recognize the most bird songs. Kate's love for all living things had come from her mom.

Dark loneliness washed over her, the feeling she'd fought for years. "Oh Mom, I miss you so much." Tears spilled down her cheeks.

She thought of Paul, someone she'd hoped would erase that hollow ache in the pit of her stomach. They had met at the gym and dated six months—until he cut it off. "I need more than you can give me," he'd said. "Your walls are too thick—you won't let anyone get close."

"Stop!" she chided herself, angrily wiping the tears from her face. "Dwelling on this will get you nowhere. Focus on your research."

She grabbed her clothes from the dining table and stuffed them into her canvas duffel bag.

4

Blue Glacier
Olympic National Park

Sunday, June 7

From her seat on the ski plane, Kate scanned the blue ice at the lower end of the glacier, and her heart plummeted. The ice had thinned and receded up the side of the mountain even more compared to last June. Lots more bare rock was exposed than she remembered when she first saw it eight years earlier.

So many people, like her father, refused to admit it, but the world was in a lot of trouble.

Her job—no, her mission—was to determine the factors causing the shrinkage of glaciers. She theorized that the heavier rainfall and the reduction of snow due to rising temperatures sped up the glacial retreat more than the temperature itself. A colleague studying glaciers in Patagonia had recently published a paper supporting the theory.

Every summer, Kate and her students continued to measure the thickness of layers in the ice tunnel that had built up over decades. Her analysis of the pollen samples they collected between each layer revealed the amounts of precipitation the vegetation received in the valleys below. A strong relationship had emerged: the greater the precipitation in the form of rain, the thinner the ice layer. This relationship was maintained even as the air temperature recordings on the glacier rose and fell.

If she could confirm and publish her theory, she hoped it could lead to more precise estimates for the life spans of mountain glaciers. Her data could help the millions of people who would be affected by the eventual loss of alpine glaciers around the world. She liked to think that by making the public aware of this, she could change attitudes and behaviors—and in her small part protect the planet and improve people's lives.

The ski plane slid to a stop at six thousand feet above sea level on the Snow Dome, the most prominent feature on the side of the mountain, where the packed snow sloped away on three sides from the nearly flat top. The summit of Mount Olympus, a cone-shaped pillar of ice-free brown rock a mile away, rose another two thousand feet.

Standing next to the plane, she took a deep breath of the crisp mountain air while Tom, the charter pilot, retrieved her duffel bag. She always felt alive and rejuvenated when she first set foot on the glacier. Arriving an hour before any of the others, she had a chance to savor the scene and couldn't help but smile.

In the brilliant morning sun the snow dazzled, a million sparkles of color dancing on the coarse, crystalline surface. A gentle breeze caressed her skin as she admired the cirrus clouds feathering the deep blue sky above the expansive peaks and valleys that appeared close enough to touch, yet were miles away. The hush—the sheer absence of sound—made her feel wrapped in a kind of peace she couldn't describe.

The roar of the engine broke the silence, and the plane lifted into the air, returning to Port Angeles for the next member of the project team.

Picking up her duffel bag and ice ax, Kate started hiking the half mile down the side of the Snow Dome toward the research station. From the top of the hill, she was always struck by how small and lonely the station appeared on its rock outcrop surrounded by snow.

Built almost sixty years before, the brown boxy structure—about the size of a two-car garage—sat in the sheltered saddle between the Snow Dome and Panic Peak, its silver-painted metal roof shimmering in the sun. A shed housing the one-hole privy, a diesel generator, and a handful of tools perched precariously a few feet from the main building. The dish antenna that linked the station to an Internet provider's tower eighteen miles away was thankfully still there, standing upright on the mast above the roof, along with the Park Service radio antenna.

Kate unlocked the only door to the building and entered the outer room serving as pantry, workshop, and storage space for hanging coats, ice axes, and climbing ropes. The musty smell hit her right away, but everything looked just as she and Frank had left it when they closed up the previous September.

Inside the entryway, three coils of climbing rope hung side by side on the wall next to four pairs of spiked crampons used for traction on ice. On the left, filling the entire side of the room, built-in shelves contained enough canned and dried food to last for months. On the opposite side, the tools they would need to calibrate and maintain their research equipment were lined up neatly on the wall above the workbench.

Continuing on through the doorway into the living quarters, Kate inspected the makeshift kitchen to her right—a small sink next to a built-in propane stove. She replaced the blue plastic bucket below the drain to catch rinse water that spilled into the sink when they washed dishes. Although Kate and Frank had adjusted to not having indoor plumbing, her new students would probably need a few days.

Everything in the rest of the room appeared to have survived the winter's fury intact but was covered with the usual layer of dust. Kate wandered past the wood table and two benches, large enough for six, and then to the built-in desk along the wall to her left. The shelves above it were filled with old geology and glaciology reference books. When she spotted the bound copy of her PhD dissertation on the shrinking of the Blue Glacier, she smiled, recalling the many months and late nights of work to complete it. On the desk, her powerful binocular microscope sat under its dust cover, ready for her to analyze the pollen samples she and Frank collected.

She rolled up the blue plastic tarps protecting the mattresses on the four bunks built into niches in the back wall—stacked two on the left side and two on the right. The dust cloud made her sneeze. As she scanned the small room from the vantage of the bunks, the black metal oil heater in the center stood out. Whenever the temperature fell, they'd fire up the heater, the only source of warmth on many cold nights over the years.

Kate was painfully aware that the heater, generator, and stove she had inherited from the 1950s burned fossil fuels that ultimately contributed to the melting glacier, contradicting everything she stood for. Her efforts to replace them over the years with solar power had failed. No money, she was told time and again. All she could do was use them as sparingly as possible.

After dropping her duffel next to her usual lower bunk on the right side, Kate headed back to the Snow Dome, pulling one of the station's fiberglass sleds to transport baggage and supplies. The three students would come individually in the same single-engine ski plane, too small to carry more than one passenger at a time, their gear, and some fresh food.

When Alice jumped off the plane, her face aglow with excitement, Kate thought back to when she had interviewed her. Alice's wide-eyed enthusiasm was the first thing she noticed about the Berkeley graduate, who'd earned double bachelor's degrees in fine arts and atmospheric science. Kate also recognized that Alice's training as a gymnast had made her strong and disciplined, two requirements for anyone on her team.

Of average height, Kate smiled down at Alice, who came to just her chin. "How was the trip?"

"Awesome." Removing earbuds from her ears, the young woman spread out her arms to take in the scene. "It's beyond beautiful up here. I had no idea."

Kate had concerns that Alice's small, youthful frame would keep the guys from taking her seriously. But she'd been wrong. At the team's orientation two weeks before, she hadn't noticed any issues.

Alice carried a shiny, new Eddie Bauer backpack, bulging at the seams, and a bulky duffel bag that felt unusually light when Kate hoisted it onto the sled. It amused her to see the things her students chose to bring.

"Did you remember the ice ax you were told to get?" Kate asked.

Alice nodded, her dark ponytail bouncing behind her. "It's in the duffel with all my art supplies."

They fell in step on their way down the Snow Dome to the station as Kate pulled the sled loaded with Alice's gear and food supplies. She didn't like admonishing her students right away, yet she felt compelled to say something. "Alice, I'm eager to see your artwork of the mountains, but remember, we're counting on you to do research."

"I know, I know. I can do both." She pushed the bangs off her face and gave Kate a disarming smile that spread to her chestnut eyes. "You'll see."

At the station, Alice stood in the middle of the room and surveyed the space. "Wow! It's smaller than I expected."

"You'll get used to it. Besides we'll be working outside most of the time. Here's your bunk." Kate rested her arm on the bunk above hers. "Throw your pack up there, and let's head back to the Snow Dome to meet Charlie's flight.

The two women had just arrived at the top of the Snow Dome, Alice pulling the empty sled, when the small red-and-white plane glided to a smooth landing on the snow up ahead.

Charlie, a sophomore at the University of Washington, the youngest student to ever work on the glacier, bounded from the plane wearing a T-shirt and strode toward them, a sandy-haired kid from Colorado without an ounce of fat on his sinewy body. His gear included a well-worn pack, no doubt used on his many trips into the mountains. He'd lashed a climbing rope and his ice ax to the outside.

Charlie greeted the two women with a broad smile, revealing a sizable chip in his front tooth that wasn't there during orientation.

Kate stared at his mouth. "Charlie, what happened to your tooth?"

"Yeah, just some bad luck. Last weekend, a buddy and I went climbing, and I slipped on a friction pitch and smashed into the rock face. Boy, were my parents pissed. They spent a fortune on braces. I'll get it fixed when I go home."

They wouldn't have to worry about Charlie's conditioning or mountaineering skills—only the hazards of a fearless teen on a mountain glacier.

Kate pointed toward his feet at a second canvas bag on the snow. "What do you have there?"

"I couldn't spend the summer without my electronics." He bent down and unzipped his bag. "Here, Professor Landry, let me show you."

"No need for formalities here," she said. "Both of you, please call me Kate."

As Charlie pulled items out of his duffel, she recognized a soldering iron, multimeter, and various electrical parts, large and small. He held up two circuit boards. "These are my Arduino and Raspberry Pi—I need them to build my remote monitoring circuits while I'm here."

"That's why we hired you," Kate said, laughing. "Let's see what creative inventions you come up with."

Charlie and Alice loaded his bags onto the sled while Tom stacked on a box of canned food and another containing fresh produce and cuts of meat wrapped in dry ice.

The three hiked down the Dome side by side, Charlie in the middle. Kate pulled the sled and fell silent as Alice and Charlie pointed and chattered about the mountains surrounding their new home. After Kate gave Charlie a brief tour and showed him his bunk, she left the two students to get settled while she went back to the Snow Dome to meet Frank's plane.

She and Frank needed some privacy to discuss how to approach their return to the tunnel. Based on its condition when they left it in September, she wouldn't be surprised if it had already collapsed.

As she thought about their imminent return to the unstable tunnel, her chest tightened—the sudden unease making her question their plan. Was it too risky to go there at all?

Frank landed on the Snow Dome shortly after noon, his arrival just as entertaining as that of the other two. Wearing his ever-present blue baseball cap, his curly hair sticking out underneath, he unfolded his six-foot-four, 250-pound linebacker frame from the ski plane. Kate knew his endurance enabled him to climb two thousand feet to the summit and hike three thousand feet down to the lip of the glacier and back to the research station on the same day without getting tired.

He carried the pack she remembered, but this time he also brought a greasy canvas bundle of heavy tools that clanged as he dragged it out of the plane and dropped it on the sled.

"Frank, what the heck? We didn't discuss those."

"I threw them in at the last minute. You never know when we might come across something embedded in the ice that needs to be chiseled out." He looked down at her and winked.

"Good idea." She pulled him aside while Tom finished unloading two large instrument cases. "Frank, did you notice the ice at the tip of the glacier as you flew in?"

"Sure did. All the exposed rocks—the glacier has receded so much since last year."

"I'm worried with all the melting the tunnel will be impassable. Even if we can get through, we'll have only two days to expose our mysterious shadow before Poole arrives. Let's get to it first thing in the morning."

They stood next to the sled and watched the plane zoom past and disappear over the side of the Snow Dome, then reappear as it became airborne.

"I've been thinking . . ." Frank pulled the sled as he and Kate walked toward the station. "Like you were saying last winter, being at the bottom of the ice near the summit, it has to be hundreds, if not thousands, of years old."

"That's all I've been thinking about."

Kate had mixed feelings. The urgency to find out before Poole landed on the glacier compelled her to consider chipping away at the ice as soon as she could grab one of Frank's chisels. On the other hand, a major find could compromise her research if this turned out to be her last chance to document the effects of rising temperatures on the Blue Glacier.

By the time Frank and Kate entered the station, Alice and Charlie had already stowed their belongings under the bunks. The room buzzed with excitement.

After giving them a chance to get reacquainted and get a bite to eat, Kate said, "Listen up, everyone. Grab your ice axes and let's meet on the rocks out front."

They followed her down the rough rock outcrop supporting the station and assembled on the snow at the base of the Snow Dome where they had just come from the plane. The June sun blazed high in a pastel-blue sky accented with a few wisps of clouds.

"After my overview," she said, "we'll do self-arrest practice using our ice axes. This is especially for you, Charlie and Alice. Learning to self-arrest could save your life." Kate bounced her ax handle in her hand. "You may have heard about the young man who fell and broke his leg while climbing Mount Olympus a couple of years ago—he was one of my students. I don't want to lose any of you to an accident."

Alice examined the ax in her hand with its long black handle and perpendicular silver blade welded across the top. "I've read about self-arrests, but I've never done them."

"Here's what you do." Kate showed them how to hold their axes across their chests with the point facing out. She climbed fifty yards up the thirty-degree incline on the side of the Snow Dome. Flopping down on her stomach, she stopped by digging the point of the ice ax into the snow while putting her full weight on the toes of her boots. The students then took turns, dropping onto the snowy incline until they could bring themselves to a stop from almost any position.

As they went back inside, Kate hoped this training for Alice and Charlie and refresher for Frank would be enough. In the last five years, she'd never lost a student, but every summer she worried that someone on her team might not make it home.

5

Blue Glacier
Olympic National Park

Sunday, June 7

That evening, after a hearty meal of steak, mashed potatoes, and fresh green beans, the students stayed at the table talking. Kate and Frank leaned against the wall across the table from Alice and Charlie. It was close to 7:00, and daylight coming through the small window above the table lit up what was left of their meal.

Alice turned to Charlie. "How do you like Seattle compared to Denver?"

"Can't compare them."

"Why not?" Frank asked.

"Because I'm inside a lot in Seattle. It's always cloudy and rainy."

"So you like Colorado better," Alice said.

"Didn't say that." Charlie grinned, his blue eyes playful.

"Boy, you're hard to pin down," Frank said.

Kate sat quietly listening to the students. This was the kind of banter that produced cohesive groups. She knew this would become a strong team, although it was barely the beginning.

"Charlie," she said, "in my classes I want students to form opinions. You'd be in trouble."

"Actually, I have opinions about both places. They're just different."

Frank laughed. "I'd vote for this kid to be in Congress. By the way, I grew up on a ranch near Sheridan, Wyoming, and it's better by far than either Colorado or Washington."

"Hold on," Alice said. "California has them all beat. It's got the highest and lowest spots in the continental US."

"Oh brother, I can't believe you guys are college students," Kate said, shaking her head. "We'll have to settle this debate later. Right now, I want to move on to what I call the Blue Glacier Ice Breaker. At the orientation, you had a chance to meet each other, and now it's time to share more about yourselves—your background, what you hope to accomplish this summer, and what unique qualities you have." She glanced around the table. "Who wants to start?"

Silence. Across from her, Alice and Charlie stared down at the table.

"I'll start." Frank tossed his napkin onto his empty plate. "This is my third summer on the glacier, and I'm glad to be here. I can't think of anywhere I'd rather be. Well, except with my family. Annie, my wife, is home in Seattle with Sammy, our incredible eighteen-month-old son." He looked off.

Kate smiled at such tenderness in a man who could have played for the Seahawks. "Being here won't be easy at times. I hope your experiences will make it worthwhile. You wouldn't be part of this group if you didn't want to better understand our planet."

"The focus of my PhD dissertation," continued Frank, "is studying the ratio of precipitation falling as rain versus snow and its effect on the downhill flow of the glacier—more rain leads to a faster flow than snow. I'm also helping Kate collect pollen samples in the ice. So far, the data we've collected supports her theory."

"I'll go next." Charlie cleared his throat, his eyes serious. "I feel lucky to be part of this team. All of you have a gazillion more years of experience than I do. I'm here mostly because of my interest in electronics and mountain climbing. I've designed and built instruments for collecting weather data and for automating my parents' house."

Alice folded her arms on the table. "That's impressive, Charlie."

"Thanks. Professor Landry—I mean, Kate"—he shot a glance at her—"wants me to automate the remote collection of data here. My goal is to design a way to monitor the glacier year-round. I'm majoring in electrical engineering, but I'm thinking about switching to atmospheric science this fall."

Everyone turned to Alice. "I'm interested in *albedo*," she said, grinning at Charlie's baffled wide eyes and raised brows. "Changes in light and dark, shadow and sunlight, reflection and absorption of light are all measures of albedo. It can determine how fast the snow and ice melt over the summer. Let me show you."

She stacked her plate on Charlie's to clear the space in front of her, then pulled out two large photographs from her backpack and placed them side by side on the table. "These are shots of the lower Blue Glacier." She pointed to the one on her left. "This one was taken last year about this time in June, and that one"—she pointed to the other one—"was taken in September. Notice how the pure white overlay of snow has almost completely melted, leaving the darker blue ice exposed. I'll measure the amount of light reflected from these two surfaces to explain the different rates of melting."

"You can use my data on the volume of meltwater," Frank said.

"Thanks. I was counting on it. And here's something else that's cool." Alice pointed to the side of the glacier on the September photo. "See this pink area? It's actually a kind of algae—did you know that?"

"Yes, Frank and I are familiar with it," Kate said, "but Charlie probably isn't."

"Algae in the snow?" Charlie shook his head. "Never heard of it."

"It grows on snow exposed to sun for long periods," Alice said. "I saw some this morning just below the research station. It has a few names, but I like "watermelon snow" because of the reddish-pink color, and it even smells like watermelon if you sniff it up close."

"Tell us why you think it's important," Kate said.

"Remember, I'm studying albedo. Current research tells us that the darker pink color of watermelon snow reduces the reflectivity of sunlight off the snow, possibly contributing to the melting of the glacier. And because the algae grows all over the world on glaciers and polar ice, we need to include it in our models to show we're losing ice faster than people had thought."

Charlie took a closer look at the photo. "That could make a huge difference."

"I'll also do some art while I'm here." Alice held up a watercolor

painting. "I captured this scene of the Olympic Mc
ricane Ridge outside Port Angeles at sunrise yesterc
tioned at the orientation, I double-majored at Berkeley
science and fine arts."

"That's beautiful. You're really good," Charlie said.

"Hey, thanks. I'm really happy with how it came out.' ‚ smiled.

Kate slid off the bench carrying plates in both hands. "It's my turn,
but let's clean up first."

They heated hot water on the stove for the dishes. Charlie washed
them in a plastic basin set into the sink and handed them to Alice, who
poured hot rinse water over them in the rack on a drain board to the
side of the sink. Then Frank dried the dishes and stacked everything
on the wooden shelves mounted to the wall above and to the right of
the sink. They finished in less than ten minutes.

Meanwhile, Kate went outside to return the half-empty quart of
milk to the metal "ice box" buried in the snow below the rocks. From
there she climbed back up to the shed to start the generator and felt
relieved to hear the rhythmic thumping of the diesel after it had sat
idle all winter. Back inside, she saw that one of the several bare light
bulbs hanging from the ceiling had burned out and made a mental
note to ask Frank to replace it.

Once everyone returned to the table, Kate took a deep breath. "Okay,
my story. I grew up on a ranch in Wyoming, like Frank. As the oldest
of four children, I was in charge of my siblings a lot. That's where my
inclination to teach came from. I like to work hard, and I don't sleep
much. You may hear me up at five o'clock—I'll try not to wake you,
but I usually read journals and write in the early morning."

She paused. "As you also know, I chose each of you to conduct
your own research to contribute to learning more about what I call
an 'endangered species'—the mountain glacier. I used to think that
if we returned in a hundred years, the Blue Glacier would be gone.
But after seeing what's happened in the last year, I'm worried that in
our lifetimes, we'll see nothing here but smooth rock and moraines."

Charlie scooted back on the bench. "You really think it's that bad?"

"Yes, sadly."

"Is there anything we can do to stop it?" he asked softly, his face grim.

"Unfortunately, no," Kate said. "But I think we can find ways to slow it down, and to do that, we need to understand how and why the ice is melting. The lives of thousands of people in South America and Asia depend on glaciers for their water supplies. We can help them plan for what's coming—and it appears it will happen sooner than later."

"There's one thing that could be done," Alice said. "We learned about it in our atmospheric science classes."

"What's that?" Frank asked, a hint of challenge in his voice.

"Of the several proposals for 'solar radiation management,' the most cost effective would be to inject sulfate aerosols into the stratosphere, like what happens naturally with volcanoes."

"What would that do?" Charlie asked.

"It causes some solar radiation to be reflected back instead of being absorbed by the Earth."

"Yes, I've read about that," Frank said. "That could help, but it would still take decades to cool enough to replenish the snow and increase the glacial ice. Worse, though, sulfates can cause acid rain."

"And wouldn't we need help from other countries to make something like that work?" Charlie asked. "We can't even get people to agree that burning fossil fuels is a problem."

"Our goals haven't changed," Kate said. "We need to document glacial melt and inform the public—but now time is more critical. Only when we understand the problem can we identify the best ways to slow down or reverse the process. Every week I read about promising research. Just this morning, I got a Google Alert about researchers studying rocks in Oman to understand how carbon dioxide in the air is converted to calcium carbonate rock, or limestone. They thought that someday the concentration of atmospheric carbon dioxide might be significantly reduced through a similar man-made process."

The room fell silent. Frank slouched down against the wall, and Charlie struggled to keep his eyes open. She was tired herself. "It's

been a long day—we could all use some rest. But I have one more announcement before we crawl into the sack. In three days, a visitor will
arrive to observe us doing our work."

Frank straightened up. "Yeah, he's doing research for NASA."

"His name is Dr. Grant Poole," Kate said, her body tensing at the
mere mention of his name. "Ignore him as much as possible. Just do
what you'd do if he weren't here."

Charlie shrugged. "That won't be hard. I've got nothing to hide."

Kate didn't respond.

6

Blue Glacier
Olympic National Park

Monday, June 8

The next day Kate got the crew started early with a gentle, but persistent "up and at 'em." After breakfast, Alice and Charlie assembled their gear, preparing to begin their independent data-collection activities.

Kate caught Frank's eye and nodded in the direction of the door, and he followed her to the rocks outside. "While Charlie and Alice are busy collecting their data," she said, "let's check the condition of the tunnel."

"I'll fetch my chisels."

"Good. I'll get a rope and two pairs of crampons, but let's wait until Alice and Charlie have left."

As if on cue, Charlie came outside, followed by Alice, both wearing jackets and backpacks and carrying their ice axes.

Kate turned to them. "We talked this morning about your assignments, but now show me your equipment, and tell me exactly where you'll be working."

Alice slid her backpack off her shoulder. "I'm climbing to the top of the Snow Dome with Charlie." She pointed toward the massive white hill that loomed over them. "I'll try to find a spot with a clear view of the Lower Glacier where I can take my first photo of the snow cover and the blue ice."

She unzipped the top of the pack and pulled out her digital 35 mm camera along with a spiral-bound sketchbook. "While I'm there, I'll make some drawings of the peaks on the far side of the valley."

"Be sure to hold on to your ice ax and stay alert as you climb," Kate said. "The Snow Dome has large crevasses on the far side. And since you're just getting used to climbing with your lug-soled boots on this snow, you and Charlie should stay roped up."

"I'll be careful."

"How about you, Charlie? Tell me your plans."

"When we get to the top of the Snow Dome, I'll look for a spot to test the acoustic ice-depth measurement system I designed." Reaching down to the backpack at his feet, he pulled out a short gray cylinder with a long green fuse attached. "I'll set these off one at a time and then use an array of these waterproof microphones." He held up a disk the size of a coaster. "Once the explosive goes off, the software on my laptop will measure how long it takes the sound to reflect off the bedrock and tell me the ice depth. It will also give me the density of the different layers of ice between the surface and bedrock."

"It should work. Just make sure you come back with all your fingers."

Charlie grinned. "I promise."

"I see you both have your ice axes, and Charlie has the rope. Do you have the other items on the list? Sunglasses, sunscreen, pocket-knife, water, snack?"

They nodded.

"Okay. We'll meet back up here at noon," Kate said. "Frank and I are going to check on a project we started last year not far from here. She pointed past the generator shed. "You could follow our tracks, but don't go there unless there's an emergency. The route crosses a dangerous ice face."

Shortly after Alice and Charlie left, Kate and Frank fastened the spiked crampons to their boots and tied the rope to the climbing harnesses they both wore. Frank tossed his bag of tools onto his back, holding it in place with a strap across his chest. Kate led as they hiked single file the quarter mile from the station, traversing the nearly vertical patch of snow and ice.

Fresh snow from the previous winter obscured the path to the tunnel mouth, so they had to stomp firm steps and use the flat adz end of their axes to chip footholds in the bare ice. Even wearing crampons, they risked slipping and falling into the steep ravine below.

A wave of guilt washed over her. Could Alice and Charlie handle the steep snow and crevasses on the side of the Snow Dome? Kate probably should have gone with them on the first trip out.

A half hour later, twice as long as normal, she reached the depression that told her they'd arrived at the entrance. It was almost completely filled in with snow. She called back to Frank, "Here's the tunnel, but now we need to get into it."

Frank stepped up beside her. "Looks like we have work to do."

He pulled a short-handled shovel from his canvas bag and pushed snow from the entrance over the side of the precipice while Kate assisted using her boots and gloved hands. Once they had cleared the way, they put on headlamps and turned to face the blue-black hole piercing horizontally through the ice. Everything had frozen solid—a welcome change from the melting ice and water flowing across the floor, so prominent in September. They might make it to the shadow after all.

After walking about halfway, Kate stopped abruptly, and Frank bumped into her. "Oh no! We're screwed," she said.

A wall of blue ice blocked their path. A large slab had fallen at an angle from the roof of the tunnel all the way to the floor. The opening dropped from seven feet to zero in the span of about ten feet.

"I was afraid of this. Our tunnel's sealed shut." She pushed with both hands against the ice, but it didn't budge. "Give me a hand."

Frank pressed into the block with his shoulder. "That's not going anywhere." He straightened up and kicked the ice in front of him. "Shit!"

They stood there staring at the wall, neither one speaking.

Frank took off his cap and raked his hand through his curly hair, then shoved his cap back on and grabbed the shovel. "There's got to be a way past this thing." He chipped at the edges, trying to free the block. Nothing moved, and he tossed the shovel down. "How about torching it?"

"Too dangerous. We might bring down the whole tunnel."

An explosion from the Snow Dome echoed around them, telling them Charlie was at work.

"Maybe a quarter stick of dynamite?" Frank laughed.

Kate appreciated his attempt to lighten the mood, but the weight of disappointment crushed down on her. Was this it? After all the months of worrying and planning, would she really have to give up?

"We knew something like this might happen," she said in a flat voice. "Let's go. Maybe we'll come up with a solution. You need to start collecting your data."

Heading out, Kate in the lead again, they were about to step out of the tunnel and traverse the ice face when Frank said, "Damn. I left my tools. I'll be right back."

As soon as he disappeared into the darkness, a series of deafening cracks came from deep in the ice, followed by a thunderous roar. The ground trembled under her feet.

"Frank!" Kate shouted as she sprinted back through the darkness, afraid of what she'd find.

She first saw the light of his headlamp and then heard his voice. "I'm okay—just shaken up. But look at this."

Turning on her lamp, she joined him in front of the ice slab, now lying horizontally along the floor. It still blocked the tunnel, but a fissure about a foot tall and two feet wide had appeared along the top of the slab. Frank leaned in and peered down the opening.

"What do you see?" Kate asked.

"The slab is only about eight feet deep. Looks like it's clear on the other side. If we chisel past this block, I'll bet we can go to the end."

A loud crack came from the ice and ricocheted through the enclosed space.

"I don't know, Frank . . ." She was still rattled from the last close call. "Maybe this is a sign that the whole thing isn't worth it. It's too dangerous. If that slab had fallen when we were inside last fall, we'd be dead on the other side. Or if it had fallen on you just now—"

"But, Kate, the tunnel is a lot more stable since it's refrozen. And we can use my chisels now."

She hesitated. "Yes, that's true. Except for this slab, the tunnel's in better shape. Okay, let's expand this hole."

While he banged with a hammer and chisel on the ice, Kate kicked the scattered bits of debris to the side. Frank had come prepared—one of his tools was a tree-pruning saw with a fiberglass handle in six-foot sections, making a total of twelve feet. That gave him the reach he needed to enlarge the opening through to the far side. After an hour, the hole was large enough for a child to pass through, but still too small for either of them.

Another loud cracking sound came through the opening they had made. "Frank, can you see if anything is happening in there?"

He bent over slightly to look through the hole. "Nothing's changed that I can tell."

Continuing to chisel, he soon made the passage large enough for Kate to wiggle through if she shed her parka.

"Here's the moment of truth." He interlaced his fingers so she could step up to the opening. She slithered in with both arms extended in front of her like a scuba diver entering a cave.

A wave of claustrophobia hit her hard, making her dizzy, and she almost yelled to Frank to pull her out. But she kept going, breathing heavily, until she dropped down headfirst on the other side, bracing her fall with her arms.

"You okay, Kate?"

She shook her right arm and opened and closed her hand. "Yeah, sprained my wrist a little."

"Watch out in there," Frank called through the opening, his voice tense. "I can't get through to help if you get in trouble."

"I'll be fine. Just wait there." Another loud crack echoed back and forth like a shot from a rifle.

"Get out of there, Kate!" Frank's headlamp blinded her as she looked back through the hole. "I'll make the opening bigger so I can get to you if there's a problem."

She felt like she was suffocating. "You're right. I'm coming out."

After he pulled her through the small opening, she leaned against the wall and took a deep breath. Frank squatted down next to her.

"We have to be smarter about this," she said, her heart pounding. She looked at her watch and saw it was after twelve. Alice and Charlie would be worried. They could resume their quest the next day.

When Kate and Frank walked through the station door, Charlie and Alice jumped up from the table, their faces clouded with concern.

"Where were you?" Alice asked. "You said to meet here at noon."

"I'm very sorry." Kate bent down to untie her bootlaces. "We were working in an ice tunnel, and it took us longer than we expected."

"What were you doing?" Alice asked.

"We were cleaning out snow and ice from the winter."

"And we ran into a problem." Frank sat on the end of a bench at the table taking off his boots.

Kate walked to the cooler they kept by the sink and pulled out a bottle of water. "I'll explain what happened in a minute. But first, tell us how it went for you this morning."

"Fine, actually." Charlie beamed. "My acoustic sounding system was awesome. The ice on the Snow Dome where I set up is about eighty-five meters deep."

"That's a meter less than we measured last summer. Scary. Your method's amazing. It would have taken us a day and a half to measure the ice depth using our old method of melting through to bedrock with a heated element on a cable."

"How'd you do, Alice?" Frank asked.

"Success. That's a killer view of the Lower Glacier from the far side of the Snow Dome. I'll be going back each week to take my series of photos. I also had time to make some sketches."

"Let's see," Kate said.

Alice pulled the pad from her backpack and handed it to her.

"Nice. You've really captured those peaks in your sketches." Kate passed the book to Frank. "How did you feel climbing over the top of the Snow Dome? I was worried."

"It wasn't too bad. But I'm glad you warned me to be careful. I did see some crevasses partially covered with snow."

"Good. You'll find there are lots of ways to get hurt up here. I want you to be extra cautious until you've had more experience. Here's another example. The tunnel Frank and I were in today is unstable. There's already been one cave-in since last fall. That's why we took so long—we were trying to clear it enough to get through."

"Why's it so important?" Alice asked. "Why not abandon the tunnel?"

"Years ago, scientists studied the layers of ice in there—like tree rings. Recently, Frank and I have been collecting pollen and spore samples there to determine how the plants in the area evolved over time. This field is called palynology. Anyway, last September he and I found something buried in the ice we really want to identify. It may be nothing, or it could be a discovery for paleontology or archeology. Until we know, I don't want you two going in there—it's too dangerous."

"I'd like to see what you've found," Alice said. "I'm willing to take the chance."

"Me too," Charlie joined in.

"Let me give it some thought. Right now, Frank and I need to install a piece of equipment for his research on the side of the Snow Dome. While we're gone, you can work on pulling the data you collected this morning into a report and planning your next steps."

She couldn't get her mind off the tunnel the whole time she and Frank hiked to his research location. The dark shape in the ice might turn out to be something ordinary like an elk or moose. Why risk Alice's and Charlie's lives? But, then again, why was she willing to risk her life and Frank's?

7

Blue Glacier
Olympic National Park

Tuesday, June 9

Early the next morning, Kate asked Charlie and Alice to join her at the table. "Frank and I talked last night, and I've decided you two can go with us, but under one condition—you'll have to wait at the mouth of the tunnel until we've enlarged the opening so we can fit through. Someone has to remain outside with a transceiver at all times in case we run into trouble while the others are inside with another radio. The second there's a problem, everyone leaves. Deal?"

"Deal!" Charlie and Alice said in unison.

Kate sounded more confident about her decision than she felt, but she couldn't treat them like children either. Besides, she could use their help clearing out the tunnel.

It was another day of nice June weather—warm, but not hot. The younger crew members sat on the rocks in front of the station while Kate and Frank roped up and attached crampons to their boots. She demonstrated to Alice how to fasten crampons and tie the knots to attach the rope to the climbing harnesses they each wore.

Using their axes for balance, the four of them inched along the narrow ledge chipped into the nearly vertical ice face above the ravine. Kate led, followed by Alice, Frank, and Charlie in the rear. At the mouth of the tunnel, Kate looked back to watch Alice taking small, tentative steps.

"This is scary!" Alice shouted, her eyes wide with panic.

"Focus on the path right in front of you." Kate wanted to tell her not to look down, but she knew that often had the opposite effect.

It was too late. Alice's foot slipped off the ledge. She leaned toward the ice to arrest her fall with her ax, but her feet slipped out from under her, and she slid off the ledge down the face. "I'm falling!"

"Frank, hold on!" Kate yelled.

Attached to Alice by the rope on the other side, Frank planted his weight squarely over his feet the way Kate did. Their crampons dug into the ice while Alice's weight jerked the rope, saving her from falling into the icy chute of the West Couloir and over a two-thousand-foot drop-off to the White Glacier.

By the time she stopped moving, Alice had slid to the bottom of the V of rope between Frank and Kate, her arms and legs splayed out against the ice.

Kate and Frank could hold her for a few minutes, but Alice would have to get back to the path on her own. She needed more experience on the glacier before she could handle such a steep traverse.

Alice tried to climb, but her feet kept sliding down the slippery ice and wouldn't support her weight.

"Lean back against the rope," Frank yelled, "and put your weight over your feet. We'll hold you." She followed his command and pulled away from the wall. Her crampons gripped the ice, and she had the traction she needed to climb.

"Walk back up to the trail," Kate yelled from the tunnel entrance. "We'll take up the slack in the rope."

Alice had a look of stoic determination as she slowly climbed up the steep incline to the path.

"You're doing great!" Charlie called out.

Back on the ledge, she paused and took a deep breath before continuing on, keeping her weight over the crampons so she wouldn't slip again. Near the entrance, she grabbed Kate's extended hand. "Whew!" She shook her head. "That was close. I could have died. I've never been so scared in my life. Thank you for saving me."

Kate held Alice's hand in both of hers and looked into the young woman's pale face. "We need to be here for each other. Are you okay?"

"I guess." Her voice trembled slightly.

As Charlie and Frank joined them, Kate said, "The important thing for all of you is to learn how to survive in this place. This was your first lesson, but I hope they're not all this exciting—for all our sakes." She wound the climbing rope in a loop under her elbow, then over her hand. "Charlie and Alice, stay here at the entrance and we'll radio you with updates on our progress."

She and Frank turned on their headlamps and walked farther into the tunnel as the luminescent blue light faded to black.

"We've made it to the ice slab," Kate said into the radio.

Frank took out his tools and started chipping the ice to enlarge the hole, alternating between pounding the chisel with a hammer and extending the long pruning saw deep into the opening. Kate kicked the chunks of loose ice into a pile nearby.

After an hour, Frank stopped. "That should do it. We can all fit, but it'll be tight. Do you want me to make it bigger?"

"No. We might weaken the ice above, and the roof could collapse. It's big enough." Kate gave the radio update to Charlie and Alice. "Going through the opening. Everything's stable."

Frank went through first and helped Kate land gently on the other side. Then she led the way toward the end of the tunnel.

Her heart pounded with nerves and excitement. It just had to be a carcass of some kind.

But she wasn't prepared for what she saw. The ice had melted enough since last fall to expose part of the body.

Frank aimed his headlamp at a clump. "I can definitely make out tufts of long, reddish-brown fur."

Kate pointed to another spot a couple of feet to the right of the fur. "Over here. Oh my God. This looks like an elephant snout. I think we've found a woolly mammoth!"

"Hot damn, Kate! Congratulations."

"I was afraid we'd never get back to this spot. I thought it could be a mammoth, but I didn't want to get my hopes up." She pounded the air with her fist. "YES! We did it." Her voice echoed off the ice.

"Yahoo! Let's give Charlie and Alice a hint."

"Sure." She pulled the transceiver from her parka pocket. "You guys awake out there? Over."

"Yep. We heard shouts. Everything okay?" Alice's voice came through the speaker.

"We're just excited. Blown away. You'll definitely want to see this. Over."

"Can't wait. Over."

"We'll come back to bring you here. Out."

Alice and Charlie greeted them with smiles, their faces bright with anticipation.

"It's unbelievable what we found," Kate said. "Turn on your headlamps and follow me. Frank will stay here with the radio."

They walked single file behind her. "We're lucky the tunnel's quiet today."

As the light-blue luminescence engulfed them, Alice looked from side to side and up at the ceiling. "Ah, this place is magical. Artists have described more than sixty-five different shades of blue—like cerulean, cyan, and cobalt. This tunnel has every one and a few they haven't named yet."

"I've never thought of it that way." Kate glanced at the ice walls, enjoying the many gradations of color through a first-timer's eyes. "It's like all the terms we glaciologists use to describe ice texture."

Charlie touched the wall with his gloved hand. "So much work must have gone into chiseling this tunnel through solid ice."

"It was quite a project back in the early sixties."

Kate helped them through the opening in the slab and asked them to wait for her on the other side. As they approached the end, the shadow darkened the entire four-by-seven-foot wall of ice. She trained her headlamp on the fur and snout.

"It's huge!" Alice reached out and gently touched the end of the trunk with her gloved hand. "What is it?"

"We think it's a woolly mammoth," Kate said with pride.

"How cool is that?" Charlie squeezed between Alice and the wall to get a closer look. "I've never seen an extinct animal before." He stretched his arms across the ice like he was trying to embrace it. "When can we get it out?"

"Hold on." Kate pulled away to get some air. She could barely breathe in the crush of the excited students. "We're all eager to get at the body, but we need a plan first."

After giving them a few minutes to study what little they could see, she said, "Let's head back to the station to debrief."

They met up with Frank, and all four of them worked their way across the ice face, Frank in the lead this time. Kate kept an eye on Alice, who moved haltingly but kept going, and their return trip went far more smoothly.

Kate's thoughts swirled. What a find! At the intersection of global warming, melting glaciers, and paleontology—she couldn't ask for a better way to get people interested.

8

Blue Glacier
Olympic National Park

Tuesday, June 9

Back at the station, Alice, Charlie, and Frank huddled around the table, all talking at once, discussing possible theories about how the mammoth could have gotten there.

Standing by the sink, Kate poured a fresh cup of coffee and tapped her mug with a spoon to get their attention. "First, this discovery must be treated with care. It's imperative we keep the creature's existence among the four of us. That means not discussing it during our radio contacts with the Park Service or with Tom, or in emails to friends and family."

They all nodded.

"And one more thing. When Dr. Poole arrives, he's not to know about the mammoth."

"Why not?" Charlie tore the wrapper off a candy bar. "Don't you trust him?"

"It's complicated . . . The short answer is no. I don't know him, so I can't trust him yet."

Alice cocked an eyebrow. "And what's the long answer?"

Kate paused. "There's a lot at stake, and no one else knows what we've found. We can leverage this to our benefit, but only if we handle it right."

Narrowing her eyes, she looked pointedly at each student. "Can you keep this between us?"

Yes, they all said.

Needing their help to gather information, she also saw a teaching opportunity. "Everyone, stay put. I want us to do something." She leaned back against the kitchen counter and folded her hands in front of her. "What are some things we might want to learn about this specimen?"

"First, is it a mammoth or mastodon—how can we tell?" Frank spoke quickly, his eyes bright with excitement. "And how'd it get up here?"

"Yep." Kate looked at Charlie. "Would you take notes, please? What else?"

Charlie picked up his tablet and started typing on the screen while everyone waited.

"What did it die from?" Alice said.

Frank ticked off on his fingers. "How old was it when it died? Is it male or female? What was its last meal?"

"Hold on." Charlie's fingers flew across his screen.

After pausing for him to catch up, Kate said, "Can we tell how close the carcass is to where it died? How far has it moved?"

"How complete is the carcass?" Frank said. "What shape is it in?"

"What about contact with humans?" Charlie said. "Any signs of being hunted?"

"This is a great start," Kate said during a lull. "Take the next three hours to look for answers. Our books here are dated, so search the Internet—our network account is private and secure. Of course, you can work together or alone. Then let's gather to share what you've found."

They scattered around the room, Charlie on his bunk, Alice at the desk, and Kate and Frank at the table. For the next several hours, they stayed glued to their laptops, stopping only to grab something to eat or periodically talk among themselves. By late afternoon, Kate had everyone reassemble around the table.

"Years of research in this tunnel haven't revealed anything like this," she said. "The far wall probably receded due to rapid melting, which exposed the carcass. What did you guys come up with?"

"I've found a few things." Charlie sat up straight on the bench. "After the last Ice Age, only scattered mountain glaciers remained. This mammoth might have been one of the last to roam the valleys below, and it somehow managed to climb to this six-thousand-foot level. We can only guess how it died."

"So how could a mammoth have died up here?" Kate waved her pen in the direction of the tunnel.

"Our mammoth might've been pursued by hunters," Frank had been straddling the bench and turned back to face the others. "Driven onto the ice of the Blue Glacier. The only route they could have taken is up the side of the Snow Dome from the Lower Glacier. Maybe fell into a crevasse and died, preserving the carcass."

"Why do paleontologists think that mammoths became extinct?" Kate asked.

"There are several theories," Charlie said. "One is that they came in contact with humans and got an illness that wiped them out. A second theory is they were hunted to extinction, and a third is the habitat changed faster than they could adapt."

Alice pointed to her laptop screen in front of her on the table. "Mastodon bones were discovered not far from here, near the town of Sequim. This journal article estimated its age over thirteen thousand years. It had a spear point embedded in one of its ribs. Looks like humans hunted these large mammals here on the Olympic Peninsula."

"So if our mammoth came across humans," Kate said, writing on her notepad, "it might have contracted an illness that killed large Ice Age mammals. Or maybe it was weakened by some disease and hunted. But we can't determine the state of its health without tissue analysis."

Kate paused, looking down at her notes. "Alice and Charlie, you can scrape and cut tissue from the end of the trunk after Frank has cleared away enough ice. Any indication of an illness would most likely show up there." She turned to Frank. "I want you to take charge of packaging the specimens we collect so Tom can take them on his supply flight next Monday and ship them to a lab for analysis."

He nodded. "Sure, no problem, but I thought you wanted to keep this from the outside world."

"I have a particular lab in mind. A friend and colleague of mine works at the Denver Museum of Nature and Science. Dr. Walter Slater is an expert in this field. I'll let him know our specimens are coming."

"Slater?" Frank's eyes widened. "*The* Walter Slater? I just read about him. He's pursuing the theory that disease may have caused the extinction of the mammoths."

"Yes, I know." Kate couldn't help but feel smug. "He'll be ecstatic about our find. Now, back to our visitor, Dr. Poole. I'll give him a tour of the glacier to keep him distracted while you collect the samples."

She rubbed her forehead with her fingers. "I'm worried about something else—what might happen if word gets out to the press about our mammoth discovery?"

"Sort of a feeding frenzy of science speculators and news media," Alice said, standing up to stretch. "I read that dozens of reporters and thousands of tourists descended on Sequim after their mastodon find."

"We can control messages coming directly from our crew," Frank said, "but once we send out specimens for analysis, we've opened up a new channel we can't control."

Kate nodded. "I've thought of that. Walter and I have had a long, professional relationship. I trust him with my life."

"I have a question." Charlie raised his hand. "Can we get acknowledgment for helping with the mammoth once you go public?"

"Oh Charlie—always thinking of yourself," Alice said, smiling.

"No, I'm serious. I'm thinking of our careers."

"Absolutely. We're a team." Kate swept her arm from Frank to Charlie to Alice. "What we accomplish is the result of our collective effort. I will make sure each of you gets credit for your contributions this summer."

9

Port Angeles
Washington

Wednesday, June 10

Dr. Grant Poole looked through the window at the tiny red-and-white ski plane sitting on the tarmac next to the fuel pump. A half-dozen single and twin-engine planes were tied down under their canvas covers nearby. There was no sign of activity in the sleepy, little airfield.

How could that ski plane take off and carry two men to the side of an eight-thousand-foot peak—and land there? He needed to trust this pilot Tom. Where the heck was he? He was supposed to have been there a half hour ago.

Grant would be the first to admit he was the opposite of an adrenaline junkie. In the safe, controlled environment of his lab at the University of California, Santa Cruz, he studied leadership styles by assigning roles to undergraduates who then worked together in various scenarios. When they finished, they'd fill out questionnaires about their interactions and accomplishments.

He simulated some emotionally intense situations, yet as he stood in the small terminal at the Port Angeles Airport at 9 a.m. headed for the Blue Glacier in the middle of the Washington wilderness, the words "safe" and "control" no longer applied.

It had taken every ounce of courage he had to get here.

"Dr. Poole." The only other person around was seated behind the counter in the small airport lobby.

Grant walked over. "Yes?"

"Tom called. He said the fog's too thick in the mountains to fly right now, but it should burn off by noon."

"That long? I'll be three hours late. Dr. Landry will wonder what happened."

"I'll call her on the radio."

"I appreciate that."

Grant returned to his seat and opened his laptop to catch up on emails. First, a message from a colleague wishing him good luck, and then another from his sister with photos from his niece's birthday party on Sunday. Smiling, he grabbed his phone.

"Hey, Nicole, I'm stuck in this tiny airport in Port Angeles. I just saw the photos—Matt always does an amazing job. It's hard to believe Emily is five now."

"I'm really glad you could make it."

"Me too." He loved seeing his niece, but it still irked him that he hadn't been allowed to join the team when they first arrived on the glacier. What was up with that? He hadn't even started and already couldn't follow his protocol.

"Emily partied so hard she caught a cold," Nicole said. "We're snuggling in her bed right now. She helped me pick out the photos to send to you."

His niece called out to him, "I love you, Uncle Grant."

"She's such a sweet kid, Nicole. You guys are so lucky."

"We are." She paused. "You'll have your own family someday soon, I'm sure of it."

He didn't know what to say.

"Grant, do your best to enjoy the summer. Think of it as a fresh start. And remember to send us an email once in a while, okay?"

"Yes, I will. And tell Emily I hope she feels better soon."

After they hung up, he went back to the photos, but his thoughts drifted elsewhere, his mind pulled like some magnetic force to the same dark scenario.

"Please, come and crew with me," Megan had said to him that day two years before. "The winds are up. It'll be fun." She loved to sail her twenty-five-foot sloop out of Santa Cruz harbor.

They'd been planning to get married as soon as he finished the all-consuming task of writing his first textbook. Both in their late thirties, they were eager to start a family.

Had he been more adventurous she might still be alive.

When she asked him to join her that day, he had looked away. "Sorry, I've got to catch up on work."

For months after she died, he hardly slept, replaying their last conversation in his mind again and again, guilt torturing him. In truth, he felt vulnerable on the open water—especially when the wind was brisk. But if he'd gone with her, he could have untangled her from the rigging when the sailboat capsized.

Would he ever be free of the horrible pain of missing her?

Grant knew he wasn't a complete coward—hadn't he tackled his academics with stamina and courage? His avoidance of outdoor adventure probably stemmed from his mother's protectiveness, like her refusal to let him try out for sports or let Nicole do gymnastics. His mom had even made his dad stop taking flying lessons because she worried he'd crash. Playing it safe became his family's approach to life, and he fell right in line.

Megan's voice came to mind again: "Grant, you need to be bold—live a little."

Theirs was a case of opposites attracting. She brought the spark and he added steady resolve—a combination their friends admired—although before Megan's accident, he began to enjoy the whiff of adventure that followed her, realizing how much he'd missed in life. Often, she would share her recent sailing feats as they snuggled in front of the fire in his rustic home nestled in the redwoods.

Since Megan's death, he'd tried to immerse himself in work, but his research seemed pointless. His published papers hadn't made a single impact that he could tell. The petty politics among the department faculty got under his skin—what a waste.

He knew he had to make a change. Megan would have been proud of him now that he'd stopped playing it safe and was heading to a glacier.

"Dr. Poole? A man's voice jerked Grant from his reflections. "I'm Tom Saunders. I'll be flying you to the glacier as soon as the fog burns off the peaks."

Grant stood and took in the short, slim man with silver reflecting sunglasses, lines chiseled in his face, wearing a red-plaid flannel shirt and blue down vest. "Yes, I'm anxious to get started. When can we go?"

Tom removed his glasses and shook Grant's hand. "Visibility should be good by early afternoon. Let's get some lunch. I know a nice diner nearby."

Grant checked his watch. Just past 11:30. He'd lost track of time. "Sure, let's go."

Over burgers and fries, Tom asked, "What made you decide to work in a remote spot like the Blue Glacier?"

"I wanted to study an isolated research team working in a dangerous setting. I came across Professor Landry's article describing her fieldwork there on the glacier." Grant poured ketchup on his fries. "It appears to be a pretty remote place."

"For sure. Takes me a half hour flying over some of the tallest trees I've ever seen to get there. And then there's all the rugged ice and rocks up top."

"I read online that a member of Landry's crew fell from the summit a couple of years ago and had to be medevaced off the mountain."

"I was the pilot who picked him up and brought him here." Tom pushed back from the table and finished his iced tea.

"So you know the risks. Anyway, I submitted a proposal to NASA to observe this team and explained how the findings could apply to crews in space or even the military."

"Sounds important."

"They agreed and followed up with a budget to cover my salary and expenses for three months."

"I hope you know what you're getting into. That glacier with all its crevasses—"

"Yeah, that's what I hear. Dr. Rollins at UW said he'd have Landry give me some basic mountaineering training. Still, I have to admit I'm a little nervous."

When Tom reached for the check, Grant beat him to it. "It's on me. This will be the last time I eat out for months." He stood and threw some cash on the table to cover their lunch and tip.

They drove back to the airport in silence. As he thought about the upcoming flight, Grant's palms got clammy.

Tom helped him snug up the four-point restraint harness before climbing into the front seat. As the engine growled and the plane's wheels left the asphalt, he gripped the back of Tom's seat so hard his knuckles turned white. "This is for you, Megan," he whispered.

10

Blue Glacier
Olympic National Park

Wednesday, June 10

Grant's mouth dropped in awe as the small plane flew over the forests and rivers of Olympic National Park. When they reached the rain forest, he could make out individual trees, which gave way to brilliant white peaks and valleys. The metallic blue Pacific Ocean stretched out to the west. Behind them to the north, he saw the Strait of Juan de Fuca, dotted with small islands.

It was spectacular, but Grant felt queasy the whole trip. What was he thinking when he ordered that large burger for lunch?

As the plane slid to a stop, Tom said, "The Snow Dome is mostly free of the crevasses that exist almost everywhere else on the glacier. It's a natural landing strip."

Waiting for Tom to unload his gear, Grant felt small and vulnerable standing next to the plane. They weren't that far from civilization, yet this place had nothing but mountains and valleys covered with snow and protruding rocks in every direction—no evidence of life any-where. The intense sunlight reflecting off the snow hurt his eyes, and he dug into his daypack for the goggles he'd just bought. Though he had expected the temperature to be in the mid-forties, it seemed much warmer than that—in fact, he was almost too hot in his new parka.

When Tom was ready to leave, he shook Grant's hand. "I wish you luck. You're a braver man than me, and I'm a bush pilot."

If only he felt as brave as Tom seemed to think.

Grant turned toward the station he had seen as they flew in and saw a distant figure in shirtsleeves climbing the side of the Snow Dome. As the person got closer, he saw a young woman with short hair and long legs marching toward him with a determined stride. Three people followed behind her, appearing to scramble to keep up.

The woman held out her hand. "Welcome to the Blue Glacier, Dr. Poole," she said. "I'm Dr. Kate Landry, head of the project team. We go by first names here, so call me Kate."

Her flat voice made him doubt the sincerity of her greeting. "Good to meet you, Kate. You can call me Grant. I'm sorry I'm late. Our flight was delayed by the fog."

"So I heard. This is Frank, our veteran. He's using our research for his dissertation." Kate waved a hand toward a man slightly taller but half-again wider than Grant. "And this is Charlie, here to develop an electronic year-round monitoring system." She pointed at a sandy-haired kid who looked barely out of high school. "And Alice, who's using the changes in the variation of color and light to help determine the state of the glacier." Kate put a hand on the pixie girl's shoulder, protective yet proud.

"Glad to meet all of you," Grant said. "I'm looking forward to learning more about your work."

In contrast to Kate's icy demeanor, Charlie and Alice greeted him with warm smiles. Frank stood apart, tucking his T-shirt into his jeans.

"How come you picked us to study?" Charlie asked.

Grant smiled. "Because you guys are in the middle of nowhere."

They all headed for the research station, with the students lined up alongside Grant and Kate a couple of strides behind.

"Do you have mountaineering experience?" Frank asked.

"Not really. Just hiking in the woods."

"You're going to have to learn fast. This place can kill you if you're not careful."

Just what Grant needed to hear. "Maybe you can show me how to be safe."

"I suppose." Frank pointed to Grant's lime-green parka. "I've never seen one that color before. You'll really stand out here on the snow."

"You think? I was told it's the latest fashion by the salesman in Santa Cruz." He caught Frank sneering and looking back at Kate. What was up with this guy?

Just then the tiny ski plane accelerated past them, the roar of the engine echoing off the surrounding mountains, and disappeared from view. After it flew off the north side of the Snow Dome, it reappeared seconds later flying toward Port Angeles.

"So let me get this straight," Grant said as Charlie opened the door into the station. "We have electricity and Internet but no indoor plumbing?"

"Yep," he said.

"If you don't have plumbing, where do you get water for drinking, washing the dishes, and bathing?"

"We melt snow." Charlie pointed to the pot on the stove. "To wash up, we use a basin and washcloth."

"Like we're camping out."

"Basically, yeah."

Primitive—a typical university budget.

Charlie walked over to a lower bunk. "You can throw your things here. I'll sleep on an air mattress on the floor."

Alice joined Charlie and Grant. "I thought this place was cozy when I first saw it, but now I'd call it cramped. We don't have much privacy—just strip to our underwear before crawling into our sleeping bags. I guess we'll know each other well before the summer's over."

What had he gotten himself into?

After sliding his duffel under his bunk, he stood and faced the two younger students, Kate and Frank still outside. "Maybe you could show me how you plan to study the glacier. I'd like to learn what you do."

Charlie grinned, and Grant couldn't help notice his chipped tooth. "Sure. Come over here, and I'll show you on my laptop." He led Grant to the desk where they slid their two chairs to face his computer.

"I collected this data on ice depth two days ago on the Snow Dome." He pointed to the bands of color indicating thickness and density of ice.

"That's dramatic. Did you use some kind of radar?"

"Nope. I designed and built this acoustic sounding system myself. It uses small explosives, so the sound travels to bedrock and back."

"Well, that's creative." He looked over his shoulder at Alice. "What kind of research are you doing?"

She brought over her laptop and pulled up a photo. "This is the Lower Glacier, the first in a series of shots I'll take every week. See the straight black line of the lateral moraine on the far side of the glacier? That shows the extent of the ice at its peak and how much it has retreated over the years due to climate change."

"So you think the glacier will eventually melt away?"

"Yes, it could happen in our lifetime."

"Seriously?"

"Afraid so. Now notice the line separating the blue ice and the white overlying snow cover."

"Yes. It's quite distinct."

"That line will move to the right up the glacier as more blue ice is exposed. The darker blue ice will absorb more of the sun's energy and lead to more melting. I'll correlate that with Frank's measurements of the water volume flowing down Glacier Creek at the tip of the glacier to determine the rate of melting."

"Alice, this is stunning."

"Think so?" Her eyes sparkled.

"I'm looking forward to observing both of you collect data."

Grant started to relax, picking up on the enthusiasm of these two young students. His outlook had improved already.

Kate entered the room, followed by Frank, and she shooed Alice and Charlie away from Grant. "Okay, everybody back to work."

She asked Grant to get the ice ax he was told to bring and join her outside. They stood on the rough rock surface, a tiny island in a sea of snow.

"First of all," Kate said, her hands on her hips, "how do you plan to do your observations?"

"What do you mean?" He raised a hand to shield his face from the bright sun.

"Are you going to follow us around every day?"

"Yes, I want to see as much daily activity and interaction as I can."

"I need to set some boundaries." She practically spit out the words.

"Like what?"

"For starters, I don't want you to interfere with our work. That means staying out of our discussions."

Grant crossed his arms and studied the rocks at his feet.

"Also, I don't want you to slow us down. We walk fast from one place to another to collect data. And we need downtime at night when we can relax and know you aren't gawking at us."

He looked up to see Kate's lips pursed with anger—or was it disgust?

"When we're not under your microscope, you can join in our conversations."

She didn't want him there, it was clear, but she also apparently didn't know the first rule of behavioral science: to avoid influencing the subjects so they would act as naturally as possible.

"Sure, I agree," he said. Her ground rules to minimize interactions fit his protocol anyway.

"Good . . . okay." Her shoulders relaxed. She seemed surprised he hadn't fought her. "Since you don't have any mountaineering experience, you'll need to learn how to self-arrest with an ice ax."

"I have no idea what that is, so you'll have to show me."

She guided him off the rocks toward the flat snow at the base of the Snow Dome, describing how it worked as they walked. "The pick is the business end for stopping yourself."

After demonstrating how to hold the ax, Kate climbed about fifty yards up the slope while he waited at the bottom. Holding the ice ax diagonally across her chest, she dropped face first. The pick and her toes dug into the snow and quickly stopped her downward slide. Then she asked Grant to do it.

Once he put enough weight on the pick and his boots to stop, Kate said, "Now for the fun stuff."

He stared at her. "You mean that wasn't fun?"

"No. I want you to picture this. You're walking on a steep, snowy slope, with a large crevasse looming below you. You lose your balance and fall backward, sliding upside down, head first on your back, toward the crevasse and sure death. What do you do?"

"Avoid being in that situation." Grant chuckled.

"No, I'm serious. Most of the time we'll be roped together, and if we're to trust you won't fall and take us to our deaths, you have to practice until you can stop yourself."

He and Kate climbed up the side of the hill again as the late afternoon shadows lengthened on the north side of the Snow Dome.

"You want me to slide down that hill upside down *and* backward?"

"Yes." The slope below them looked even steeper than before. He started fantasizing about hitching a ride on the first plane off the mountain. "Okay, he said, "here we go," and flopped onto his back with a thud.

He rocketed down the hill, struggling to maneuver his feet. By the time he managed to point them downward, he was at the bottom, still on his back—he never did use the ice ax to slow himself down.

Standing, he brushed off the snow and climbed up the hill. Was Kate smirking? He could swear she enjoyed watching his awkward efforts. But, damn it, he had come to observe her team, not to climb Mount Everest.

On the second try, he brought both his legs up at once, thinking he could do a half somersault to get them pointing down faster, but the world spun as he flipped, end over end. He landed with a thud on his stomach, knocking the wind out of him, but at least he'd made it onto his belly.

"Good work, Grant. You're getting it."

Hearing the approval in her voice, he decided on the third try he'd master it and scrambled with renewed energy up the side of the hill. This time, though, he threw himself backward with too much force and hit his head on the dense snow. Somehow, he stopped his downward slide before reaching the bottom of the slope.

He sat up with a groan and rubbed his head. "Damn, that hurt."

"Okay, that's good." Kate walked down to him and put out her hand to help him to his feet. "Now we can explore the glacier without worrying about you pulling us off the mountain."

"Thank God," he muttered under his breath.

They hiked back to the research station in silence. As Kate reached for the doorknob, she said, "You showed you could learn some mountaineering back there."

"You think so? I admit I was a little nervous."

"Ah, you did great."

Maybe his first chilly impression of her had been wrong.

"I have to take care of some business inside." She opened the door but blocked the entrance and pointed to a steep mountain behind the station. "Why don't you climb up Panic Peak? You need the conditioning, and the view from the top is worth it. Just be careful—you're still learning to self-arrest."

Staring in disbelief at the summit, Grant gulped with fear. Regardless of what Kate had said, in his mind he had just flunked his basic ice-ax arrest training. Was she trying to kill him? Even though the peak seemed close, a steep, narrow incline led to the summit, and it dropped off sharply on both sides.

Grant's boots slid a little with each baby step he took in the dense snow. Panic Peak was the perfect name. Fighting an impulse to retreat, he kept his eyes straight ahead, not daring to look sideways for fear of losing his balance. When he mustered the courage to glance to the east, he saw nothing between where he was headed and the blue ice of the glacier far below. Nearby to the west was a drop-off to another glacier.

His heart thumping wildly, he stopped to suck in a chestful of thin air and consider what to do. Just two ways to go—keep inching up or go back the way he came. He was determined not to give in to fear, so he continued on and finally reached the top, where he peered tentatively straight down to the Hoh River, thousands of feet below. Even at this distance, he could hear the steady sound of rushing water.

How terrifying to be this high—but thrilling too. And he had been so close to chickening out.

On his way down the narrow band of snow, the sole of Grant's boot slipped on a patch of ice, and he landed on his stomach, skidding head first, snow up his nose and in his mouth. My God, he was headed off the cliff!

He plunged the point of his ax into the snow, threw his legs in an arc downward, and dug in his toes, stopping just short of the edge. He made it.

Shaking with relief but smiling, he lay on his stomach in the snow to catch his breath before making his way back to the station.

Kate and her students were gathered inside, seated at the table. When everyone avoided eye contact, he knew they'd been talking about him.

"That's a fantastic view from the top of Panic Peak."

"I thought you'd like it," Kate said offhandedly, passing a piece of paper to Alice.

She didn't ask how the climb went or anything that most people would say to acknowledge how challenging it must have been.

That evening Grant's arms and back were sore. What a long, exhausting day. Kate's on-again-off-again hostility troubled him, and the students' stealthy glances told him they were up to something.

After dinner, needing some time to think, he excused himself and walked cautiously to the rock outcrop west of the station, where he could see all the way to the Pacific Ocean. The last salmon rays of sunlight touched the horizon as he took in the stark landscape.

Within minutes, the purples, blues, and reds reflecting off the snow deepened and spread into a blazing sea of color unlike anything he had ever seen. His breath caught in his throat. Back home in Santa Cruz, he had watched many beautiful sunsets, but none of them came close to this.

He wasn't a religious man, wouldn't even consider himself spiritual, but the sight of all that beauty after such a stressful day nearly made him weep.

If only Megan were there to see it.

Alice and Charlie said the glacier would disappear completely in a few decades. He couldn't fathom it.

There was no sound, no wildlife—the wind had no leaves to rustle or branches to whistle through. It was so quiet that soon he noticed the subtle, repetitive whoosh of his own heartbeat. The uninterrupted stillness made him feel more alone than ever. Despite the magnificent display before him, his gut started churning, telling him he'd left his comfort zone, probably for the next three months. But he had sought out adventure, right?

11

Blue Glacier
Olympic National Park

Thursday, June 11

The next morning Grant woke up disoriented, feeling like he was stuffed in a large shoebox. Slowly he remembered he was in his bunk in the niche below Frank's, next to Charlie on his air mattress.

He fought to pull his pants on over his underwear while lying on his back in the sleeping bag. As he swung his legs around to stand, he kicked Charlie and had to grab Frank's bunk to keep from stumbling.

"Oh crap," Grant said under his breath. "So sorry."

Charlie rolled over to face him. "Hmm?" he muttered.

"Alice was right. This place is crowded."

Kate, working at the desk, rose and approached him, her finger on her lips. "Shhh," she whispered, shaking her head.

"Sorry," he blurted out like an idiot.

Alice uncovered her head from the sleeping bag. "Could you please be quiet? Some of us are trying to sleep."

"No shit," came from Frank's bulky form.

"Sorry," Grant said for the third time.

"Jeez, I feel like a counselor at summer camp," Kate said, no longer whispering.

She returned to her reading, and Grant took a seat next to her. She ignored him. Opening his laptop, he tried to focus on refining his observation protocol.

Perfect. The day couldn't have gotten off to a worse start.

—————

After breakfast, Frank, Alice, and Charlie headed out the door with ropes and ice axes, leaving Grant and Kate alone in the station.

"I expected to start my team observations today," he said.

"Frank's working with Charlie and Alice to get them prepared for their research."

"That's important for me to observe."

"I'm sure you wouldn't find it interesting."

"I need to be the judge of that."

Kate was definitely hiding something. First, she delayed his arrival, and now she was being deliberately vague about what her team was doing.

"Listen, Grant. You can observe Frank and me doing fieldwork tomorrow and Charlie and Alice on Saturday. But you could use more orientation, so today I thought we'd go to Athena's Owl."

"Where's that?"

"It's a rock outcrop a couple of miles south of here. She rubbed sunscreen over her freckled face and offered him the bottle. "Here, you'll need this. You're still pink from yesterday."

They headed outside, roped up, and started climbing the Snow Dome. Although he was in decent shape, he struggled to keep up with her.

They hiked south to a rocky ridge at the top of the Snow Dome, where they stopped and looked down.

"Here's a clear view of the Lower Blue Glacier about a thousand feet below us."

"It's beautiful. I can see the line between the blue ice and the white snow that Alice showed me."

"It's also upsetting. See how much bare rock is exposed at the tip? That's all due to rising temperatures."

He scanned the valley below. "Have you seen a big difference over the years?"

"Yes, it's dramatic. The ice depth is less, and the tip pulls back more every year."

"When Alice and Charlie told me this would all be gone within the next fifty years, I couldn't believe it."

"That's a big part of the problem. Unless people are directly and immediately affected, they can't wrap their heads around global warming. Up here, we're on the front lines."

Of course, he knew about the controversies and had read about the weather changes around the world, experiencing them himself. But to see the impact in this pristine setting through Kate's eyes made him realize just how real and alarming it was.

They turned and climbed up into the basin between the summit of Mount Olympus and the East Peak, then came to a stop. "This is called the Cirque," Kate said, stretching out her arms. "Alice and Charlie will be coming here tomorrow to measure the ice depth."

They kept hiking across the relatively flat basin, skirting around a couple of massive crevasses while dragging the climbing rope between them. At the top of a long, steep slope of snow, she pointed ahead. "We're going to untie from the rope and glissade down to the base of Athena's Owl."

Grant swallowed hard. "What do you mean 'glissade down'?"

"You know how to ski, right? Well, when you glissade, it's like skiing, but without any skis."

"Actually, I've never skied."

Her eyebrows shot up. "Really?"

"I'm more of a summer hiker," he said as breezily as he could, too embarrassed to admit he'd been afraid to try.

"Okay, I'll show you." Kate jumped onto the top of the slope. Standing with her knees bent and feet together, she held the ax with both hands on her left side and leaned against it. When she pushed off, she pointed her feet first left, then right while moving swiftly down the steep, snowy slope.

From the bottom, she looked up and shouted, "Your turn."

Telling himself he could do it, he began picking up speed down the slope. About halfway down, his feet hit a patch of hard, frozen ice.

"Hop over that crust," she called out.

But Grant's feet had stopped sliding as his toes dug into the rough surface, sending his upper body head first down the hill.

"Ice ax!" Kate yelled from below. He had clung to his ax and now dragged it across his chest into the self-arrest position he had practiced. Rather than shooting past Kate down the side of Mount Olympus onto the rock outcrop below, he came to a stop at her feet.

She clapped. "Great work!"

"Well, that was really fun—until it wasn't."

He rose slowly to his feet, and she guided them toward a steep spire of tan-colored rock on the side of another snow-covered mountain.

As they stopped to take in the scene, Kate said, "That peak is called Athena, and the outcrop is our destination, Athena's Owl. The two horn-like protrusions make it look like a large owl. We better rope back up so I can help you climb."

She took the lead, and within minutes, they were sitting next to each other at the top.

"The ridges and mountains look like frozen ocean waves," he said. After taking in the scenery for several minutes, he shifted his gaze to the attractive woman sitting next to him.

She turned to him. "What?"

"Nothing." He smiled and looked back at the snow-covered peaks. She was a puzzle—strong and full of knowledge, but so defended personally. Maybe with time he might get her to open up a little. He'd like that.

She reached into her backpack and pulled out an apple and pocketknife. He grabbed the peanut butter sandwich he threw together before they left.

"Would you like some?" she asked, handing him a slice.

"Gee, thanks." He searched her face. Maybe it was a peace offering.

Soon they climbed off the outcrop and back up the side of Mount Olympus. It took them considerably longer to slog up the slope than the few minutes to glissade down. Grant's chest ached from the exertion, and sweat trickled down his face. Eventually, Kate steered them to the side of the Cirque below the rocky pass leading to the Snow Dome.

At their feet was an unusual patch of light-pink snow. "What's this?" he asked.

"Smell it."

He bent over and scooped up a handful. "Hey, this smells like watermelon."

Kate laughed. "Because it's watermelon snow."

"Watermelon snow?"

"It's actually algae that forms in snow banks exposed to ultraviolet sunlight, primarily in harsh environments—that's why most people don't know about it. You can often find it high in the mountains on snow patches in the Rockies and here in the Olympics—even on Arctic ice."

"What does it taste like?"

"Try it."

Grant took a mouthful. "Mmm, it even tastes like watermelon."

"What?" Her head jerked back in surprise. "Never tasted like anything before." She scooped up a mouthful. "Just snow—no flavor at all."

He grinned. "Ha. Made you eat some too."

Kate shot him a dirty look, then slowly smiled. "Yeah, yeah, you got me."

She turned to resume walking when her watch started beeping. Grant checked his—it was 3:00. "What's the alarm for?"

"Frank and I arranged to check in on the radio." She unclipped the small black transceiver fastened to her waist. "Blue Glacier base, this is Kate."

"Frank here, we're all back in the station—mission accomplished."

"Good. Grant and I are in the Cirque about to head back."

"Well, not all good. We have a problem."

"What's wrong?" Kate asked, her voice filled with concern.

"Alice freaked out in the tunnel. Charlie and I managed to get her out, but she's still really upset. I don't know what to do."

Grant moved closer. "You have to calm her down. Slow her heart rate."

"Frank, what's she doing? Where is she?" Kate asked.

"She can't sit still—keeps pacing around the station, hugging herself—and says she just wants to go home. At one point, she said her chest hurt like she was having a heart attack."

"That sounds serious, Kate," Grant said. "We need to quiet her. Do you have any sedatives?"

She didn't respond to him, but pushed the transmit button. "Frank, look in our first-aid kit. You'll find a bottle of Benadryl—it's a sedative as well as a decongestant. Have Alice take a spoonful. And get her to lie down."

"Copy that. When will you be back?"

"In about thirty minutes. How's Charlie?"

"Not so good either. He caught a cold—he's been sneezing and coughing all afternoon. And he says he has a sore throat."

"Give him some Benadryl too. We'll be there shortly. Kate out."

The silence hung awkwardly in the air.

"What was that about with Alice?" he asked.

Kate closed her eyes and took a deep breath as though she were counting to ten. She finally faced him. "It doesn't concern you."

"I've had clinical training. Let me help. What do you think triggered the panic attack?"

"Thanks for the offer, Grant, but I can handle this." She started marching up the rocky pass leading from the Cirque to the top of the Snow Dome.

"What are you hiding, Kate?" he yelled after her. "You're stuck with me. You have to trust me."

She came to a halt and looked down at him. "No, I don't have to trust you," she yelled. "Your grant from NASA entitles you to what I say it does and no more." She stormed ahead until the hundred feet of rope between them went taut.

He had little choice but to trudge behind in silence, wrestling the whole time with what to say to her when they reached the station. He didn't want to blurt out something he'd later regret.

Frank was waiting for them on the rocks.

"How's Alice?" Kate asked.

"She's been asleep for the past ten minutes or so," he said, his voice low. "I'm glad you're back. It was tough for a while."

"I don't want her going back there." Kate nodded to the west.

"Frank, what happened?" Grant looked over her head, making eye contact with Frank.

"Grant, please go on inside," Kate said. "I need to talk with Frank privately."

He detached his end of the rope and stomped past the two of them, muttering, "What is going on here?" When he entered the living quarters, he saw that both students were asleep—Alice in her upper bunk and Charlie on his air mattress, making rasping sounds as he breathed.

He sat in a desk chair quietly fuming. Why did Kate refuse to let him help?

Before him lay one of Alice's photos of the pink bands on the lower glacier, reminding him of the watermelon snow. Opening his laptop, he searched for the term and clicked on a link. Uh-oh—a teaspoon of this snow contained about a million cells, and they recommended not eating any—it caused diarrhea. Wonderful. He squirmed and smiled wryly to himself—too late now.

When Kate and Frank came in, they gave him a cursory nod but said nothing, then got busy coiling ropes, stowing their climbing gear, and greasing their boots. The three of them fixed their own meager dinners of sandwiches and chips. When he attempted to talk to either one of them, he got only one-word answers.

Grant finally gave up and stepped over Charlie and went to bed. Staring up at the top bunk, he felt a mixture of anger and confusion. How could he do his job under these conditions? Right now, he couldn't count on Kate to allow him to observe any of them. He'd like to think she was professional and reasonable enough to keep her word, but she had been so unpredictable.

And what the hell was in that tunnel?

12

Blue Glacier
Olympic National Park

Friday, June 12

There was no denying that Charlie was getting worse. At the breakfast table the next morning, the poor guy kept coughing, nearly choking at times. He was making a valiant effort to rally, but Grant knew he was struggling. His eyes had the redness and glassy look of someone with a fever. He needed to stay in bed.

As for Alice, though calm, she was certainly not the bubbly woman he had met two days before. What a rocky beginning for them both.

Kate talked about the day ahead, and while not throwing any camaraderie his way, she at least included him in the conversation. "So that's it for our plans today. Grant will observe Frank and me on the Snow Dome, and Charlie and Alice will collect ice-depth data in the Cirque."

As volatile as she could be, Kate was a woman of her word after all.

They all gathered their backpacks and equipment and met at the base of the Snow Dome. As they roped up, Charlie doubled over in a violent fit of coughing.

Kate went over to him. "Charlie, c'mon, you're way too sick to work."

"I'll be okay," he croaked.

"You sound terrible." Alice reached up to put a hand on his shoulder.

"I'm good." He blew his nose. "Besides, we have to collect the ice-depth data in the Cirque so I can begin work on my year-round monitoring system."

Kate studied him as they stood huddled in the snow. "Don't push it. No more than a couple of hours."

Frank and Kate teamed up for the traverse to the top of the large icefall between the Upper and Lower Glaciers to check out Frank's equipment they'd installed on Monday. Grant hiked close behind observing their interactions, starting to feel more comfortable on the terrain.

As they approached the edge of a large open crevasse above the icefall, Frank yelled out "Oh no, my strain gauge!" and ran ahead.

Kate scurried alongside him and gasped. A ten-foot-long, three-sided aluminum tower teetered precariously on the snow, one end sloping into the opening.

Frank looked around frantically. "We have to grab it before it's swallowed up."

Kate threw down her backpack. "The crevasse has opened a lot in just the last few days. Let's move, or we'll lose the instruments and your ice flow data."

Grant stood by her to help but had no idea how.

"Anchor me with a good belay," Frank called to Kate. He pulled a short coil of rope from his backpack. "I'll see what I can do."

Kate drove the shaft of her ax into the snow until only the head was exposed. She wrapped the climbing rope around the shaft and knelt, one knee holding down the head of the ax against the pull of Frank's weight as he crawled on his hands and knees to the gauge dangling over the crevasse.

"Grant!" she barked at him. "Don't just stand there—lean on my back. I need more weight to anchor him."

He leaped over and pressed against Kate's back, his arms awkwardly wrapped around her for balance. Meanwhile Frank tied a nylon cord around the instrument package, still fastened to the tower, and inched backward, away from the far end of the structure.

Within seconds, the ice supporting the end of the tower gave way.

"Ahhh!" Frank shouted as he fell from sight over the lip of the crevasse, jerking the climbing rope taut.

"Oh my God," Grant whispered. He tightened his arms around her, as if his strength could help Frank hang on.

"I'll maneuver sideways to the tower," Frank yelled. "It's wedged at a near-vertical angle." Silence stretched forever before his muffled voice reached them again from the opening. "It's too unstable to support my weight. We could lose everything."

"You're going to have to climb up," Kate shouted, so close it made Grant's ears ring.

"Can't do it . . . rope's dug in at the top."

Kate's fingers turned white from grasping the rope. "Hold on, Frank. We'll get you some ascender handles." She turned her head. "Grant, dig through my backpack. Feel for a pair of metal handles with loops of braid attached. Hurry!"

How would she hold Frank's weight without him? He needed to trust her. Letting go of her, he raced over to her backpack and rummaged through it. "Found them." He yanked out the handles and held them above his head.

"Lower them to Frank using a piece of nylon line from my pack." Kate, gritting her teeth, strained to get the words out while keeping the ax in place.

Grant had only one chance. He knelt at the edge and felt the soft snow give way below his knee. His heart jumped to his throat. Another half inch and he would have plunged over the lip.

"Come on, Grant." Kate's plea propelled him to action. He backed away to where the snow supported his weight.

Lowering the handles, he saw Frank's body suspended in midair and the yawning blue-black crack in the ice extending down to oblivion. The "jaws of death"—a cold, solitary way to die if either of them fell.

Frank fastened the handles to the climbing rope. One held his weight as he put his boot in the loop and then slid the second handle up the rope as high as he could. He alternated from one loop and handle to the other, climbing to just below the rim.

"Lie on your stomach, Grant," Kate yelled. "Reach for Frank's hand to help him over the lip."

Grant swiveled his body around and grabbed Frank's gloved hand. An image of the glove slipping out of his grasp made him reach down with his other arm and pull up with strength he didn't know he had—Frank outweighed him by fifty pounds. Once Frank rolled up over the edge, they both lay motionless on their backs in the snow, breathing heavily.

Frank turned to Grant. "I owe you one."

"Not really. Kate told me what to do."

"Well done, Grant," Kate said, approaching them.

He sat up. "Science here is a lot different from my lab in Santa Cruz."

"And more exciting, I bet," Kate said, and all three laughed.

While she and Frank pulled up the tower and strain gauge and repositioned them across the crevasse in a more stable spot, Grant recorded their actions on his tablet—a relief to be doing his job.

Megan's face flashed before him. He had saved Frank, and he could have saved her—he knew that now. But that just made him feel worse.

As he worked, small explosions echoed off the row of peaks along the east side of the Lower Glacier.

"Sounds like Charlie is busy," Kate said. "I hope he's okay. I'm eager to know the ice depth. It was about eighty-five meters thick last year, about the same as the Snow Dome. Based on recent trends, I predict it's at least a meter thinner this year."

By the time Grant returned to the station with Kate and Frank, it was mid-afternoon, and Charlie and Alice had already come back from the Cirque. Both of them leaned against the wall at the table, their eyes closed.

Charlie convulsed in a rumbling cough. Grant felt his forehead. "You're really hot."

"Let me take your temperature." Kate retrieved the first-aid kit from the entry room and took out a plastic thermometer. "We've never had to use this before." She inserted the tip into a disposable cover and placed it under Charlie's tongue. He struggled to keep it in place between coughs.

When the thermometer beeped, she read the display. "Oh, Charlie. It's 103.1."

"I'm so sorry . . . Kate," he choked out the words. "I feel like crap . . . You were right . . . I should have stayed here this morning."

Hunkered down in her parka, Alice said, "I've got chills, and my throat is sore too." She followed her announcement with a coughing fit.

She had the same glassy look Charlie had. Kate took her temperature—101.5—gave them both some ibuprofen, and sent them to bed, then motioned to Grant and Frank to head outside.

"I'm really worried about those two," she said. "I need to call Tom right away to see if he can fly Charlie to the hospital in Port Angeles. And he might have to take Alice too. But we have—"

Frank cut her off, pacing nervously. "Now that Alice has his cold or flu, or whatever it is, I'm not comfortable sleeping so close to them—though we're probably all infected at this point."

"I'm not comfortable either," Kate said. "The three of us can sleep in the entry with the door closed. But listen, we have another problem on our hands. I just checked the weather—an intense storm is heading up the coast toward us, expected to hit in the afternoon. I sure hope Tom can fly up first thing in the morning."

13

Blue Glacier
Olympic National Park

Friday, June 12

Standing on the rocks, Grant overheard Kate through the open door talking to Tom on the radio. "Evacuate Charlie . . . having trouble breathing . . . fly first thing? . . . I can't thank you enough . . ." After ending the call, she spoke with Frank in hushed tones, but Grant couldn't make out any of it. He was just about to go inside when Kate joined him, a deep frown on her face.

"I've made a decision I hope I won't regret." She took a deep breath. "I need your support to complete our research agenda this year. We're losing Charlie, at least for a while, and probably Alice. Our funding is already under threat, and unless we show some big results, they'll shut us down."

"What can I do?" Maybe she would finally tell him what everyone had worked so hard to hide.

"I want to show you something we've discovered in the tunnel. We think we know what it is, but we're not sure yet. It could be huge, and I need to be able to explore it more openly. But here's the thing. I want our team to get full credit for it, and we're not prepared yet for public disclosure. Are you willing to comply with that?"

"Of course, you can count on me."

She eyed him closely and tilted her head slightly, as if she wasn't sure he was telling the truth. "Unfortunately, some people have had their contributions stolen."

"Your secret is safe with me. What do you think you've found?"

"I'll let you see for yourself. I'm curious what you think."

Asking for his opinion? That was a switch.

"It's getting late," she said, "but we need to go before the storm hits tomorrow. Alice is wrapped in a blanket drinking hot tea, and Charlie's asleep. Now is a good time to go."

Grant, Kate, and Frank roped up and put on crampons to cross the ice face. Frank looked upset, his face dark with anger. When Kate talked to him, he refused to answer. This was the first sign of trouble Grant had seen between the two of them.

When they set out, the sun hung low in the sky below long bands of high cirrus clouds, the precursor to the storm. The entire ice face glowed orange, highlighting little irregularities in the surface in alternating shadow and sunlight.

Even with the spiked crampons, Grant felt wobbly on the thin ledge. The sheer ice drop-off below led to a narrow chute, what Kate had called the West Couloir. Beyond that lay nothing but air.

At one point, his foot slipped. "Shit!" He grabbed at the ice next to him, adrenaline shooting through him. His ax dangled precariously from the safety loop he'd put around his wrist. For sure, he'd slide over the edge this time.

"Grant, put your weight squarely over your feet," Kate called back to him. "The crampons will hold you."

His skin prickling with fear, he followed her instructions and continued creeping across the ice face. "Man, this surprise better be worth it."

He finally reached the tunnel entrance and took a deep breath before following Kate inside, Frank close behind.

"Headlamps," Kate said.

Grant could make out the sheen on the surface where the ice contacted the warmer air, but their combined lights didn't penetrate the darkness ahead. Their muted voices echoed back at them, triggering his chest to tighten, and he swallowed to squelch the rising panic. One foot in front of the other. He forced his legs to carry him forward as they made their way down the tight passageway.

"He didn't earn the right, Kate," Frank said from behind.

She glanced over her shoulder. "Take it easy. This was my call."

"He'd better not tell anyone," he shot back.

Stopping, Grant turned so his and Frank's headlamps seared into each other's faces. "I told Kate that I'd respect your damn secret. So back off."

Frank, his fists raised, lunged at Grant as if he were about to punch him.

"Stop it, you two," Kate yelled. "Let's just get this over with before it's too dark to see going back."

After they had gone about twenty-five yards, she stopped in front of what appeared to be a shelf of solid ice with a narrow opening above. "This is the hard part. You'll have to slide on your stomach across this ice to the open tunnel on the other side."

"Are you serious?" Grant stepped closer to peer into the tiny space. "I don't like this. No wonder Alice had a panic attack. I'm almost there myself. You're sure it's safe?"

"No. This slab has already fallen, but we think it's reasonably stable after the winter freeze."

Grant hesitated and looked down the opening once more. "All right, I'll go."

Kate led, putting her arms out in front of her and slithering through the gap. Climbing up and into the small hole behind her, Grant struggled to move ahead, wiggling his shoulders and hips as they pressed against the ice on both sides. At one point, he didn't appear to be moving at all, convinced he was stuck. But then he could see Kate's headlamp getting closer, and he dropped to the floor of the tunnel in a heap.

He rose slowly to his feet. They'd never escape in time if anything happened. This was nuts. His chest tightened even more.

At the end, only a few more yards from the ice slab, Kate stopped and pointed to something in the ice.

Then he saw it—reddish-brown hair and a trunk protruding from the surface. Grant's concern about the tunnel evaporated in a gasp.

"What is that thing?" He lifted his hand as if to touch it. "It looks like an elephant's trunk, but hairy. It's not a—?"

Kate nodded. "A woolly mammoth. That's what we think, anyway."

"It's . . . it's . . . it's incredible," Grant stammered.

"We were as surprised as you."

Frank joined them. "Grant, you have no idea how rare this is. Other mammoths have been found frozen in the soil, but never embedded in clear ice like this."

"So what happens next?" Grant asked Kate.

"Verification. Yesterday the students chipped enough ice to get tissue samples. We're planning our next steps."

"I bet this will get a lot of people excited."

"Yes, but for now, this stays among us."

"You're in an elite group." Frank's sarcasm was unmistakable.

Kate turned and nudged Grant back toward the entrance. "Let's head back while we can still see."

Near the mouth of the tunnel, he heard a deep rumble. "Christ, what's that noise?" As he rushed ahead to the opening, the other two stopped to listen.

"That's just the normal slow movement of the ice," Frank said. "If that had been a sharp crack, we would have beaten you to the entrance."

"Whatever it is, I'm not comfortable standing under all this ice." His voice rose in pitch.

In spite of the afterglow of dusk in the sky, it was too dark to see clearly across the ice face without their headlamps. Kate's light bobbed as she worked her way along the ledge in front of Grant.

His leg muscles turned to rubber when he thought about the hazardous traverse he would have to repeat—this time with little light. After taking a couple of steps on the narrow path, he froze, aware of the steep drop-off to the icy chute below. But he didn't dare try to go back.

Kate had arrived at the gently sloping snow below the station and turned to watch his progress.

"Grant, keep going," she shouted.

"I'm not sure I can do this." His legs began to shake.

"You're roped in. We won't let you fall." Frank's voice came from several feet behind him.

His encouragement helped Grant get moving again. Within minutes, he stood beside Kate on the smooth snow, his breathing slowing to normal, watching Frank's approaching headlamp.

As the three of them neared the station, Grant grabbed Kate's arm. "Can we talk?" Frank gave him a sideways glance and continued inside.

"Can this wait? I need to check on—"

"Why wasn't I briefed about your discovery before I got here?"

"We waited until you arrived to reduce the risk of disclosure. And we wanted to verify what we had first." She turned to go into the station, but he blocked her path.

"But, Kate, none of you are trained paleontologists. You have no experience documenting something like this."

"That's obvious, Grant."

"More important, you're risking your whole team by entering a tunnel that's already begun to collapse."

"Oh boy, you're on thin ice here!" Kate said, raising her voice. "Science isn't always clean—you should know that. Some hazards are justified." She leaned forward so her face was just inches from his.

He blinked and stepped back against the station door. "Kate, I'm only saying—"

"We need to deal with whatever nature throws at us—and you're not telling *me* how to run *my* project." She pointed her thumb at her chest. "You can leave tomorrow after Tom picks up Charlie if you want." She glanced over at the last hint of light in the western sky and back at him. "I know what I'm doing. Please take that observer role you talked about. Then maybe we can get through this summer, okay?"

"Look, a couple of hours ago, you wanted my opinion, and now I'm giving it to you." He shook his head. "I'll have to delay any preliminary reports to NASA on your work until you've gone public with the mammoth."

"Do whatever you have to as long as you don't disclose what we've found. Let's get inside before the students think something's wrong."

She reached around him for the door. "I thought I could trust you—I'm not so sure anymore."

While Kate checked on Charlie and Alice, Grant and Frank dragged their sleeping bags into the entry room, away from the sick students, and laid them out head to toe in the narrow space. Kate threw her air mattress and sleeping bag in line with Frank's and closed the door, her face tight with anger.

Well, she could just be mad. All he did was tell the truth. She'd simply have to get over it.

14

Blue Glacier
Olympic National Park

Saturday, June 13

Charlie and Alice coughed violently behind the closed door for most of the night. Kate dozed off but couldn't stay asleep and slipped out of the entry long before dawn. The winds rocked the station as she sat at the desk in the dark, a myriad of thoughts running through her head.

She was used to taking charge and fighting her way through everything, solving problems, grabbing what she wanted. That's what led to this rare Blue Glacier opportunity for her at such an early age, long before she had reached tenure.

But that approach wasn't going to magically cure her students right now. Somehow she felt responsible for what had happened—Charlie and Alice seemed so healthy and vibrant when they first arrived, and now they both had to go to the hospital. Their families depended on Kate to take care of them, and she'd let them down.

All she could do was get the young students the care they needed. Thank God for Tom.

But what if the rest of them got this horrific virus? What then?

She wouldn't think about that.

As for Grant, she hated involving him, but it was the right thing to do—besides, what choice did they have? They had worked too hard to walk away from this extraordinary discovery. She had to accept his help, as hard as that was for her.

It would probably surprise people to know that as much as she bulldozed her way through everything, she hated conflict. It left her worn out, second-guessing herself, jittery inside. Still, she had no intention of letting Grant take over.

The cables holding the station in place whistled as the gusts intensified. Kate opened her laptop to check the weather, and in the light of her screen, she could see Frank coming through the entry door.

"Couldn't sleep?" she whispered.

He shook his head and sat next to her.

"Look, Frank, about telling Grant—"

"Hey, forget it. You're right—we had to include him. And we can probably trust him. He seems like an okay guy."

She moved her laptop toward him. "This doesn't look good. It's a severe weather bulletin from the National Weather Service."

Grant joined them, still buckling his belt. "Boy, it's crazy out there. It feels like the wind is going to rip off the roof."

"And it's going to get worse," Frank said. "This area has had only a couple of storms with barometric pressures this low. One of them swept across the Olympic Peninsula with ninety-mile-an-hour winds and caused eight deaths. This storm may be worse due to record warming over the Pacific this year."

"What does this mean for Charlie's evacuation?" Grant leaned in for a closer look.

"It doesn't look promising," Kate said. "Last night the weather service predicted the storm wouldn't hit until afternoon, but this morning there are already sustained winds of thirty miles an hour in Port Angeles, gusting to forty-five. They're always stronger up here."

"And they're from the west," Frank said. "That will create a dangerous crosswind on the Snow Dome."

"Do you think Tom might have to cancel his flight?" Grant asked.

Kate nodded. "I'll call him on the radio right after sunup."

Grant pointed toward Charlie at the sound of his coughing. "How's he doing?"

"Not good. He's fighting to breathe . . ." The words caught in her throat. "And Alice is too. Tom should take them both—if he can get here."

"I thought his plane could handle only one passenger," Grant said.

"That Aviate Husky has plenty of power," Frank said. "And Alice doesn't weigh much. It'll be cramped, but Tom should be able to pull it off."

Kate stood up from the desk. "Let's check on them."

Turning on a battery-powered lantern, she knelt by Charlie's air mattress and gasped. "My God! His face is blue. He's suffocating!" Her stomach lurched.

Grant felt Charlie's forehead. "He feels even hotter than he did yesterday."

Kate gently touched Charlie's face with the back of her hand. "You're right."

Frank took the lantern and stood next to Alice's bunk. "Her lips are blue too."

"I'll take their temperatures again."

As Kate removed the thermometer from Alice's mouth, the young woman rose up on one elbow and began a spasm of deep, wet coughs, then collapsed onto her pillow, gasping. Frank jumped back and glanced at Kate, wide-eyed. "Alice is wheezing like Charlie did last night."

"I have more bad news," Kate said. "Charlie's temperature is now 104.2, and Alice's is up to 103."

Frank moved to a desk chair. "There must be something we can do for them." He typed on the laptop. "Okay, the blue lips are a symptom of 'cyanosis.' They both need oxygen—which we don't have." He stopped and raked his fingers through his hair. "Man, I'm beat. I got up way too early." He went over to the cooler for a bottle of water and returned to the desk.

"This site says to give them lots of fluids and ibuprofen for the fever and prop them up with pillows to help drain their airways. If their temperature reaches 103, you should call a doctor. At 106 or above, it can cause permanent neurological damage, so you should go to the ER."

"But what if there is no ER?" Kate asked. "What should we do?"

"In an emergency, you can lower the body temperature with cold compresses or ice."

"If their fevers get worse, we'll have to cover them with snow."

"The rest of these sites say the same thing . . . There isn't much more . . . we can . . . do . . . till. . . Tom . . ." His voice trailed off.

"What's wrong, Frank?" Kate asked, knowing the answer before he spoke.

"I feel so tired and weak, and my throat hurts. Hell, I'm getting sick too."

"Oh no, Frank. Why don't you lie down and rest until Tom comes? Use Grant's bunk."

Would this nightmare ever end? Right now, she had to focus on the two younger students. She replaced Alice's sweaty clothes with dry ones while Grant did the same for Charlie. For the next couple of hours, Kate and Grant used washcloths and water from a basin to cool the students' foreheads as best they could.

Near dawn, they both took a break and sat at the table. When Frank started coughing in his bunk, Kate dropped her head in her hands. What was happening to them?

At first light, she radioed Tom, who told her he'd attempt the flight in spite of the impending storm. "Tom, I can't tell you how relieved I am. Please be careful."

After what seemed forever, she heard the faint buzz of the plane's engine as it drew near. "There he is." She reached for her jacket. "Let's get them to the Snow Dome."

She went over to Frank. "I wish Tom could take you too, but you know he'll barely have room for Alice. I'll find out when he can come back."

"I couldn't move anyway," he said, coughing.

Kate bundled the two students in blankets, both of them barely conscious. Grant carried Charlie outside, and Kate followed close behind with Alice in her arms.

Closing the door, Kate stumbled as the wind blasted her. The clouds had thickened and lowered, making her nearly cry out in despair. Tom might not be able to land.

At the sleds, Grant gently lowered Charlie onto his back. The young man reached up to him. "Thanks, man," he whispered.

"Hey, you get well."

As Kate tucked the blanket in around Alice's petite, limp body in the sled, the young woman opened her eyes, looking up at her like a frightened child. "Am I going to die?" she asked.

"Oh Alice, you're going to be fine. Tom is flying both you and Charlie to the hospital in Port Angeles." It broke Kate's heart to see her so helpless. "You'll be back in no time. Now just rest."

By the time Kate and Grant pulled the two sleds to the top of the Snow Dome, Tom had already landed and taxied back. He jumped out, and she hurried to greet him. "I'm so glad you made it. How was the flight?"

"Bumpy as hell. But I like that," he said with a broad grin. Then he glanced at the sleds and his face fell. "Looks like these two are in bad shape."

"Tom, if it weren't an emergency, we wouldn't have asked you to fly in this weather."

She crouched down across from Grant and helped him lift Alice into the space behind the passenger seat where baggage would normally be stowed. Tom anchored her with the webbing used to hold down cargo.

Alice looked especially small, staring blankly at the others standing nearby.

"You get better, Alice," Kate said. "I'll call your parents."

"Thank you. I'm sorry for all this." She could barely hear Alice's weak voice in the wind.

Grant lifted Charlie over his shoulder and lowered him gently into the passenger seat behind the pilot. Charlie opened his eyes, then closed them again.

Tom finished buckling in Charlie and moved to get into the plane. "Wait," Kate said, "Frank's also in bad shape. Is there any way you could come back for him?

He shook his head, his brow creased with concern. "I'm so sorry. This wind is already pushing my plane's limits. I don't know when I can get back."

"I understand. Be safe. And thank you again."

After working together shoulder to shoulder with Frank for three years, she felt sick to her stomach at the thought of losing him.

"Oh, I almost forgot." Kate ran back to Tom and held out a small ice chest containing the vials of mammoth tissue packed in ice. "Could you please have the contents of this cooler repacked in ice and sealed for overnight shipment to the lab in Denver? The directions are inside."

"Sure, no problem."

Tom climbed in, fastened his harness, and started the engine. After saluting Kate, he taxied to the upper end of the smooth snow and turned to face downslope. Soon the plane sped past and over the edge. Wind gusts pushed at their backs.

"I hope Tom has enough power to get airborne," Kate shouted against the wind. It was very possible the Husky would blow sideways off the snow and onto the rocks. Staring at the horizon where the plane had dropped out of sight, she soon heard the engine a split second before it reappeared, airborne.

Grant let out a sigh of relief. "He did it."

The plane flew down the valley toward Port Angeles, its wings jerking right and left, hammered by the wind. The dark clouds raced across the sky, so low they obscured Panic Peak. Kate watched the plane until she could no longer see it. Now Charlie and Alice would get the care they needed.

Then she turned to face her next challenge: getting back to the station and making Frank as comfortable as possible until Tom returned, whenever that would be.

15

Blue Glacier
Olympic National Park

Saturday, June 13

Grant braced himself against the wind as they fought their way back to the station. Never in his life had he felt so exposed to nature's fury. The earthy smell in the air told him the skies would break open any second and dump rain, or maybe snow with the falling temperature.

At the station, Kate reached for the doorknob. "It's locked. Shit! And the key's inside." She stomped her foot. "I can't believe I pulled the door shut without checking first."

She banged on the door. "Frank!" She banged again.

Nothing.

"He's asleep, Kate. And he probably can't hear us with all this wind." Grant fumbled in his jacket. "Maybe I can get my pocketknife into the latch." She stepped aside, and he tried to wedge the blade in far enough to release the lock. His hands shook so badly he could barely hold the knife. They had to get inside to help Frank and get out of this weather. The blade bent, then broke in his desperate effort to jimmy the lock.

"Damn it, Grant!" Kate shouted over the wind. "We don't have time for this." She picked up a large rock and marched to the side of the station.

He heard shattering glass and the rock hitting the floor, then she threw open the door—just as the first sheets of cold rain blew across the outcrop.

The storm clouds made the interior so dark Grant ran to the shed to fire up the generator. The bare light bulbs flared to life, throwing beacons across the rocks, revealing sheets of rain as he ran back inside.

Kate was kneeling down next to Frank. "Are you okay? Frank?" He groaned and opened his eyes. He had that unfocused look Grant had seen in Charlie and Alice. Whatever this illness was, it was coming on even faster now.

"I feel like hell." He sat up and coughed violently, almost gagging. His breathing was shallow and labored.

After lighting the heater to counter the plummeting temperature, Kate powered up the Park Service radio. "Hoh Rain Forest Visitor Center, this is the Blue Glacier Research Station," she said, the mic pressed to her lips. "We're declaring an emergency. We need help."

Up to this point, Kate's take-charge actions had given him some measure of comfort, but the new tremor in her voice increased his own panic.

No sound came from the radio.

She adjusted a knob, filling the station with hissing static. "Mayday, Mayday, Mayday. Anyone in the Park Service, please respond!"

Her foot tap-tap-tapped like Morse code against the side of the desk as she stared at the radio. Were her sunken cheeks and the circles under her eyes a reflection of the stress and lack of sleep—or a sign that the virus had spread to her? Grant was terrified at the thought of all of them getting seriously ill on this remote mountain.

"Do you think the storm knocked the ranger's radio off the—?"

BOOM! The explosive sound, like a clap of thunder, shook the roof.

"Oh no! The antenna!" Kate jumped to her feet.

They both rushed to the door and forced it open against the wind. The broken antenna tumbled against the rocks of Panic Peak and bounced out of sight into the ravine below, their radio and Internet gone.

Now they were completely on their own.

16

Hoh Rain Forest
Olympic National Park

Saturday, June 13

As he took off, Tom threw the control stick from side to side and pumped the rudder pedals, fighting the fierce crosswinds to keep the Husky from blowing onto the rocks or flipping over. The left ski caught the edge of a crevasse just before liftoff and dangled by a single cable, banging loudly in the slipstream against the side of the plane. He could probably make it to Port Angeles before the ski damaged the airframe, but he looked for places to set down in case they weren't so lucky.

Between Glacier Meadows at the tip of the Blue Glacier and the Hoh River, the steep valley walls were covered with rocks and thick heather. The tall spruce trees on the valley floor would tear the plane apart. He could slow the plane to stall speed and drop gently enough to be caught by the upper branches. But he and his passengers would be left hanging in the thick forest canopy a hundred feet above ground.

In an instant the banging stopped. Silence. Then a sharp jolt. The plane shuddered and the nose dropped. Tom pulled back on the stick, but the nose barely moved, the airspeed gauge climbing to the "never exceed" line where structural damage could occur. When he pulled back on the throttle to reduce the airspeed, there was still no change. The nose continued to point down at a steep angle toward the water, rocks, and trees lining the valley floor.

Maybe the ski had broken free and hit the tail. The blow must have damaged the elevator hinge somehow. He would have to land immediately or lose control altogether. Pulling the throttle to idle and engaging the flaps, he raised the nose so their landing wouldn't destroy the propeller and probably the entire plane.

He headed for a band of open space between the massive trees and lined up directly with the river itself. If he ditched in the rushing glacial meltwater, they'd all get hypothermia and likely die. A wide gravel bar downstream ran a good hundred yards—he could try to land there, if he could make it. The trick would be to bring the two main wheels down on the wet gravel without bogging down and flipping the plane upside down.

Heavy rain blocked his view to the side, but the blast from the propeller kept his windshield clear. The treetops were getting dangerously close as they lost altitude.

"Hold on a little longer," he said out loud.

Throwing the control stick right and left while adjusting the rudder pedals, Tom kept his eyes on the gravel bar ahead. He lined up to land as he would on final approach to the runway back home in Port Angeles. He had only one shot—it had better work.

Before touching down, he switched the radio to the international emergency frequency of 121.5 MHz and called "Mayday," realizing the minimal chance of anyone hearing.

As he committed to the landing, he spotted a mother bear and her cubs at the side of the water and revved the engine to warn them. The plane glided in, the gravel bar zooming about six feet below. His wheels touched down as the bear and her cubs bolted into the woods.

The two main wheels and remaining right ski skittered along the wet gravel. He pulled hard on the stick to hold the nose up as high as possible to minimize the weight on the wheels. When the forest at the end of the gravel loomed closer, he released the back pressure. The bare left wheel with the missing ski sank to its hub, spinning the plane and almost flipping it into the fast, icy current.

His body flew against the restraint of the harness and then sideways against the door. Tearing into the raging current, the propeller blade buckled. The tremendous force of the sudden stop nearly sheared the engine from its mounting bolts.

He switched off the magnetos, his heart beating fiercely. Never had he come so close to death as a bush pilot. Turning around, he saw both passengers had endured the rough landing, thanks to their seat belt and cargo harness, but they were asleep or unconscious, he couldn't tell.

Although he'd saved everyone from a fatal crash, they were trapped in the woods in a raging storm next to a roaring glacier-fed river. From here, the visitor center at the Hoh River trailhead was a five-mile trek, challenging in good weather, and the radio frequency on the aircraft required a direct line of sight to be received.

Once the Husky settled onto the gravel, he flicked the toggle on the emergency locator transmitter to trigger the repetitive beacon that would alert the FAA of an emergency. He cursed himself for not replacing his old unit with something that could have been monitored by satellite. The odds of an airliner flying directly overhead and detecting his signal were slim to none.

The plane sat precariously close to the river. He hopped out and scrambled up the bank to find a safe place for himself and his passengers. Up ahead, at the edge of the forest, a narrow, level area was their only option. Using plastic tarps from the plane and branches scattered about, he hurried to construct a rough lean-to, knowing the river could engulf the plane at any moment.

Racing back to the plane, he dragged Alice up the bank to the shelter. She moaned as he removed her from the plane, while Charlie remained limp and unresponsive the whole time. Both their faces had a frightening blue color. They'd never be able to travel on foot. Their only hope was if someone picked up his emergency radio transmissions.

The trees above them whistled as torrents of rain sprayed their shelter. A corner of the tarp broke free from one of the branches and flapped in the wind. Huddled between two massive downed trees, Tom re-anchored the tarp, wincing at the loud crack of a branch splitting somewhere above them.

Exhausted, he leaned back against the log and stretched out his legs. Alice's sleeping head rested inches from his foot and Charlie lay alongside her. All he could do was hunker down and pray rescuers would find them.

17

Blue Glacier
Olympic National Park

Saturday, June 13

Frank lay ashen-faced, shivering with fever, his breathing a low, wet growl. Kate held his hand, visions of her dying mother flashing in her mind—her hair gone, her face gaunt. Kate had felt frightened and helpless then too. What if they couldn't save Frank? The meager supplies in the first-aid kit offered few options.

At the very least, they could make it more comfortable inside and cover the window she had smashed to get into the station. Rain sprayed the floor with each wind gust. She held up a sheet of plastic while Grant hammered tacks around the window frame. They worked in silence as she tried to figure out what to do.

The relentless, deafening rumble of bands of rain pounding the metal roof fueled her desperation. A buzzing sound on the shelf above the desk drew her attention—Charlie's static electricity detector. As the electric charge in the air increased, a spark gap in a mason jar attached to an outside antenna changed from a periodic pop to a buzz that rose steadily in pitch.

Dear Charlie. When he hopped off the plane less than a week ago, he looked so excited, his face one big grin. By now he and Alice would be getting good care at the medical center in Port Angeles. Suddenly, a flash lit the station, followed by a nearly simultaneous explosive BAM!

Kate ran to the window. A bolt of lightning had split one of the boulders twenty feet from the building. The buzzing jar went silent.

"There's no way Tom will be able to power through this for a second rescue flight," she said, more to herself than to Grant. When her student had broken his leg two years before, she radioed for a medevac and Tom was there immediately. Not this time.

Frank let out a moan, and they both went over to him. Grant felt his forehead. "He's burning up."

"Oh, Frank." She put the thermometer under his tongue, then gasped when she removed it. "It's 105.4!"

"We need to pack him in snow immediately." Grant threw on his coat and headed for the entry.

"Use the buckets in the shed—and hurry."

Within seconds, she heard a loud bang. "Grant?"

"It's okay," he shouted. "The wind caught the door and almost broke the hinges."

Kate brought over a basin of cool water and placed a wet washcloth on Frank's forehead. They had to be able to help him. "Frank, can you hear me?"

No response.

When Grant rushed in minutes later, he carried two large buckets of snow, his parka dripping a trail of water on the floor. "That's a ferocious storm out there," he said.

"Hang your coat by the stove to dry and help me get Frank out of his clothes." She unbuttoned his shirt while Grant stripped him down to his underwear and rolled him on his side so she could put a tarp between his body and the sleeping bag on the bunk.

They packed the coarse granules around Frank's legs and torso. Kate dipped a washcloth into some of the melted snow to wet his parched lips and squeezed a small amount into his mouth to revive him.

Their efforts seemed to be working. Frank even opened his eyes and tried to sit up, but then fell back, his skin now sickeningly blue. Soon he closed his eyes again and stopped moaning.

Grant grabbed a wrist and felt for a pulse. "His heart has stopped!" The color drained from his face.

"What? That can't be." She felt his pulse, then climbed into the bunk and straddled Frank's legs. There was no time to move him.

Brushing off the snow, she began rhythmic compressions of his chest, counting to a hundred, praying she was doing it right. Had the CPR instructor said one hundred or fifty?

"Check your watch and call out every minute," she said.

Frank let out a moan.

"It's working!" she shouted. She kept the frantic compressions going for another five minutes, but he made no more sounds. Soon she started to get dizzy, her breaths shortening in exhaustion. Grant touched her back. "Let me take over."

She nodded. Her hands shook as she lifted them from Frank's chest.

Grant squeezed into the lower bunk and gave Frank steady compressions for another five minutes and then felt for his pulse again.

"Kate . . ." The sadness in his eyes tore at her heart.

"No!" She climbed back on Frank's legs and resumed compressions, fast and erratic, her eyes closed, willing his chest to expand on its own.

Firm hands grabbed her shoulders, and she jumped. "Kate, I'm so sorry," came Grant's soft voice close to her ear.

He had to be mistaken.

She turned to Frank's pallid face and his blue-gray lips. He couldn't be dead—the man who had more stamina than anyone she had ever known. "He looks like he's asleep, like he'll sit up and complain about the weather or something. Oh how I wish he would."

Sliding off the bunk, she stared down at him, a flurry of images going through her mind. Frank in the front row of her classroom and in the graduate office leaning back in his chair, his feet on the desk, combing his fingers through his curly hair. The time they enjoyed a beer together, just the two of them, on a Friday night down the street from the university. The blue cap he always wore. And Annie—

This couldn't be happening.

Grant stood beside her, neither of them moving, the rain beating against the station.

She had to do something—or she'd fall apart. "Let's clean up this snow before it melts all over the place." Using her hands, she shoveled the snow onto the floor and then covered Frank with a blanket, all but his face. She couldn't bear to cover him completely.

Grant swept up the snow and dumped it into the sink. "Does he have a family?"

"A wife and son—just a year and a half old."

"Oh God."

She shuffled to her desk chair, tears streaming down her face. Grant sat next to her. Every time a gust hammered the building, it shuddered slightly, and she flinched. Between gusts, the wind howled around corners and through cable restraints. If this continued, the cables could chafe clear through, and the station would topple down to God knows where. Only the steady chug-chug-chug of the generator provided reassurance amid the tempestuous clamor.

Closing her eyes, she went numb, the way she did when her father came from the hospital with the news of her mother's death. She glanced over at Frank's still form and then at Grant slumped next to her in his own trance.

"My God, Kate," he whispered. "This can't be real, can it?"

"I'm afraid so," she said, barely able to form the words. "This aggressive illness has ravaged my crew."

"I can't imagine how it must feel to have your students struck down like this, your summer research cut short." He put his hand on her shoulder, but she pulled away and stood up.

"You're right," she said, walking to her bunk and lying down. "You have no idea. I care about these kids like they're my own. I'm prepared to invest my heart and soul in them. To you they're mere subjects to observe—at arm's length."

"I'm sorry you feel that way. They matter to me. They're good kids." He paused. "Kate, we have to get out of here before we start getting sick too."

She didn't respond. Wrapping herself tightly in her arms, she turned to the wall only to bring up the memory of Frank's grad-student apartment strewn with toys, and the lasagna he and Annie had cooked to celebrate the end of last summer's work. What would she tell Annie? Sammy would grow up not knowing his dad—all because this mission had gone horribly wrong.

The floor squeaked as Grant paced around the cramped room, the high-pitched noise clashing with the tumult of the storm outside. She covered her head with her pillow so she wouldn't have to listen anymore.

He stopped next to her bunk. "You and I haven't come down with the virus yet, but that could change any minute." Crouching down, he said, "How long do you think it will be until Tom's plane can get back to us?"

She sat up and used her sleeve to wipe away the tears. "Days, with this storm."

"How long to hike out?"

"Twenty hours—probably more. The path's rough enough without all this wind and rain. It would be hell in the dark, not to mention slippery."

Grant put out his hands, as if weighing their options. "So we stay here, waiting to get sick or blown off the mountain." A harsh blast of wind rattled the building, underscoring his point. "Or we take our chances on the trail." He strode across the room and sat in a desk chair facing her. "Kate, this illness is a time bomb."

She stared at him, hearing his words, but nothing made sense. She couldn't think straight. It was all too much . . . too fast.

Kate looked over at Frank and back at Grant. By tomorrow, the two of them could be near death themselves. But Grant wasn't an experienced climber. Still, they'd be trekking downhill, so he'd probably make it. "Okay," she said, rising slowly to her feet. "Let's get out of here while we can. We may have only a few hours left." She pulled a backpack from under her bunk and began to assemble what they'd need.

By midnight the wind had calmed down slightly with only occasional gusts, and the rain had slowed. She and Grant dressed in three layers under their parkas and put on rugged waterproof pants over long underwear.

Kate felt like she was slogging through glue, her arms and legs almost impossible to move.

They each loaded their backpacks with a change of clothes, a sleeping bag, a half-dozen power bars, a sandwich bag of trail mix, some beef jerky, and three liter bottles of water. That would give them enough provisions to get to the Hoh Rain Forest Visitor Center, twenty-five miles down the trail. They could get help there.

Kate also threw in a small first-aid kit and lashed a two-person tent across the top of her pack. Grant tied two rolled-up foam pads to his.

About 1 a.m., after strapping headlamps to their foreheads, she turned off the stove and said good-bye to Frank's motionless body while Grant shut down the generator.

When they stepped off the rocks and onto the edge of the snow, Kate stopped to take a last look at the station through the thick fog and drizzle. "I'm sorry, Frank. So, so sorry. When we get to the visitor center, I'll call Annie." Her voice broke, and she sucked in a breath. "I hope I'm doing the right thing." A tear slid down her cheek, and she wiped it away.

18

Blue Glacier
Olympic National Park

Sunday, June 14

Grant fumbled with his gear as they roped up. Being tied to Kate was reassuring—the only thing between him and his fear of dying alone on a frozen mountaintop. He'd do anything to reach civilization.

Their bright headlamps barely pierced the fog. As they walked, they remained far apart, the rope in between, so if one of them fell, the other could self-arrest to prevent both of them from sliding down the mountain or into a deadly chasm. Kate set a compass heading to avoid going in circles.

"We'll use dead reckoning and follow a southeast heading," she said. "It should take us safely down the side of the Snow Dome and miss the icefall to the south and the couloir's vertical drop to the north."

Grant skidded along the snow's surface, now refrozen into a sheet of ice. He tried to break through the crust heel first with each footfall, but in one place his foot didn't penetrate, and he fell spread-eagled on his back, only stopping by holding his ice ax to his side. His calf muscle rewarded him by knotting into a painful cramp. He got up and limped on.

When they came to the outcrop of rocks near the base of the Snow Dome, Grant felt relieved to have solid ground under his feet. But he took a bold stride and both feet slid out, and he landed hard on his back again, this time unable to breathe. Already he regretted insisting they hike down the mountain in the dark.

Kate returned to where he lay on the rocks. "I felt a tug on the rope when you fell. These wet rocks are treacherous."

"No kidding."

The slope became more gradual, and the snow gave way to the rough surface of bare ice. The crevasses on the Lower Glacier were like wrinkles or parallel cracks—much more frequent and closer together than the massive, cavernous ones on the Upper Glacier. As Grant leaped from one ridge to the next over the icy surface, he tasted bitterness, afraid he would fall victim to whatever lay in the shadows his headlamp couldn't reveal through the mist.

The constant noise, like water flowing down a giant drain, sent chills through him, prompting him to zip his parka to his chin. He imagined falling into a stream of icy water and being carried off in a relentless current that turned him blue as it sucked his last breath.

What would be worse—waiting to die from the terrifying disease that had just killed Frank or freezing to death because he fell, broke his leg, and lay helpless? The morbid images kept appearing.

And how insane to trust Kate's dead reckoning compass headings in these near-zero visibility conditions. "Dead reckoning"—even the term made him shudder.

A sharp crack and thunderous rumble made the ground shake and Grant's chest vibrate. His heart leapt like a panicked rabbit.

"Freeze!" Kate yelled, though they were already stopped. "We're right below the damn icefall."

From somewhere behind, an enormous mass crashed with a deafening impact, sending a rush of wind past them. He held his breath as a million small ice shards cascaded around his boots.

A block of ice slid into Kate's side and knocked her down. "My leg!" she called out as the rope between them pulled taut and nearly yanked Grant off his feet. Then all grew hushed save the steady running of water below the ice.

"Are you hurt?" he shouted, hurrying to her side.

"Just shaken up, I think." She first propped her weight on her hands, then her knees, and Grant helped as she forced her way to her feet, testing her leg.

"That was too close," he said.

Kate adjusted her gloves. "We need to get the hell out of here." She checked her compass heading in the light of her headlamp. "Let's go due north down the glacier. That will take us away from the icefall and toward the tip."

They moved carefully across the ice, jumping over the openings until she stopped, waiting for him to catch up. "This is crazy," she said. "We're going to kill ourselves hiking in the middle of the night."

"I agree. Totally bad idea. Let's go back."

"Are you serious? After we've come this far?"

"What's the alternative?"

"We brought a tent. Let's pitch it on a patch of snow and wait till dawn."

He never expected to camp in the snow, but she was right. They wouldn't survive if they kept going in the dark.

Grant stayed close to Kate as they crept down the glacier until they came to a place where the rough ice was covered over. "This smooth snowfield should work. No danger of ice blocks crushing us."

After putting up the tent and rolling out the foam pads, they laid their sleeping bags on top and crawled in together—an uncomfortably close arrangement, especially given the tension between them the last few days. They each faced the tent wall on their respective sides and turned off their headlamps.

Grant closed his eyes, but he was too churned up to sleep. Frank's horrible death and their near miss below the ice fall kept replaying in his head.

When Kate started sobbing softly, her shoulders shaking against him, he rolled over and pulled his arms out of his sleeping bag to comfort her, but stopped himself. She had pulled away earlier, and he didn't want to make things worse.

At last, he started drifting off. All around them, the water still cascaded under the ice, but mercifully the wind and rain had stopped.

19

Blue Glacier
Olympic National Park

Sunday, June 14

A deep coldness spread through Kate's legs, and her shoulders and back felt stiff and sore. She needed to get out of bed and do some work before everyone else woke up. They had to go back to the tunnel today and check on the mammoth. Then Frank's blue face flashed in her mind, and she remembered. There would be no more trips to the tunnel for him. Her insides twisted with such force she thought she'd vomit.

When she tried to roll over, she couldn't move. Sometime during the night, Grant had wrapped his arms around her from behind. As she wiggled to break free, he stirred and stretched full length so his feet pushed against the bottom of the tent and his head almost poked out the flap.

His eyes opened with a look of surprise that melted into a smile. "Good morning, Dr. Landry."

"Morning." She yanked herself out of the sleeping bag, her head heavy from crying and lack of sleep. As it was, they had been in the tent under four hours. She unzipped the tent flap and glanced up at the sky.

"How does it look?" Grant kicked his legs free.

"The fog is still thick, but at least there's daylight." When she crawled out to get her bearings, her heart sank—there was a whiteout in every direction. She could barely make out the fuzzy shape of one of the rock outcrops lining the base of the Snow Dome just twenty yards away. They'd need more than compass headings to navigate. "I'll use the GPS today."

Sitting in the tent, comparing the topographic map of Olympic National Park with the tiny map on her GPS screen, she entered waypoints in the device's memory. These points should take them safely off the glacier and down to the Hoh River Valley.

Grant dug through his backpack and pulled out a power bar. "I'm sorry I pushed so hard to leave the station. It nearly got us killed."

"Hey, I agreed, didn't I? And we didn't—we don't—have time to waste." She grabbed a handful of trail mix and forced it down, her stomach still roiling with nausea.

After taking a final look at the map, she folded it and put it in her backpack and the GPS in her parka pocket. "The hike is still hazardous, but at least we won't get lost."

"Do you feel okay?" he asked. "I mean, do you have any chills or a sore throat?"

"No. You?"

He shook his head. "Let's get moving while we can."

They packed their tent and sleeping bags in minutes and resumed their trek down the Lower Glacier. As Kate stepped from the crests of ice separating each crevasse, the surfaces varied randomly from scattered rock fragments to smooth water-covered ice.

It was exhausting to have to focus on where to best place her boot with each step. But it wasn't enough of a distraction to take her mind off Frank. Surely, none of it had happened. In the light of day, it was easy to believe he was still alive, waiting for them at the station.

Grant followed a couple of steps back. "How's it going?" she asked.

"I'm stepping wherever you do. It's not too bad, but I'm groggy from so little sleep."

The sound of hundreds of rivulets of meltwater, combining into ever bigger streams below, told her danger was nearby. "We have to steer clear of the glacier's tip or we might slide into the opening. If we fall in, we'll be washed away and dashed onto the rocks."

"Then let's get out of here. It freaks me out just thinking about it."

Soon they came to a solid gray wall rising up into the fog—the lateral moraine that had formed along the east side of the retreating glacier.

As they climbed the steep slope side by side, loose rock and sand debris everywhere, Grant slipped several times, even when using his ice ax. Once they reached the narrow knife-edge top, they saw nothing but more whiteout. The entire valley had filled with fog so dense that they could hardly see their feet.

She turned to Grant. "I've gotten us off the glacier, and I'd like to think we're home free. But I'm afraid we've got some rough terrain ahead."

"It can't be any worse than hiking on glacier ice, can it?"

"In some places, yes—especially in the fog."

The steep path over the moraine plunged down the back side to the heather, wild flowers, and small evergreen trees of Glacier Meadows—all reduced to indistinct gray shapes in the fog.

As much as Kate loved working on the glacier, she welcomed the comfort of being surrounded by plants—particularly after living on snow, ice, and rocks for days. But the fuzzy outlines of all the bushes and trees in the fog made it difficult to make out the path. Would they ever see the sky again?

The crashing roar of Glacier Creek defined their boundary to the west as it emerged from under the ice to cascade over rocks. To avoid it, she had to go into pure bushwhack mode, pushing branches aside, trying to walk in as straight a line as possible. Once, she brushed past a large branch and it snapped back, catching Grant in the face.

"Hey!" he shouted.

"Sorry."

Rivulets of water from the storm ran everywhere, and puddles had formed in every depression, obscuring the faint traces of trail even more. When they appeared to be making some forward progress, they came to a shallow pond of meltwater.

"Damn," Kate said. "We'll have to find a way around."

She turned right and tried to maintain the heading based on the GPS as she pushed through underbrush, coming to one dead end after another.

After circling around a wide bush, she climbed over a rock outcrop and discovered the faint evidence of an established trail. "Finally. Here's the Glacier Meadows Campground." She pointed to the fire pits and flat, open spaces nearby for pitching tents. "Any campers who might have been here are long gone," she said.

"At least we're getting closer to civilization." Grant shifted his pack on his back.

"The map says the Glacier Meadows Ranger Station is just past the campground and over the next hill. They'll have a radio, and we can find out about Alice and Charlie, make arrangements for Frank's body, and notify his family." Her boots moved faster on the pathway.

What emerged through the fog instead was a rustic, wooden platform with no sign of a building or even an abandoned tent. "Not much of a ranger station." She tried to swallow past the knot in her throat. "Should have known." The last time she was there, she'd been a grad student. "The Park Service hasn't been fully staffed for a long time. Obviously, they don't use this anymore."

Not saying anything, Grant stared at the platform, his forehead lined with worry.

"It's okay," Kate said, wanting to reassure him—and herself. "We'll find someone eventually."

"How much farther?" he asked.

"Eighteen miles." She looked up from the GPS at the sky. "Let's push on. We might make it before dark." She splashed off through the puddles and continued down the trail, Grant close behind.

How ironic. She never wanted Grant to come to the station and now she didn't know what she would have done without him. Not once on their difficult journey had he whined or complained, in spite of so little rest. He kept her going when all she wanted to do was curl up in a ball, fall asleep, and forget.

This soft professor from a fancy California beach town proved a lot tougher than she and Frank thought. They had been wrong about him.

20

Glacier Meadows
Olympic National Park

Sunday, June 14

After they left the ranger station tent platform, the roar of Glacier Creek receded behind them. Kate's rapid stride widened their separation, and the route seemed to take them back uphill. Grant had to stop. "Hold up a minute," he shouted, bending over to catch his breath. "I thought we followed the stream *down* to the Hoh."

"We can't. The water flows through a deep, narrow gorge. The valley falls steeply, so the trail stays pretty high."

"I'll try to keep up."

Farther down the trail, they came to a steep, treacherous slope of slippery mud, loose gravel, and water. At times, the soles of Grant's boots were so encrusted he had to stop and scrape them off on rocks. Even without ice, the terrain seemed determined to do him in.

Soon the beaten track disappeared yet again into the thick fog as it dropped steeply down a ravine. He crept along, positioning his boots crosswise to the path to keep from slipping. When he finally reached the bottom, he let out a groan at the jumble of loose boulders and broken rocks before them.

They pushed on, Grant stumbling once again—it felt like he was walking on giant marbles. At one point, he fell sideways onto the protruding stones, but except for a bruised shoulder, he wasn't hurt. Walking on all fours was the only way to move forward without falling.

When he caught up with Kate, she had reached the far side where a nearly vertical wall strewn with gravel and loose rocks rose into the sky. This time they lucked out with a ladder—two metal cables with wooden crosspieces ascended above them. It would have been impossible to climb the face without it. Grant counted ten rungs but suspected more continued out of sight.

Kate had reached the fourth rung when she called down, "This is scary as hell. The soles of my boots are slippery. They barely stay put."

"Take your time."

When she climbed to the fifth rung, Grant grabbed the cables and started up as gravel began to rain down. He shielded his head with one arm while holding onto the cable with the other.

"Watch out!" Kate shouted.

He looked up in time to dodge a softball-sized rock that sailed past him into the ravine.

Then Kate fell in slow motion toward him.

"Oh no!" He held on tightly with one hand and tried to grab her with the other. The best he could do was cushion her fall as she bounced off his side and tumbled down the steep slope below the ladder and onto the rocks at the bottom of the ravine.

Grant jumped from the ladder and slid in the gravel down to where she lay on her back. "Oh my God. Are you okay?"

No response, even though she stared up at him. Then her face scrunched in pain. "I couldn't breathe."

Blood flowed from a gash on her forehead. "Kate, you have a nasty cut." Rifling through her pack, he found the first-aid kit, grabbed a large bandage, and pressed it against her scalp.

"Help me sit."

He grasped her upper arms and gently pulled her into a sitting position on the rocks against an upright boulder.

She winced. "Ouch! Careful."

"Where does it hurt other than your head?"

"I'm not sure . . ." She wiggled her hands and feet. "I don't think anything's broken, but my hip and knee are really sore."

"That was an ugly fall." He handed her a water bottle, and she took a sip.

As they sat together, more rocks and gravel fell down the slope toward them. "We have to get past this ravine soon," he said. "It's too dangerous to stay here long." After a few minutes, another large rock shot by them. "We really need to go."

"My head is pulsing."

"Let me see if we have something." He found some ibuprofen in the first-aid kit.

Kate swallowed two tablets with a gulp of water and leaned back with her eyes closed but kept talking. Her head injury didn't seem severe, though he couldn't be sure.

"Let me help you stand up."

When he lifted her by her arms, she let out a cry. "Ow! My hip." She rubbed her side. "I must have come down hard on it." She leaned on him and rotated her leg.

"I'll support you." He put her arm over his shoulder, and she hobbled slowly across the boulders to the bottom of the ladder.

"Let's sit for a minute," she said. "I have an idea." They sat side by side on the gravel away from the mud. "You can belay me, the way I did for Frank when his strain gauge fell. This time, hold the rope around your back to provide an anchor."

He glanced up the ladder and back down to her. "Okay. I'm game. I learned how to use the ice ax, so I should be able to do this." He pulled the coiled rope from the top of his pack, and they each tied an end to their climbing harnesses they'd worn on the glacier.

Grant grabbed the cable and stood on the first rung. "Stand to the side. I don't want you to get hit again." He climbed steadily to the top while she waited below. To avoid being pulled off, he tied himself to the highest rung and sat facing out, both feet resting on the rung below.

He ran the rope from Kate behind his back and then through his gloved right hand, serving as a brake across his chest. "Belay on," he shouted.

"Climbing," she said from below.

As she lifted one leg at a time and paused, he pulled the rope snug around his waist. Minutes passed with each step. Once again gravel fell on them, and he worried another large rock might come flying down.

Partway, she stopped and called up weakly, "I feel . . . faint . . . I'm not sure I can do this."

"You're so strong, Kate. You can do it. Concentrate on the rungs. Go one more. I'll hold you." His hand began to cramp from gripping the rope so hard.

All of a sudden, the rope around his waist pulled in so forcefully he thought it would slice him in half. She must have slipped. But in the next instant he could breathe. He had to concentrate to pull up the slack and keep up with her. He'd never felt such victory as he did when she reached him at the top of that ladder.

But they weren't done yet.

They had to leave the ladder and scramble the last twenty feet over loose rock to the trail above. He stayed in front, still assisting Kate with the rope tied between them, and climbed to the top on all fours. When he reached the path, he pulled her the last few feet. She grimaced in pain, but climbed steadily up to him.

Both of them were panting when Grant grabbed her hand. "Not many people could have pulled that off."

"Maybe so, but you did all the pulling." They both laughed weakly.

When they made it to solid ground, they sat wearily on a rock above the ladder. They both drank some water, then Grant took a bite of a power bar and handed her a piece. As they sat and their sweat started to cool, she began to shiver.

"Kate, we need to keep moving to stay warm. Maybe we can still reach the visitor center before dark. We have to try."

If he could get Kate up that ladder, he could get her the rest of the way. He handed her another bite of power bar and gently pulled her to her feet. "Come on. I'm ready for a shower and a warm dinner."

He watched her limping as she took a few steps. "Can you walk okay?"

"I think so. Take it slow." The limp seemed less severe once she took a few more steps.

"Give me the GPS—I'll lead." He held the small instrument while she showed him how to flip through the screens.

The trail was little more than a shallow bench carved in dirt and gravel along the steep hillside, now made slippery by runoff from the storm. He had Kate walk behind him with one hand on his shoulder to give her stability. After a half mile, they had to stop—an enormous, uprooted spruce tree blocked their path.

"Stay here." Grant helped her sit. "I'll look for a way around."

He left the trail on the downhill side.

"Grant, don't go—"

He cut her off. "I'll be right back. I want to get us around this thing."

The steep hillside, covered in slippery mud, dropped off into the fog. As he rounded the end of the tree, his feet slipped out from under him and he started to slide. "I'm falling!" He rolled onto his stomach, desperately grabbing at whatever he could as he continued slipping faster down the hill.

"Use your ax!" she shouted.

Reaching back, he yanked his ax from the side of his backpack and pulled it across his chest, stopping his slide just feet from the edge. Thank God Kate had drilled him so hard. Her training had saved his life—again.

On his climb back, he slipped some more. By the time he reached Kate, his new parka was soaked and covered in mud. He began shivering—from fear and relief as much as the chill.

"I tried to warn you," Kate said, "but you were in too big a hurry."

"Warn me how?"

"Not to go down. You cross on the uphill side. The valley falls off hundreds of feet to the river, but you wouldn't have known that."

Grant took her hand and climbed around the downed tree on the uphill side, which gave them something to brace against. She seemed more sure-footed with the solid support. "You still have a lot to learn about the mountains, Grant. But I like your gung-ho attitude."

He studied her profile. Was she serious? No one had ever described him that way before.

They continued down the trail at the rate of a thousand vertical feet per mile according to the GPS. When they reached the Elk Lake

Campground, they stopped briefly. The GPS showed sixteen miles to the visitor center.

Worn out from lack of sleep and the strenuous hike, Grant couldn't stop shivering. And when he looked over at Kate, he saw her bandage was now soaked in blood.

They both needed shelter and medical attention—fast.

21

Hoh River Trail
Olympic National Park

Sunday, June 14

Kate followed Grant down the path, descending the steep, rocky slope into the rain forest. They were soon surrounded by the massive trunks of gigantic red cedar, Douglas fir, and Sitka spruce.

The river's sound intensified, going from something like wind blowing to crashing waves. By the time Kate reached the edge of the Hoh River on the valley floor, she had to shout for Grant to hear her. "How many more miles?"

"Twelve," he shouted over his shoulder. "Every mile feels like ten. And now it's raining again."

"No, that's from the trees—they'll drip for days after the rain."

"Whatever. I'm freezing." His body drooped, and he started shuffling his feet.

"I got soaked through by a cold rain last year on the glacier during an unexpected storm—I know it's miserable."

The unrelenting sound of the river and Grant's worsening condition made her want to hurry, which was impossible with the newly fallen trees, even without her injuries. Getting around each obstacle required going deep into the tall ferns and bushes and then finding a way back to the trail.

Eighteen hours had passed since they'd left the research station, but it seemed a lot longer. After another two miles, they came upon a rustic, wooden building, a cabin of sorts, the windows shuttered.

"This is the Olympus Guard Station," Kate said, joining Grant on the porch. She groaned when she saw the padlock on the door. "We have to find a way inside and get you out of this wet and cold."

His teeth chattered so much he couldn't talk, his face an eerie bluish-gray.

As daylight waned, they walked around to the side where Grant found a chest-high shutter with a half-inch gap from the frame. He tugged on the boards until the shutter broke free, exposing the window underneath. They both removed their backpacks and pushed up on the window, managing to get it open. After crawling in, Kate reached down to help Grant, and once inside, he continued shaking, even more. She'd never seen anything like it.

Was he suffering from hypothermia and fatigue—or the deadly virus—or both?

The cold, dark, musty ranger station offered little more than a summer shelter—unfinished planks made up the floor and walls. In the light of her headlamp, Kate saw that one room held a desk and chair with a counter in the corner, and the second had a single bed and mattress. There was no fireplace or stove.

They'd have to use their bodies for heat.

She stood before Grant and looked up at him. "You're hypothermic, and we have to get you warm. You might not make it otherwise."

He nodded, his eyes in a distant stare.

"You need to strip off those wet clothes."

"Are you nuts? I'll freeze to death." He backed away and was about to crawl out the window.

"No!" She grabbed his arm, worried that the hypothermia was making him confused. "Grant, it sounds crazy, but I know what I'm doing. Please take off your clothes."

He eyed her with suspicion and began to peel off his dripping clothes. "You don't give me much choice." Stepping out of the soggy pile on the floor, he pulled dry underwear from his pack while she opened her sleeping bag and laid it on the bed.

"Here, lie down." She covered him from head to toe with his sleeping bag and then shed her own clothes down to her underwear and climbed in next to him. Holding onto his clammy, shivering body from behind, she gritted her teeth to keep from pulling back, goose bumps sweeping over her.

After what felt like hours, heat started filling the space around them, and his shaking subsided.

"I hope this is okay with you, Grant," she whispered. "You were out of it and so cold."

"More than okay. You're really warm."

She wanted nothing more now than to escape into sleep, to escape Frank's death, her throbbing head and hip, and fatigue so heavy she felt pressed into the bed.

As she dozed off, she couldn't help but notice how well she and Grant fit together, like two puzzle pieces.

A painful tingling jolted Kate awake. Her arm had fallen asleep. Grant's steady breathing told her he had dozed off too, and she didn't want to disturb him, but she had to move her arm. Slowing slipping it out from under him, she almost made it when he stirred.

"Kate?" He turned over. "Are you okay?"

"Yes—sorry—my arm fell asleep."

"Nothing to be sorry about. You saved me—and more than once. I owe you my life."

She felt awkward suddenly and moved to get out of bed.

Grant reached over and touched her in the darkness. "Don't go."

"I'm going to put some clothes on. I think you're thawed out now." She fumbled until she found her long underwear and sweatshirt at the end of the bed and crawled back in next to him. He was already snoring softly.

Kate woke when the light of dawn filtered through the fog and dimly lit the small room. She stretched, causing Grant to open his eyes and blink.

"What time is it?" He staggered over to his pack and checked the time on the GPS. "Can you believe it's 5:20? We slept eight hours."

"Yes, I believe it," she said, putting on her pants. "We were exhausted, and I still feel tired and sore. But we better get started. If we leave now, we can get to the visitor center before it closes."

"At least I'm warm. Thank you, Kate."

"Hey, you were in bad shape."

He pulled his long-sleeved underwear over his head. "Ten more miles to go. Ugh. First, let me see your head." His headlamp shone in her face. "Looks like the bleeding has stopped." He took out an alcohol wipe from the first-aid kit and gently wiped her wound.

She smiled, touched by his thoughtfulness.

"Our last bandage," he said, ripping open the sterile wrapper and taping the gauze over the spot.

He took a sweatshirt and nylon shell from his pack and slipped them over his head. "I'll tie my parka to my pack. It'll dry eventually."

Sitting on the bed, they shared some trail mix and beef jerky and emptied another water bottle, leaving one liter apiece. Grant climbed down from the window and gave Kate a hand.

As they continued along the trail toward the visitor center, she was grateful that their latest crisis had a happy ending. Thank God Grant had survived. She would never forget the feel of him lying beside her.

22

Hoh River Trail
Olympic National Park

Monday, June 15

Grant kept his headlamp on long after sunrise to keep from tripping on roots and rocks. The forest seemed more threatening to him in the dim morning light, the fog still as thick. The chest-high ferns on both sides and otherworldly shapes of intertwined branches overhead made it feel like he was walking through a tunnel. He couldn't imagine woods more dense than this temperate rain forest, except perhaps the jungles of South America.

The night before with Kate kept playing in his mind. He had found her attractive from the beginning, though her curt behavior had made romantic feelings unimaginable. But something had changed since then—there'd been a thaw. She had let herself be vulnerable. And she'd shown such caring and concern. Holding him the way she did was a gift, warming his body and his soul.

It was now 10:30, and they'd been hiking for twenty-one hours— thirty-three hours since they'd left the research station. He glanced at the GPS and saw they still had about five more miles to go before reaching the visitor center.

Kate hadn't said much since they left the Olympus Guard Station. She was still limping, but they were walking faster than they did the previous day. "How are you doing?" he asked.

From behind, she said, "My hip and head hurt, but other than that, I'm okay."

"I'm beginning to think we escaped the virus. It's been a couple of days, and neither one of us is sick."

"Maybe. It's such a frightening illness—we know nothing about it."

"But why would the students get it and not us?"

"They spent hours in the tunnel collecting samples, and we were in there only a short time. Maybe it has something to do with the mammoth."

"What are you saying? That the carcass contains some kind of virus?"

"It's possible. Just a few days ago, I read an article about frozen caribou bodies melting from permafrost in Siberia. They actually had live smallpox spores—a real concern."

"You and I were in the tunnel too."

"Yes, but we weren't cutting into the tissue of the carcass like the students. Maybe the virus is transmitted through direct contact with the flesh."

When they rounded the trunk of an enormous spruce with spooky, moss-covered branches, something caught Grant's attention—a flash of yellow after miles of monotonous gray rock, brown bark, evergreens, and ferns. He stopped. "Hold up a minute."

To his right lay a swath of yellow plastic. He walked over to it and saw part of a poncho mostly covered by branches—its edges held down by rocks. As Kate approached, he bent to lift one corner and jumped back. He lifted the plastic again and revealed a petite woman's body.

"My God!" Kate gripped his arm. "That's Alice."

"But how's that possible?"

"They never made it to Port Angeles." Kate's voice rose in panic. "Where are the others?" She began to walk in a circle. "Charlie?" she called. "Tom?"

Ten feet into the woods, he found a blue tarp covering another lifeless body. "It's Charlie."

She turned to look. "He was just a kid. And Alice—" She buried her face in his shoulder and sobbed.

Grant didn't know what to say or do except to hold her while she cried, her body shaking. She didn't pull away.

When her sobs subsided, he said softly, "The plane must have crashed. Let's look around." He held her hand as they walked to the river. In the diffuse light of the fog, he could just make out the bulk of a large object. The plane.

"Tom? Tom!" he shouted. "It's Grant and Kate!" They both shouted until they were nearly hoarse. There was no sound but the water cascading over rocks.

Grant turned to inspect the wreck. The propeller was bent, and one of the skis was missing—there was a frayed cable where it had been attached. The side of the fuselage bore deep gouges and dents. And then he saw the large chunk missing from the tail where the loose ski had struck. Otherwise, the plane was largely intact.

But no sign of Tom.

Grant shouted to Kate above the river's tempest. "Looks like Tom made a forced landing. I'm guessing they survived, but the virus was too much for Charlie and Alice. Tom protected their bodies the best he could."

"You're probably right." Her voice broke. "Grant, do you realize *everyone* exposed to the mammoth has died? Tom might be infected—the virus might be contagious, even though we haven't gotten it—yet. Let's keep looking for him."

Grant hurried to where they'd found the bodies, searching for clues and hoping the rugged pilot would walk toward them from the woods. Instead, he saw the trampled ferns and branches across a huge log of an improvised shelter, but still no Tom. Kate circled deep into the forest calling for him.

Back at the plane, Grant opened the door and saw the radio headset on the seat and a clipboard with Tom's preflight checklist tucked down near the floor, but no note or clue to his whereabouts. He was about to close the cockpit door when he noticed the small ice chest containing the specimen bottles on the floor behind the pilot's seat.

"The mammoth samples," Kate said, coming up behind him. "I almost forgot about them." She grabbed the cooler and opened it. The two plastic vials floated in the melted ice water. "We have to get these to the lab right away."

Grant tied the cooler to the outside of his backpack. "If Tom tried to walk out, he could have easily gotten lost. Or maybe he got injured in the crash, and he's lying hurt somewhere. Hell, he might have had a run-in with a bear."

"Or he could have made it to the visitor center and alerted the rangers. We need to get down there ourselves."

They picked up their pace as much as Kate's injuries would allow, both of them quiet and somber as they headed down the narrow, foggy path.

23

Hoh Rain Forest Visitor Center
Olympic National Park

Monday, June 15

By the time they had walked five hours from the site of the plane crash, Kate's legs trembled with fatigue. She couldn't speak, too overwrought by what they had just seen. Charlie, Alice, and Frank now dead—and maybe Tom. No, he had to be alive—the man could survive anything.

But what if he had caught the virus too?

Even though they showed no symptoms, she and Grant had to be tested. Illnesses could remain dormant in a host and then erupt suddenly. They needed to know for sure.

The trail signs became more frequent, and the footpath grew wider and more established. Her pulse sped up as they neared their destination and the end of their harrowing journey. They'd finally get help.

Kate had never met the rangers face to face, but she'd communicated with them daily using the Park Service radio to report weather conditions. How would they react to their news—illness, death, and plane crash? And what would she say about the mammoth? How could she keep control of it and the excavation, especially now that it might be the prime suspect in the deaths of her three students?

If she told them about the discovery, the story would get in the papers and swarms of people would soon be traipsing all over the glacier. She wouldn't be able to continue her research with the chaos of film crews and enthusiasts everywhere.

The truth would come out eventually, so for now she would put off revealing it as long as possible. She needed to contact Dr. Slater first and have the samples tested, and she needed more time to think. It might turn out that the mammoth had nothing to do with the deadly virus.

The path opened to a clearing and an empty paved parking lot. Kate thought again about the rangers. "Hold up a minute, Grant."

He turned around. "What's wrong?"

"Our contact with the rangers—we don't know if we're sick, and we might infect them."

"Of course. What do you want to do?"

"Why don't I go in and ask someone to meet us outside?"

"Good idea." Grant nodded toward the squat structure surrounded by massive trees at the edge of the parking lot. "Is that tiny thing the visitor center?"

"Uh-huh."

"Looks like a double-wide trailer. I expected something like a lodge with rustic beams."

"This isn't Yellowstone. But it'll be dry and warm."

She opened the door with her gloved hand and hobbled past the gift shop, her backpack and gear groaning and squeaking as she clomped in her muddy boots. A young, trim ranger walked in through a doorway behind the counter in green pants and a gray shirt, the typical Park Service uniform, his tie undone. He looked up and his eyes widened as though he wasn't expecting visitors. No one else appeared to be around.

She stopped several feet away. "I'm Dr. Kate Landry, head of the Blue Glacier Project. We've just hiked down from the station on Mount Olympus, and I need to talk with whoever's in charge."

"I'm Michael Long. I've heard you on the radio giving the weather data. Pleased to meet you. You want Chief Ranger Johnson. Just a minute." He headed through a doorway behind the counter into what appeared to be a large office or workroom.

"Hi, Michael," she called out. "I recognize your voice. I'll be on the porch."

Soon Kate and Grant were joined by a big bear of a man wearing a similar Park Service uniform. "Hi, I'm Ben Johnson."

She and Grant backed away as he approached, not responding to his outstretched hand. "I'm Dr. Kate Landry, and this is Dr. Grant Poole. Please excuse our rudeness, but we might be coming down with something, and we don't want to infect you."

Ben pointed at Kate's bandage. "What happened to your head?"

"You know the rope ladder up the ravine below Glacier Meadows?"

"Sure, very steep."

"I got hit by a rock climbing it."

"That's bad. Looks like you could use a fresh bandage. I can get you one. You might need a stitch or two. I understand you just hiked down from the Blue. We couldn't raise you on the radio. I was afraid the wind had blown your little station clear off the mountain. How can I help you?"

"Yes, we lost our radio and Internet in the storm. Sir, we need a couple of things. First, our pilot's missing, and it's critical we find him. He was forced to land upriver near Five Mile Island and may have come through here in the past twenty-four hours. His name is Tom Saunders. Have you heard from him?"

"No. Do you know for sure he survived?" Ben said.

"Yes. He was transporting two of our students to the hospital. They were seriously ill with an aggressive flu-like virus—we might have been exposed to it too."

"What happened to the students?"

"They . . . they . . ." Kate couldn't get the words out.

Grant stepped forward. "We found their bodies near the abandoned plane," he said softly.

"Jesus!" Ben took a step back.

"We think Tom might have gone to get help," she said, her voice thick with emotion. "We couldn't find him, and we're afraid something has happened to him."

"So you two think you're sick? Do you know how this bug spreads?"

"No we're not sick—at least not yet. There's a good chance we got lucky. And we aren't sure how it spreads. But this illness killed Frank, another student—we left his body back at the station. We need your help to get tested right away in case we're infected."

"I suppose now Michael and I are at risk." Ben exhaled loudly. "First, I'll call my doctor at the Forks Community Hospital and see what he suggests."

Ben pulled out his smartphone and flipped through the screens. He left a message with a Dr. Fitzgerald to call him back as soon as he could.

"Now let's try to locate your pilot." Ben paused, glancing past Kate at the forest and back. "Before we search for him in this fog, why don't I contact his home base? See if they've heard from him. Would that be the Port Angeles airport?"

Kate nodded. "Tell them to be careful when they find him, and to contact us."

Ben held the phone to his ear. "Hello, I'm Ranger Johnson calling about one of your pilots—Tom Saunders—have you heard from him? His plane went down . . . uh-huh . . . I see . . . He may have a contagious infection, so avoid physical contact and call me immediately if you locate him. Yes, I'm at the Hoh Rain Forest Visitor Center . . . thank you."

After hanging up, he said, "No word from Tom, but when he didn't return, they started to worry. Then the FAA office in Seattle called them to report that an airline pilot had picked up his Mayday."

"So is someone looking for him?" Kate asked.

"No, they said the Civil Air Patrol would start flying as soon as the weather cleared. Now that they know the location of the plane, they'll organize a ground search."

"We have a couple more favors to ask," Grant said. "Could you get us some ice for our drinks?" He pointed to the cooler on Kate's backpack. "And any chance you have some real food we could eat? All we have is trail mix."

"Sure." Ben turned to go in.

"On more thing," Kate said. "We need to arrange for a package to be shipped overnight. It's urgent."

"Huh?" Ben pivoted and frowned. "That's a little strange. You hike down a glacier, possibly infected with a deadly illness, because you have a package for FedEx?" His eyes narrowed. "What aren't you telling me?"

She hesitated, searching for what to say. When she looked to Grant for help, he raised his eyebrows and nodded, silently urging her to speak.

Kate cleared her throat. "I can see why you think it's strange. We practically killed ourselves getting here, and the first thing we ask for is mail service."

"Bingo."

She scowled at Ben. "Sorry, but that's all I can tell you. Grant and I may be dying, and we need your help."

"Dr. Landry," he said, his voice booming. "I'm responsible for the Hoh Rain Forest Visitor Center, this park, and everyone who comes to visit. Either you're going to be up front with me or you can keep walking to Forks, an hour's drive from here."

Kate straightened her back. "Hold on. I apologize. We're trying to be responsible scientists. Please trust us—we can't say anything more right now."

He frowned, then disappeared into the building.

Grant scoffed. "You really handled *that* well, Kate."

"You just stood there—why didn't you speak up?"

"It isn't my place to reveal the mammoth, but you can't ask for help and not discuss the elephant in the room. Top priority is getting tested—"

Ben came through the door with two plastic grocery bags, placed them on the concrete, and backed away. "There are your ice cubes and some bread and sandwich meat. I put a few gauze bandages in with the food. Dr. Fitzgerald's lab tech will arrive first thing in the morning. For now, consider yourselves quarantined. You can stay in one of the campsites." He pointed toward the trail. "But don't leave the perimeter of the campground. And I don't want you contaminating the lavatory and showers. Use the woods if you need a toilet."

"Yes, but what about shipping our—?"

He turned and the door closed behind him.

"We're lucky Ben let us stay here." Grant picked up the bags, and they walked down the trail toward the campground. "He could have called for an ambulance to take us to a hospital isolation unit somewhere."

"We don't know that he hasn't."

Kate was too tired to object to being quarantined in the camp-ground. Besides, they would learn soon enough if they were infected.

They picked a site in the deserted campground and set up their tent. Grant packed the ice cubes around the two vials of mammoth tissue in the cooler while Kate made sandwiches. Ravenous, they scarfed down the food—plain white bread and cold turkey had never tasted so good.

After they ate, they collapsed on their sleeping bags. Lying next to Grant, she stared up at the top of the tent, as the gloom from the foggy forest faded to darkness. "I pray we get the help we need in the morning."

"For us and for Tom."

24

Hoh Rain Forest Visitor Center
Olympic National Park

Tuesday, June 16

Despite his exhaustion, Grant tossed all night, convinced he was infected, and, if so, what about Kate? What would become of the two of them? What if she was right about the mammoth?

As he crawled bleary-eyed from their tent, a ranger emerged through the fog carrying a cardboard box and set it on the picnic table, then backed away.

"Hello again," Kate called out from the tent opening. "Michael, this is my colleague Dr. Grant Poole."

Grant waved. "What's in the box?"

"Breakfast. I told my wife about the two of you, and she wanted to make sure you had plenty to eat. I walked it over from our house nearby."

Lifting the lid, Grant pulled out containers of scrambled eggs, hash browns, ham, orange juice, and two covered coffee cups. "This is awesome. Thanks, man."

"Enjoy." Michael turned and disappeared in the fog.

They dove in, neither one speaking. Afterward, they sat at the table drinking their coffee, waiting for the lab tech to arrive. In the light of day, Grant's fears had receded some. Whatever killed Frank seemed quick. Maybe they'd be okay.

Finally, the lab tech lumbered up the trail dressed head to toe in a bulky, white hazmat suit, looking like an astronaut.

"You're not taking any chances." Grant stood and approached her.

"Darn right. Let's get this over with quick. The Hoh River is flooding, and I have to get these samples back to Forks before they close the road. Happens a lot." She collected throat and nasal swabs and blood samples from him and then Kate.

When the tech started to pack her gear, Kate asked, "Would you be willing to test a tissue sample for possible pathogens?"

"Maybe. What have you got?"

Grant pulled out one of the plastic vials from the ice in their cooler and handed it to the tech.

"What is this?" She held it up and stared at the gray chunk of flesh through the plastic.

Kate didn't skip a beat. "Some flesh from a bear we discovered buried in the glacier. The three people who died had taken samples from it for our research. We're concerned that the animal is somehow related to their deaths."

"I'll take it, but Dr. Fitzgerald will have to authorize the analysis."

The wait was making his skin crawl. Grant walked from their tent to the edge of the deserted campground and back several times, his head spinning with worry. He came from healthy stock—he had that in his favor—after all, his grandfather was still alive at ninety-five.

"Sit still, Grant," Kate said. "You're making me nervous."

Shortly after noon, Michael returned to their campsite grinning broadly. "Good news," he said. "The results came back negative—you're not infected."

Grant's knees nearly buckled with relief.

"You can come into the visitor center now. Dr. Fitzgerald wants you to call him."

Ignoring Michael, he gave Kate a long embrace.

"Thank God," she said, holding him tight.

They put their gear in the tent, except for the cooler with the tissue sample that Grant kept, and followed Michael into the lobby. He led them past the gift shop and counter into the employee workroom behind it, where windows ran the length of the room and framed the dense ferns and tree trunks outside. It was a well-lit modern workspace with a rectangular table in the middle. Two desks supporting flat-panel computer monitors and keyboards were lined up against the wall below the windows.

"Can we use a terminal to get to the Internet?" Kate motioned to the desks.

"Sorry, our web access has been down since the storm."

"Well, then can we meet Ranger Johnson? Is he here?"

"No, he's putting signs and tape across the trails to keep visitors from stumbling upon the students' bodies."

Grant wandered over and peered into an open doorway leading to an office piled high with stacks of journals, books, and nature magazines.

"That's Ben's office," Michael said. "He loves doing research. Would have made a good professor."

He picked up one of the phones in the workroom and dialed. After talking with the receptionist at the Forks Medical Center, he turned to Kate standing nearby.

"Dr. Fitzgerald will answer in a minute. Do you want me to put this on speaker so you can both hear?"

"Sure, thanks."

Michael pressed a button on the phone and left, closing the workroom door.

"This is Dr. Fitzgerald."

"Hi, this is Dr. Landry. Dr. Poole and I have you on speaker."

"Your lab test results came back negative for any dangerous pathogens."

"Michael told us," Kate said. "We're so relieved."

"But Dr. Landry, the bear tissue you asked us to analyze tested positive for an influenza virus."

She slowly shook her head. "I'm really sorry to hear that."

"Dr. Fitzgerald," Grant said, "did your technician explain that three people might have died from contact with the tissue sample?"

"Yes. And that's why we used the standard precautions in packaging and transporting it. We couldn't determine the exact strain, so I sent it to the Washington State Public Health Laboratory in Seattle for further testing. Although it's animal tissue, we need to determine if it's a threat to humans."

"A good call." Kate dropped into one of the desk chairs. "We don't want anyone else getting sick."

After hanging up, she sighed. "We are so incredibly lucky, Grant." She grew silent and had a sad, faraway look. "Not so Frank, Alice, and Charlie." Her eyes locked on his. "But we still haven't answered why you and I didn't get sick like the others."

"I know. I've been afraid all this time we would."

"Me too," she said. "We were both exposed in the tunnel and to the sick students. Maybe the pathogen isn't airborne—maybe it takes direct contact with tissue or blood."

He wandered to the far end of the room, glancing out the windows at the tree trunks shrouded in fog. There had to be an explanation, but it would take those with different training than theirs to figure it out.

"I can't believe that our mammoth—the discovery of a lifetime— could be a killer. This was one time when I didn't want to be right. And what does this mean for our research?" She fell silent for a moment, then said, "If anyone can help us, it's Dr. Slater. Now that we have access to a telephone, I'm going to contact him to see if he'll analyze the other sample." She dialed his phone number from the shipping instructions she'd attached to the cooler.

Slater answered her call. "Walter, it's Kate Landry. We uncovered something in the glacier that you might be interested in. We think it's a mammoth . . . I know, incredible . . . Would you be willing to test for the age and identity of a tissue sample? . . . Yes, but until it's confirmed, let's keep it between us. Then we'll make a joint announcement."

While Kate talked, Grant, rummaged through drawers for packing material.

"You should receive it in a day or two," Kate said, "as soon as we arrange an overnight shipment. But listen, this is very important—you must take precautions against a deadly pathogen it might contain."

She ended her call and turned to Grant. "Dr. Slater is on board.

What an extraordinary scientist. Probably about sixty and still doing fieldwork—an age when most paleontologists are in their lab. Instead, he's doing field studies on the extinction of mammoths."

"Sounds like the kind of person you want as a partner," he said. "While you were on the phone, I found everything we needed to pack our last specimen for shipment." He held up a small cardboard box. "I sealed the vial in a plastic freezer bag filled with ice, put that inside a second Ziploc freezer bag, and insulated everything with newspaper."

"Good job. Maybe Michael can help us get it shipped."

"Now that you've talked to Dr. Slater, how about calling your boss and Frank's wife?"

"I've been thinking about them. Those are going to be tough calls, so I'll use Ben's phone." Taking a deep breath, she walked over to the corner office and closed the door.

When she reemerged several minutes later, she was wiping tears from her cheeks with a balled-up tissue. She slumped into the chair next to Grant, and he reached over and put his hand on her arm.

"Oh, that was painful," she said. "I've known Annie and Frank for three years. She's in shock. I told her we'd let her know when we recovered his body from the station."

"Does she have anyone to help her through this?"

"I asked her that. She has some close friends who'll come over."

"What about your boss?"

"He understands the basic situation."

"Did you tell him about the mammoth?"

"No, Grant. He doesn't need to know until I'm ready to tell him. Nothing has changed until we get the results from Slater's lab." The impatience in her voice was unmistakable. "The more people who know about it, the more we risk people getting exposed and sick. He knows our students are dead, and the project is terminated. He'll notify Charlie's and Alice's parents, and I'll meet with them when I get back."

A loud knock on the door startled them both. Ranger Ben threw the door open so hard it banged against the wall. They both jumped up.

"Okay, you two. What the hell is *really* going on?"

25

Hoh Rain Forest Visitor Center
Olympic National Park

Tuesday, June 16

Had Ben been listening at the door? Grant quickly replayed the last few minutes in his mind. They'd been talking quietly, nearly whispering, so Ben couldn't have heard them. Something else must have happened. "What do you mean?" Grant asked.

"Dr. Fitzgerald said you had his lab analyze something you claimed came from a bear. It contained a flu virus so threatening he sent it to Public Health in Seattle. He asked me if it came from the National Park, and I had to tell him I knew nothing about it."

"He told us that too," Grant said. "What's the problem?"

"*What's the problem?*" Ben mocked. "Are you shitting me? You two don't get it. I have the well-being of thousands of visitors to consider. We've closed off the Hoh River Trail until the bodies are recovered, but that's only a temporary fix. And there's your missing pilot. My biggest problem is the source of all this."

"We've told you everything we can," Kate said.

Ben shook his head. "I gave you the benefit of the doubt. I took the chance that you might be infecting us." He glowered at them. "You either come clean, or I'm placing you both under arrest."

Grant looked at Kate. She had to stop being so stubborn about this. "You need to tell him everything."

She shook her head slightly, her eyes pleading with him. To Ben, she said, "I understand your concern, sir, but the ramifications—"

She stopped as the ranger's face darkened and the veins on his neck stood out.

Grant had no intention of letting them get arrested for withholding evidence. To hell with her secret. Staring at her while talking to Ben, he said, "The package we told you we wanted shipped is a—"

"Grant, please!" Kate shouted.

"—tissue sample from a woolly mammoth—frozen in the glacier."

"Oh great." She threw up her arms and dropped into the chair.

"What?" Ben said. "You found a mammoth with flesh intact somewhere in the Olympic National Park?"

"Yes we did," Kate said, an edge to her voice. She turned to Grant, her jaw set. "This is my story to tell." Then to Ben, she said, "What I'm about to say has to remain strictly confidential."

"I'm listening, but no promises. I'll do what's necessary to protect my rangers and visitors to this center."

Kate gestured for them to sit down and then started at the beginning, when she and Frank first discovered the mammoth last year.

As she talked, the ranger's expressions changed from baring his teeth to blinking in astonishment. "Do you think this prehistoric animal is what's making people sick?" he asked.

"It seems that way, but we won't know for sure until more samples are analyzed. Can you help us?"

Ben cocked his head toward the door. "One of my rangers is heading to Port Angeles in a few minutes, but he has to leave right away. They're about to close the Hoh River Road to Forks. The flood waters are undercutting the pavement, and it needs to be repaired. Is your sample ready?"

In three quick steps, Grant reached the refrigerator and retrieved the box from the freezer compartment. "The specimen's packed in ice and ready to go."

"You don't waste any time." Ben studied the label on the package. "Museum in Denver, huh? Let me catch the ranger." He headed out to the lobby.

The door was barely closed when Kate shot out of her chair. "Dammit, Grant, you had no right to tell him." She put her hands behind her back and paced in front of the windows. "Now that he knows, we don't have a clue what he'll do. You might have destroyed my last chance to save my research."

Grant thought of all of Ben's books and journals. The man respected science and research. "I think we can trust him."

"I hope you're right. You must understand how important this—"

The door flew open and in stormed Ben again, this time his mouth compressed into a thin line. "Well, folks, this whole thing gets worse by the minute. I just got off the phone with Dr. Fitzgerald. It turns out Public Health informed him your mammoth contains a deadly strain of influenza virus."

Kate froze and Grant braced himself for another explosion.

"Dr. Landry." Ben strode up close to her. "What's your plan for studying the mammoth?"

She stepped back. "I haven't had time to develop one," she said in a sharp tone. "I'll be collaborating with Dr. Slater at the Denver Museum of Science and Technology, one of the world's leading scientists—"

"And you expect to hear back when?"

"Within the next couple of days."

"That may not be soon enough. And if this virus is so deadly, why are you two alive?"

"We don't know," Grant said softly, eager to diffuse the situation. "We've been trying to figure that out."

"Let me know when you do," he said, his voice cold. "I want the exact location of this thing because we'll have to send a crew to destroy it for the safety of the park's visitors."

"WHAT! Destroy the mammoth!" She screamed so loudly Michael closed the door to the lobby. "It's a one-of-a kind discovery. You can't do that. There's no way in hell I'm going to tell you where it is." She pointed at Grant. "And *you* better keep your mouth shut."

"Dr. Landry, until you disclose the animal's location or come up with a credible way to study it safely, you two aren't free to leave this park. Think about it. You have until tomorrow. You can stay in the campground, but if you try to leave, I'll have you arrested." He walked out and slammed the door.

Grant and Kate stood in silence. Finally, he touched her arm. "I know you need to protect your discovery, but he has a point."

She pulled her arm away and sat down. "You're not helping. We have to wait for Dr. Slater's results and then come up with a plan."

"We better hear from him tomorrow or we're in trouble. I'm not happy either, you know."

When she didn't respond, he walked to the door. "It's getting late. Maybe Michael can help us round up some dinner."

"I don't have much appetite," she said, staring at her hands. "How will we ever get back to the research station and the mammoth? Tom is the only pilot I know with the guts to land on the Snow Dome."

"Our immediate problem is Ben. He might have us arrested in connection with the death of the three students, not to mention for refusing to tell him the location of the mammoth."

"Now I've really lost my appetite."

Michael fetched a bucket of chicken from the café five miles down the road, but they both picked at it. Kate said little, clearly still angry. It was all so surreal. After everything they'd been through, they could actually end up in jail.

When they headed out for the campground, the lobby was dark. They walked in silence the hundred yards or so past the empty parking lot through the ferns to their tent in the deserted campground.

Grant was relieved to feel the warm water of a real shower in the bathhouse a few yards from their tent—something he hadn't expected to experience for a couple more months while on the glacier.

Back at the tent, their close sleeping arrangement felt awkward now. Kate had showered earlier and crawled into her sleeping bag without a word while he was in the bath house. When he returned, he took the hint and pulled his pad and sleeping bag to the ground outside.

Lying there, the dampness of the fog drifting over him, Grant knew he had been right to divulge the secret to Ben. Everyone would find out soon anyway. This whole thing had gotten way too big for the two of them. But he also knew it would take a while for Kate to forgive him.

26

Hoh Rain Forest Visitor Center
Olympic National Park

Wednesday, June 17

A drop of water fell on Kate's face, waking her. In the dim light penetrating her tent, she reached up and touched the condensation above her head. Unzipping the flap, she saw the same blurry shapes and washed-out colors that had surrounded them for the past three days. Thankfully, the fog would discourage tourists, and Alice's and Charlie's bodies would remain undisturbed.

The weight of her sadness was almost too much to bear. Something good had to come from their deaths, but it didn't look promising. Even if Ben allowed them to leave and they somehow managed to get back to the station, would the tunnel still be there? If so, how in the hell would they extract the mammoth?

As she stepped outside the tent, Grant woke up and she muttered a quiet "good morning." Now that her anger had subsided, she regretted being so hard on him the day before.

Yawning, the two of them headed toward the visitor center, Kate still limping slightly from her bruised hip. Their path wove through grass and tall ferns and between the trunks of colossal trees. A flock of ravens squawked loudly from tree limbs in complaint at the intruders to their forest.

She headed straight for the ladies' room door in the covered area outside the visitor center entrance. In the mirror, she combed out her messy hair with her fingers, but she couldn't do much about the bandage over the spot where the rock had hit her. She gingerly lifted the blood-soaked gauze to reveal the inch-long slice in her scalp on the right side just inside the hairline. Fortunately, it had closed and would be covered by hair, so no scar. She taped on a fresh bandage.

As soon as Michael unlocked the visitor center doors from the inside, Kate charged into the brightly lit lobby, Grant behind her. Michael told them to wait and then disappeared into the workroom. She drummed the counter impatiently and scanned the posters of mountain scenes and wildlife on the walls.

When he returned, Michael was beaming. "Breakfast is served. I knew you still didn't have a way to get food, so my wife insisted on cooking again." He ushered Kate and Grant to the table in the center of the room where he'd placed a platter of bacon, pancakes, and syrup.

"Wow, Michael," Kate said, "it's really kind of you and your wife."

Grant pulled his chair next to hers. "We can't expect you to feed us forever. We'd like to pay you to bring us some lunch and dinner from the café where you got the chicken last night."

"Of course. I'll see that you don't starve."

Kate poured syrup on her pancakes. "Can we get on the Internet?"

"Help yourself. It came back up this morning."

After breakfast, she sat at one of the computers and logged onto her email account, notifying Dr. Slater he could now report his findings to her online.

"Grant, it might take a while before we hear back from Slater. I'm going to Google the 1918 influenza pandemic—this blue virus might be something similar. We've seen how horrible it can be up close."

"I'll join you."

He turned on the other computer, and the room fell silent, except for the clicking of their keys and the humming of the refrigerator in the corner.

"Oh my God," Grant said. "It's estimated that nearly fifty million people died worldwide in the 1918 pandemic. Some authorities estimate it could've been double that."

"That's partly because of World War I—people traveled across the country, Europe, the Atlantic."

"True. But think about how much more we travel today. Remember the Ebola scare. Here it says that the strain originated in China, the result of a rare genetic shift in the flu virus."

"I'm getting more nervous with every article. The symptoms then are eerily close to what Charlie, Alice, and Frank had. The difficulty breathing and blue tint of the face were signs of oxygen deprivation as their lungs filled with fluid. And get this: 'In 1918 these symptoms often appeared shortly after contact with an infected individual. Sometimes people developed the flu on their way to work and never returned.' The virus could also attack the brain, leading to hallucinations and coma."

"Listen to this, Kate. Most of the fatalities were young—between fifteen and thirty-four, just like our students. Do you think we might have been spared because we're at the high end of that range? And Tom is outside it, so maybe he's okay."

"I hope you're right. Even then, a release of this mammoth virus into the human population could potentially kill thousands—or millions."

Close to 11:00, Kate checked her emails, and Dr. Slater had just gotten back to her. With a mixture of hope and dread, she opened it and read out loud.

Dear Kate,

The overnight package you sent arrived early this morning, and our team began immediately to sequence the genome of the specimen. We used our new nanopore sequencer, which processed the genetic profile in about two hours—incredibly fast, right? We then compared the profile to that of mammoth specimens we've studied in Siberia, and we got a match. You definitely found a woolly mammoth.

We can't determine the age without a precise carbon-14 analysis requiring specialized equipment we don't have here. We will prepare your sample, removing all contaminants, and forward it to the Accelerator Mass Spectrometry (AMS) Laboratory at the University of Arizona. We should receive an accurate age in a day or two.

Personally, I would like to know whether this mammoth had contact with Paleolithic humans. Such a coexistence could support my theory that contact with humans resulted in cross-species disease that contributed to the extinction of large fauna in North America, including the mammoths.

Based on your phone call, we wore hazmat suits to ensure our staff wouldn't become inadvertently infected. The risk of a live pathogen remaining viable after this length of time is extremely low, even though the host was frozen, but we did, in fact, find some live virus, so we forwarded a sample to the Center for Disease Control for more precise analysis. We noted, with some interest, that the virus seemed to be found on the surface of the specimen and also on the container. We're not sure of the significance of that.

We have to assume that the infection your students got, somehow came from the mammoth carcass. Future exposure to the carcass must be handled with an abundance of caution. The CDC treats any new strain of virus as a serious threat to the population—especially one that is linked to a fatality.

Meanwhile, I would like to offer my services to take charge of the paleontological study. This will require careful removal and preservation of the carcass for scientific research. As you know, I've had experience in leading similar expeditions in Siberia.

I would be happy to clear my calendar for the next week or so to meet with you on or near the Blue Glacier.

Yours truly,
Dr. Walter Slater
Senior Vertebrate Paleontologist
Denver Museum of Nature and Science

She and Grant sat in silence for several minutes, and then she rose and walked to the window, her heart pounding with excitement. "It's great to have confirmation. Amazing he could analyze the tissue so fast." And Walter offered to help her—what a wonderful gift.

"He's using the latest technology." Grant focused on the computer screen in front of him. "I just searched 'nanopore sequencer,' and it promises to revolutionize genetic analysis. AMS dating is the most accurate. Only a handful of places do it—University of Arizona being one. Your Dr. Slater's on top of things."

"And his discovery of a virus confirms what Dr. Fitzgerald told us yesterday. Now that two public health labs have gotten involved, time is critical." She returned to the computer and quickly typed an email response. "I offered to share with him any journal articles and publicity that may come from documenting this find. His experience and skills would be invaluable."

"Do you think you two could develop a plan for extracting the mammoth that would satisfy Ben?"

"We better come up with something. Otherwise, we're Ben's prisoners."

"But the tunnel's in such rough shape. How are you going to study the mammoth safely?"

"I've been worried about that, but I think I have a solution. When I was a geology undergrad at the Colorado School of Mines, I had a professor who specializes in underground tunneling and construction. I can get in touch with him. He'll have a way to reinforce the tunnel. They do this sort of thing all the time."

"With ice?"

"Well, no. But it should be easier than rock." She turned to Grant. "Our bigger concern is the virus. I'm sure this place will be crawling soon with people from Public Health or the CDC."

"Are you prepared for that?" He poured himself some coffee and brought back a mug for Kate.

"No. How can we possibly disclose what we know about the illness and the location of the mammoth without starting a panic—or a stampede of publicity hunters?"

"Do what you did with Dr. Slater." He motioned with his hand to her screen. "Swear them to secrecy and trust they'll do the right thing with the information."

"But too many people know already—our time is limited before it's the whole world."

"Kate, this whole situation has become too complicated for us to handle on our own."

Michael popped his head into the workroom. "There's someone here for you: Dr. Lillian Lee. She drove down from Washington State Public Health in Seattle."

"Crap. It's starting already."

Grant stood and shut the door to the lobby. "What are you going to tell her?"

"I sure as hell won't reveal the mammoth—she'd say it has to be destroyed. I'll think of something."

"She's sworn to protect the public at all costs, and she'll be looking for the source. We *must* tell her—or Ben will."

Kate slammed a book on the desk and stood so fast her chair fell with a crash. "Goddamn it, Grant," she whispered loudly. "We have to stall her. At least till we sort this out."

He recoiled, then moved toward the door. She flew around the table into his path and put her hands on his chest to stop him. "I can't let you do this." She'd fight him physically if she had to.

"Kate, you have to deal with the threat." He grabbed her shoulders. "You say your research is critical to adapting to glacial melt and slowing the process. Yet you're willing to risk a pandemic that could wipe out millions of people? You're not thinking clearly."

"Are you calling me incompetent? How dare you." Blood pounded in her ears. She knew she should stop, but she couldn't help herself. "You know what? You're fired. I never wanted you to come here in the first place."

He thrust out his chest. "Really? Well, you can't fire me. NASA hired me through your boss. And I knew the minute I arrived you didn't want me here. You want all the publicity for the mammoth for yourself. Well, you can have it. But I won't let you kill people in the process."

"So now I'm killing people—is that what you think?" she yelled.

"You know what I meant. Jesus. Calm down." He held up his hand.

Michael opened the door. "What's taking so long? Dr. Lee's growing impatient."

"All right, Grant," she said through gritted teeth. "But we're not done. This is *my* show. You'd better follow my lead."

"Or what, Kate? Remember, I'm not the enemy here. I'm on your side."

27

Hoh Rain Forest Visitor Center
Olympic National Park

Wednesday, June 17

Walking through the lobby, Grant tried to shake off his anger. At last the truth had come out—he hadn't misread Kate's disgust when he first arrived. But he thought they had moved past that, especially after the night in the cabin. Of course, she wasn't herself—who would be after what had happened? Neither was he.

Ahead of them on the couch sat Dr. Lee, a slender, middle-aged woman with long, dark hair in a gray suit, white blouse, and burgundy scarf, a laptop open beside her. After they introduced themselves, she said, "That was quite a storm. They were doing emergency repairs on the highway from Forks as I drove in this morning."

"Yes," Grant said, "we experienced the storm firsthand on the glacier and then hiking down here." He asked Dr. Lee to join them in the workroom, where he sat as far apart from Kate as possible on the opposite end of the table.

Dr. Lee looked at Grant and then Kate. "Before I get to the reason I'm here," she said, "I couldn't help but pick up on the tension between you. Is it related to anything I should know? Maybe about the deaths of the students?"

Grant shot a glance at Kate. "Dr. Landry and I disagree about the best way to report the deaths. You need to know—"

Kate cut him off. "Dr. Lee, as head of the Blue Glacier Project, I think I should speak for our team." The doctor's head swung toward her end of the table. "Dr. Poole is a visiting scientist who has been with us for only a week."

"Please call me Lillian," she said. "Look, I didn't mean to aggravate the situation. I want to hear what you both have to say, but let me start by explaining why I'm here. Can we proceed?"

Kate stared down at the tabletop with folded arms and nodded.

Grant paused, surprised by Kate's sudden change in demeanor, then said, "Yes, please go ahead."

"My office at the Washington Department of Public Health received a report of a previously unknown strain of influenza virus forwarded to our laboratory from a physician in Forks, Washington. Coincidentally, a similar report came from the CDC this morning based on a sample from the Denver Museum of Nature and Science. Both samples apparently came from the same source. Do you know about this?"

"Yes, we requested the tests," Kate said. "We thought they might be contaminated."

Lillian typed notes on the laptop opened in front of her. "Since we know this virus has resulted in confirmed fatalities, my office has implemented the Influenza Pandemic Protocol, which authorizes me to take charge of the outbreak."

"We're glad you're here," Grant said. "The illness is so serious we hiked down from the Blue Glacier during the recent storm to get help."

"The bodies of two of my students are next to the trail," Kate said. "We need them to be picked up right away. We left a third in the research station on the Blue Glacier."

"The CDC is alarmed," Lillian said. "They've deployed a Disaster Mortuary Operational Response Team, or DMORT. You'll probably hear that acronym a lot over the next few days. They're bringing a portable morgue unit for processing and transporting the bodies. It should arrive anytime, and they like to keep a low profile to not cause panic. Their mission is to ensure all bodies are handled properly so the disease doesn't spread and to provide a secure facility for conducting autopsies." She looked in Kate's direction. "You can pass the information about your dead students along to the DMORT staff when they arrive."

She typed for a few minutes, then looked up. "Given the lethal nature of this illness, can I assume that neither of you has shown signs of it?"

"That's correct," Kate said.

"When did you have your last flu shot, if at all?"

"In November, at the start of flu season," Grant said.

"January," Kate said.

"Do you require your students to get flu shots? Does the university?"

"No. We strongly recommend it, but it's not a requirement."

"Hmm. I suspect your three students didn't bother then. Who got sick first?"

"Charlie, then Alice, then Frank," Kate said. "All three were working together for several hours in a small ice tunnel gathering data."

"Uh-huh. Was Charlie sick before he entered the tunnel?"

"No, as far as we know. Frank told me Charlie started coughing and sneezing once they were inside. Alice came down with it the next day and Frank the day after that."

Lillian typed quickly. "Other symptoms?"

"Sore throat, high fever, and a wheezing cough. Extreme fatigue. Their lips turned a scary blue as well."

"Okay." She stopped typing and leaned back in her chair. "Now, Kate, where did those tissue samples come from? One report said they came from a bear—is that correct?"

Kate flinched—no more easy questions. She glanced over at Grant, her face pale. He nodded at her, urging her with his eyes to tell the truth. "Well, Lillian," she said softly. "I need to begin by—"

Michael opened the door, and voices from the lobby spilled into the room. "You have more visitors."

Four men and a woman all geared up in rugged outdoor clothing and backpacks strode into the room. The tall fortyish man in the lead introduced himself. "I'm George Friedlander, Olympic Mountain Rescue. The FAA alerted us two days ago about a Mayday message from a pilot whose plane is now missing."

Grant stood and shook his hand.

Kate remained seated. "You guys certainly took your time. We already found the plane."

"Yes ma'am. We were told that flight operations at the Port Angeles Airport got a call from a Ranger Johnson that the plane had been located. It was impossible to mount a search until now because the road was washed out and closed since yesterday. We came as soon as we could get through." Friedlander walked over to Kate. "Tell us what you found."

"Yes, I apologize," she said, her voice softening. "It's been a tough few days. We found the plane about five miles upriver—along with the bodies of the two students it was carrying. There's no sign of the pilot."

"Mr. Friedlander," Grant said, "we're in the middle of an interview about the illness that took the lives of three students." He gestured with his hand. "This is Dr. Lee from the Washington State Department of Public Health."

Lillian nodded and gave a quick hello. "You must *not* go to the plane," she said. "The bodies are contaminated with what we believe is a contagious virus. The CDC is sending a team to process them to keep the disease from spreading. The pilot may be infected as well."

Through the open door to the lobby, Grant spotted a truck pulling into the visitor center parking lot with bold lettering on the side: "National Transportation Safety Board." Three men approached the counter and told Michael they were there to conduct an accident investigation on the downed aircraft. Hearing that, Friedlander and his crew left the workroom and crowded into the small lobby.

Then a Seattle TV van pulled up, followed by the CDC portable morgue unit.

Grant groaned. Kate leaned across the table. "That's a *very* low profile, Lillian—a van marked 'Portable Morgue Unit' parked by the front door next to the TV news crew."

Lillian excused herself and raced out to deal with the public relations disaster in the parking lot.

Kate buried her head in her hands. "This is my worst nightmare." Leaping from her chair, she strode over to Grant, her arms waving out to the lobby. "It's total bedlam out there. How do we know if we can trust any of these people? One or two, maybe, but they're coming in droves. I could use your help."

She sounded nervous, but he couldn't let her off the hook so easily. "Really? Hmm, that's not what you said a few minutes ago."

"Okay, okay." She put her hand up. "I was totally out of line. I blew it—you have every right to be angry with me. I'm sorry."

He didn't respond.

"Grant, group work is your expertise—can you please run interference for me?"

He glanced at the scene unfolding in the lobby. Representatives of the various government agencies spoke with one another, the volume of conversation rising. The TV reporter roamed through the crowd, trailed by her cameraman, and asked questions, writing notes in a pocket-sized spiral notebook.

He nodded. "I'll see what I can do."

When Grant went into the lobby, he stood close to Michael behind the counter so he could be heard over the din. "Can you corral people here while I take the heads of each agency into the workroom? We'll try to sort this out."

Michael gave him a thumbs-up, then put his fingers between his lips and produced a deafening whistle. The room went silent. "Team leads, please follow Dr. Poole," he shouted and pointed to him. When the reporter fell in line, Michael put up a hand to stop her. "Ma'am, I have to ask you to wait here." The woman argued with him as the leaders filed into the room.

After closing the door, Grant introduced himself as one of the scientists working on the Blue Glacier Project. "Dr. Kate Landry has asked me to develop a coordinated plan among the six of us here." He asked everyone to give their names, organization, and reason for being there.

At the head of the table, a man leaned forward on his crossed arms. "I'm Ramone Rodriguez from the National Transportation Safety Board, or NTSB. My team has orders to locate the downed aircraft and document the cause of the forced landing."

On a flip chart mounted on an easel, Grant wrote "NTSB" next to Rodriguez's name and his intended objective.

Friedlander sat with his chair pushed back and looked up at Grant. "I'm George Friedlander from Olympic Mountain Rescue. We're here to locate and rescue the missing pilot."

Grant continued to list names and missions on the chart.

At the other end of the table sat a distinguished-looking gentleman with black hair streaked with gray. He wore dark green medical scrubs. "My name is Dr. Raj Singh. I'm in charge of the Federal Disaster Mortuary Operational Response Team—DMORT for short."

As soon as they heard the word "mortuary," Rodriguez and Friedlander exchanged glances with furrowed brows.

"Our team's here to retrieve the bodies of two young adults," Dr. Singh continued. "We'll also ensure that the virus from their bodies doesn't pass to anyone else."

Next to Dr. Singh, Lillian introduced herself. "I represent Washington State Public Health. Our job is to document the source of the virus and see that it's fully contained."

After Kate introduced herself, Lillian raised her hand.

"Dr. Poole, wouldn't it make more sense for Dr. Singh or me to take charge? This is clearly a medical emergency because of the risk of an uncontrolled epidemic."

Dr. Singh nodded in agreement.

Friedlander pulled his chair closer to the table. "We can't afford to wait. Mountain Rescue needs to get into the field immediately—the life of the pilot is at stake."

Dr. Singh held up his hands, palms out. "No one should go near the bodies or the contaminated aircraft without protective gear and after all surfaces have been disinfected."

"Hold on." Rodriguez stood up. "Are you saying that the NTSB can't examine the wreckage for its investigation until the health department says we can? We're losing valuable information as the crash site is compromised by the passage of time."

Lillian pointed across the table. "Sit down, Rodriguez! You're out of line. We're dealing with a health emergency of potentially major proportions."

"I can't believe this." Friedlander pointed at Lillian. "Just because you have a "Dr." in front of your name doesn't automatically put you in charge. We have some major grandstanding going on over some bodies when the life of the pilot is at stake. The longer we argue, the more likely we'll find him dead too."

"Look, we didn't come here for a team-building exercise," Rodriguez said to Grant. Others nodded in agreement. "We have work to do."

They all stood and shouted at once across the table.

Grant glanced at Kate, and she rolled her eyes. By God, he said he'd help, and he would, whatever it took.

He yelled to get their attention, and when that didn't get them to stop, he slammed his hand on the table. Everyone jumped and the room went quiet. "Listen, you all have important jobs to do. Dr. Lee, what's your professional judgment about how we should proceed?"

"*Everyone* should wear hazmat suits just in case. Whether Tom is found dead or alive, we have to assume he's infected until we can confirm one way or the other."

"Because this virus is particularly virulent," Dr. Singh said, "the crew analyzing the plane crash better wear protective gear too."

Rodriguez shook his head in disgust. "You've got to be kidding."

"We don't have suits," Friedlander shouted, "and even if we did, it's too hot to hike in them."

Lillian turned to Grant. "We need to exclude these crews altogether if they're unwilling to protect themselves and the public from infection."

Dr. Singh came to her side. "I agree. These people are dangerous."

Just when things couldn't get crazier, the door to the workroom opened. Dressed in his uniform and wearing his hat, Ranger Ben Johnson looked like Smokey the Bear as he strode purposefully to the front of the room.

Ben's skeptical attitude would surely poison this unruly group. The disappointment on Kate's face mirrored what Grant felt. Their efforts to preserve the woolly mammoth and her research had failed.

"Welcome to the Hoh Rain Forest Visitor Center," Ben said in a firm, official voice. "I understand you're here because you have a job to do and you want to get started. I know you need information from Dr.

Landry and Dr. Poole." He motioned to Kate and Grant. "These two scientists have my highest respect, trust, and confidence."

Grant and Kate exchanged surprised looks.

"The situation that led each of you to our visitor center is complicated and serious. If we, and I mean *we*, are to resolve the issues at hand in a way that benefits everyone, then I insist you work with Dr. Landry and Dr. Poole to create a plan respectful of your needs and those of their Blue Glacier Project. Is that understood?"

Grant glanced around the room as Ben spoke. His authoritative voice and words did the trick. Everyone quieted down and took their seats.

28

Hoh Rain Forest Visitor Center
Olympic National Park

Wednesday, June 17

Kate would attempt to live up to the endorsement Ben had given her. She dared not blow it—her research, her career, and solutions to climate change were all at stake, not to mention the lives of thousands exposed to a potential pandemic. Nodding to the ranger, who had taken a seat in the corner, she glanced at Grant now in her former spot at the table.

He had come through for her, even after she had treated him so badly in the workroom. Smiling, he turned around to support her with a discreet fist-bump in his lap.

"Dr. Poole and I will answer your questions, but first I'll try to connect the dots that brought you here." She hesitated. "Before I tell our story, I must ask each of you to agree to strict confidentiality."

The four responders seated around the table agreed, nodding, but Dr. Singh added the caveat "unless I must act on your information to fulfill my mission."

Another concession. She had no choice but to accept his condition— they needed his help. Grant had been right. The events had become too difficult for them to figure out on their own.

Again, she launched into the mammoth story and described the students' deaths and Tom's disappearance. The details hadn't lost any of their gut-wrenching pain in the retelling.

"Amazing," Friedlander said when she asked for questions. "That sounds more impressive than the bones of the Sequim mastodon found down the road."

What a relief to hear something positive.

But then Lillian spoke up. "Although this is fascinating, what does it have to do with the illness and deaths we're here to investigate? Are you telling us you think the mammoth made your students sick?"

"I can't say for sure. I do know our students were healthy prior to their exposure to the mammoth. I also know tissue samples from it contained an unknown strain of influenza virus." She looked pointedly at Lillian. "Maybe you can tell us whether a mammoth, thousands of years old, could contain a live virus."

Before she could respond, Singh said, "It seems unlikely a virus could survive and be viable after such a long time—even remaining frozen."

"I have to agree." Lillian scanned the room, all eyes on her. "To my knowledge, no influenza virus has remained potent after thawing from a frozen state. An unsuccessful attempt was made to infect ferrets with material collected from frozen bodies of Native Alaskans who had died in the 1918 influenza outbreak. But two labs have confirmed a previously unknown strain of flu virus in the tissues taken from the mammoth carcass."

"And recently," Dr. Singh said, "anthrax spores melting from a reindeer carcass in Siberia caused at least one death."

"So Dr. Landry," Lillian said, "The recent data tells us we must take seriously the possibility that this mammoth is, in fact, the source of the virus that killed those students."

Friedlander lifted his backpack onto the table. "While you two argue about the theoretical origins of the virus, we need to find the pilot—he's at risk but also an imminent threat." He pushed back from the table. "My Olympic Mountain Rescue crew is ready to find the pilot. Just say the word."

"And my people need to recover the bodies before the damned TV reporters find them," Dr. Singh said. "Can we speed this up?"

Grant rose from his seat and, standing next to Kate, flipped the chart on the easel to a blank page. With a marker, he printed "Immediate Actions" on the top in large letters. After ripping off that sheet and taping it to the wall behind him, he turned to the next sheet on the easel and wrote, "Long-Term Actions."

"Okay, let's have it," he said. Everyone called out at once, firing directives at him so fast he had to scribble to keep up.

Lillian and Singh concurred that the emergency teams could proceed as long as anyone in direct contact with the bodies, the plane, or the pilot wore a hazmat suit. Singh had brought four extra suits and offered to give two each to Mountain Rescue and the NTSB to carry until needed.

The DMORT crewmembers had their own suits. They would handle direct contact with the bodies. This included using a strong chlorine bleach solution to disinfect the sites where the bodies had rested and the interior of the downed aircraft. The deceased would be transported in sealed body bags to the portable morgue unit parked at the trailhead.

Mountain Rescue and the NTSB offered their own action steps. Thirty minutes later, the project leaders of each team had clear tasks to carry out. Everyone pushed back their chairs and stood to leave.

Kate still wasn't convinced she could trust them. "Wait. Again, do you agree to keep this to yourselves? If word gets out, the result could be—and I'm not exaggerating—a worldwide outbreak on the scale of the notorious 1918 flu pandemic."

All of them threw out a cursory yes as they hurried into the lobby.

Grant sucked in his breath and turned to her. "Whew. That was an accomplishment. But now someone needs to deal with the media. Ben would be the logical choice."

"Agree."

The ranger was about to walk out the visitor center door when Kate rushed over to him. "Hey, Ben." He stopped and turned. "Would you be willing to handle the press? I don't think they'll be pacified for long with 'no comment.'"

"Of course. I could issue a press release from the Park Service—something like 'We are investigating three mysterious deaths, and visitors aren't allowed until we know the source of the problem.'"

Ben went to his office while Michael tried to maintain order in the lobby. The responders had gathered around their leaders to hear the plans and their excited voices kept rising. Michael had to whistle a couple of times to keep the noise down.

Kate and Grant were still in the lobby when some of the crewmembers left to prepare for their hikes up the trail. The reporter was rebuffed by one person after another as she asked them questions. The team leads had kept their mouths shut as they had promised.

But when Kate saw more reporters arriving, she hurried to Ben's office. "More media people have arrived. How is the press release coming?"

He looked up from his computer. "It's printing. I'll give them the handout and meet with them in a minute."

As the DMORT, public health, and NTSB responders got their equipment ready and opened and shut their vehicle doors, the rhythmic throb of an approaching helicopter made everyone look to the sky. Within seconds, the chopper descended into the vacant area on the far end of the parking lot.

Everyone in the lobby rushed outside to watch the helicopter drop out of the intense blue sky. The fog had now burned off, but the tall trees surrounding the parking lot made the landing perilous. Kate ran out too, concerned it might be more press. Instead, someone she knew stepped out of the helicopter.

She would recognize that bald head with the fuzzy curls above the ears anywhere—Dr. Walter Slater, her friend from the Denver Museum of Nature and Science. Finally, she would have serious help recovering her woolly mammoth.

29

Hoh Rain Forest Visitor Center
Olympic National Park

Wednesday, June 17

Grant followed Kate outside, worried the arrival of the helicopter would derail his hard-fought plan before it had even started—the situation was already chaotic enough. No longer a mere observer, he had become a key player in keeping things on track and didn't want to let Kate down. He'd been useless far too much in his life.

"Walter!" Kate shouted over the helicopter's whine. "It's so good to see you." She extended her hand to the short, stocky man. "I want you to meet my colleague Dr. Grant Poole. He joined us on the glacier to study our research team." She turned to Grant. "Walter and I have known each other for years."

He shook the paleontologist's beefy hand. "Very pleased to meet you, sir." The famous Dr. Slater couldn't have looked more unassuming in his rumpled khakis and T-shirt. He had some of the bushiest eyebrows Grant had ever seen.

As the three of them headed to the visitor center, Walter excused himself and went to the men's room while Grant continued on with Kate into the lobby. He took her arm and guided her to a corner. "Did he tell you he was coming?"

"No," she whispered. "When I replied to his email, I took him up on his offer to help, but I had no idea he'd be here today."

"This will complicate things, especially with Lillian and the health department."

"I know. But we need a strong advocate for the mammoth."

Walter joined them and pointed back outside. "What are all these people doing here? Did you hold a press conference?"

"Absolutely not." Kate glanced at the responders and all their gear on the walkway. "Any public announcement will come from the two of us. They're here because of the plane crash and deaths of my students—also to prevent an outbreak. We have lots to do before we're ready to go public."

"Then let's get to work." He picked up his well-worn canvas duffel and followed her into the workroom.

Lillian was still typing on her laptop but stopped as the three joined her at the table. After introductions, Grant turned to Walter. "How did you get here so fast? You received our shipment and analyzed the tissue sample in Denver just this morning."

"After I got Kate's urgent request for help, I had my assistant book the first available flight and arrange to charter the helicopter and pilot at the Seattle airport. I went directly from the museum to Denver International without stopping for my gear. I'll have to buy everything locally if we go to the glacier."

"I understand there's a sporting goods store in Forks," Lillian said, "about an hour's drive away."

"Good. I'll have to arrange for a lift when the time comes."

"Let's get you briefed on where things stand now," Grant said.

Walter already knew some of the story from Kate's phone call and emails, so they picked up from there, filling him in on more of the details of the last few days. Then Grant walked over to the flip charts on the wall and summarized the plan the team leads had created.

The paleontologist slowly shook his head. "I've extracted frozen mammoths in Siberia, although I never had to wear a hazmat suit before. It'll be a challenge."

Lillian closed her laptop. "I don't know what you have in mind, Dr. Slater, but any contact with this mammoth is unacceptable. The carcass is melting from its frozen state in a chamber with virtually no air circulation. It's almost impossible to work with it without contracting and spreading the virus. We can't risk it."

Walter lowered his head and peered at her from under his bushy eyebrows, his chin firmly set. "I get your priority, Dr. Lee, but you need to know that protecting the mammoth is *mine*. This specimen sounds like something we've never seen before. It could help account for the mass extinction of all large mammals."

Grant glanced around the table. What was up with all these people? Wasn't anyone willing to work together? A bunch of prima donnas. "Lillian," he said, "what if Walter is cautious?"

"It's not as simple as that. The virus doesn't care if the person who breathes it is cautious or not. It remains just as deadly."

Kate's eyes darted between Lillian and Walter. "No one wants another fatality—God knows, I've lost three students. But from all the research I've been able to do, this mammoth discovery is unique. Lillian, there has to be a way to preserve it for science, and Walter has the expertise to do this. I want to figure out a way to give him the opportunity."

Lillian shook her head. "The risks of an outbreak are just too great. Contact with the mammoth has already resulted in at least three deaths, and there could be more. I'm sorry—it must be destroyed."

Kate's face fell. "But you don't understand—"

The doctor held up her hand. "What is there to understand? That specimen has the potential to wipe out millions of people."

Grant dragged the flip chart easel to the head of the table. "Lillian, you said it would be *almost* impossible to come in contact with the mammoth without spreading the virus. Almost. That tells me it's complicated but doable. Give us a list of all the protocols that would have to be followed."

Lillian let out a deep breath. "A lot would need to be done."

"Like?" He stood poised to write on the chart with the marker.

"First, everyone would have to wear a hazmat suit. That includes a disposable hood, safety glasses, a respirator, disposable double gloves, a wrap-back disposable gown, and disposable shoe covers."

"Okay. What else?"

"When exiting the tunnel after working on the mammoth, everyone must discard their protective gear in a biohazard bag at the entrance."

"And?"

"All hand tools used to work on the mammoth would need to be decontaminated before being removed from the work area."

"Is that it?"

"Yes."

Grant turned to Walter. "What do you think?"

"Done." Walter nodded at Lillian. "And we'll have you, or whoever you trust, check our equipment and procedures before we get started."

She pursed her lips. "I'll agree, but only as long as there isn't a *single* breach of these protective protocols. They're required as a component of the Washington State Department of Public Health Pandemic Response Policy. They're not my criteria, although I think they're essential." She looked at Kate. "I must warn all of you, if a breach occurs, that carcass will be soaked in gasoline and burned to destroy any possibility of an outbreak. And those exposed will be quarantined in an isolation unit."

Walter leaned forward, about to say something.

Grant willed him to let it go. They were teetering on the edge with Lillian as it was, and Walter could blow it completely for them.

Kate reached out and put her hand on the paleontologist's arm. "Walter," she said softly, "you know how long you've been searching for something like this. I need it too. You've already taken similar precautions back in your lab. Do what Lillian asks."

He crossed his arms and sat back in his chair. "I'll do this for you, Kate. And you're right—for both of us. Let's see what you've found, and we'll go from there."

Back from the brink, they moved on to more mundane topics, like who would go to the glacier and how they'd make the steep climb and get all the supplies to the research station.

"Not to worry," Walter said, laughing. "Have you forgotten? I have a helicopter."

So Kate, Lillian, and Walter would fly to the research station the next morning, and Grant would stay behind and arrange to get back to Santa Cruz. He could barely tolerate the thought—how could he leave now? But what else could he do? He'd just be in the way on the Snow Dome.

Grant looked at Kate, the calmest he'd seen her in days now that Walter was there and they could return to the station. She was in efficiency mode, busy making a list of food, supplies, and outdoor gear they'd need. "Lillian," she said, "you won't last an hour on the glacier in those business clothes and dress shoes. You and Walter have to go shopping."

Michael gave them directions to a couple of stores in Forks where they could buy boots, parkas, rainproof shells, and ice axes, along with the food they would need. Lillian arranged for a supply of disposable personal protective equipment and disinfectant to be delivered to her at the visitor center the next morning.

From the lobby, Grant and Kate watched as the unlikely pair walked to Lillian's car, the short, frumpy scientist beside the intense, well-dressed doctor. They'd spend the night in a motel and return early the next morning.

As they drove away, Kate turned to him and smiled.

30

Hoh River Trail
Olympic National Park

Wednesday, June 17

After Grant and Kate returned to the workroom, Dr. Singh stuck his head in the door. "Dr. Poole, can we talk to you for a minute?"

"Sure, come on in."

Singh disappeared, returning with Rodriguez.

"We could use your help, Grant," Singh said. "Ben told us you wouldn't be going to the glacier in the morning. Could you lead us to the plane and the bodies? It would save us time."

He didn't hesitate. "I'd be happy to take you. Give me twenty minutes to pack my gear at the campground."

"Really appreciate it. We need to leave as soon as possible. It'll be getting dark in just a couple of hours. Friedlander's Olympic Mountain Rescue crew has already left to hunt for the pilot."

Kate said nothing after they left, focusing on her laptop. Hell, she was hard to figure out. Was she sorry or relieved to see him go? He asked her to program waypoints in her GPS so he could lead the first responders to the plane while he went to pack his things. She agreed and said he should take their tent, since Michael had offered to loan her one for the night.

When Grant returned wearing his backpack, he saw her through the glass doors. She walked out to meet him on the porch and took his hand. "We'll be gone when you get back tomorrow. I want to thank you for all your help."

He lowered his pack to the pavement and stepped close to her, so close he could smell the shampoo in her hair. "We've spent day and night together," he said softly into her ear. "Wish we'd had a chance to talk about everything—over a beer or something."

"I wish we could have too."

Grant turned to see the DMORT crew waiting by the sign marking the start of the trail. "They're leaving. I have to go." He swung the pack onto his back and snapped the waist and chest strap fasteners. "Good luck with the mammoth. Maybe we can get together once this is all over and you're back in Seattle." He doubted that would happen, but it was worth saying.

They hugged briefly, and Grant hustled to catch up to the men already walking single file past the sign as the setting sun shone on the tops of the tallest trees. Before the trail veered off into the dark shadows of the forest, he looked back at Kate and lifted his arm in salute. She held her arm high in return.

Grant took the lead, followed by Dr. Singh and his three-man/one-woman mortuary team, then Rodriguez and his NTSB investigation crew of two additional men. They all wore hiking boots and rugged clothes, and the designated individuals carried hazmat suits in their backpacks. The DMORT people had matching green jackets, and the NTSB crew wore dark blue jackets with the federal government patch.

Within minutes, they were greeted by the massive trees and sweet, musty smell of the forest. Focusing on his stride, Grant walked fast to set the pace for a crew of young men and women in peak condition, though he wasn't eager to see the two students' bodies again.

At a small waterfall, they stopped for a brief break. Checking the GPS, he saw they had come about two miles, three more to go. They still had some late-afternoon daylight, but it would probably be dark by the time they reached the plane.

As they were about to continue on, Singh's handheld radio came to life. "DMORT, this is Mountain Rescue," the male voice on the radio announced.

"Singh here. Go ahead."

"We found the pilot," announced an unemotional voice on the speaker.

"And?"

"He's dead."

"Damn," Grant said. Kate would be devastated.

Singh brought the radio to his lips. "Where was he? What happened to him?"

"His body was about a mile east of the visitor center. Looks like he got disoriented in the fog and went about a hundred yards off the trail and into the undergrowth. Appears to have been pretty sick—same blue-gray color to his face and neck Dr. Landry described."

"Don't touch or move the body—the virus is highly contagious. Stand by a minute." He talked with his crewmen behind him, then returned to the radio. "Have someone from your team wait by the trail to take us to the body. I'm sending a man with a stretcher and body bag to meet you and handle the retrieval. One of your people will have to wear a hazmat suit and help my man transport the body."

So that confirmed it—Tom never had direct contact with the mammoth, so he must have contracted the virus from Charlie or Alice. Lillian would make it even harder for Kate and Walter, knowing now that the virus spread from infected individuals through the air and appeared to pose an even greater risk than they had first feared.

Since the portable morgue unit was at the visitor center, Grant and Singh agreed that the man from the mortuary team would also inform Ben, who would then tell Kate about Tom's death. Better that than having her hear it over the unsecured Park Service radio.

They moved on. When they came to a log spanning a rocky ravine with a small stream at the bottom, he crossed with both arms extended, nervously focusing on the log in front and not the rocks below. Looking back, he marveled at how briskly the others walked across, seeming to have some internal gyroscope for balance.

On one of their short breaks, he spotted an owl not ten feet from him sitting motionless at eye level on a large branch. Even with its huge round eyes staring directly his way, he would never have seen it had he not stopped. An NTSB crewman spooked the bird, and it spread its massive wings and flew silently deep into the forest.

The bird reminded Grant of Athena's Owl, the rock outcrop he and Kate had climbed days earlier. They had just begun what could have been an exciting summer together. Who knows what might have developed between them?

"Magnificent bird," the DMORT man standing next to him said. "Amazing to see it so close in the wild. I've heard Native Americans think owls portend death."

"Let's hope not—there's been enough of that," Grant said, moving on up the trail, the others falling in line close behind.

As the forest darkened to deep shadows, everyone in the party turned on either a headlamp or flashlight and kept a steady pace, scanning both sides of the trail. Grant glanced back and saw the string of lights behind him, like headlights he would see in his rearview mirror while driving down the highway.

"According to the GPS, we're getting close," he said. "I'll recognize the clearing. It's where the path skirts around a huge tree."

"We've got something here!" A member of the mortuary team shone his flashlight beam on a yellow plastic poncho. The group gathered around the spot. The poncho was slightly mounded and anchored at the edges by river rocks—as Grant and Kate had left it.

"Here's the other one," said the NTSB crewman standing over the blue tarp.

"Don't lift the covers or disturb the bodies," Singh said. "We'll take care of them in the morning."

"Let's look for the plane," Rodriguez said.

"It's this way." Grant headed off toward the gravel bar and river. The crashing rumble of the river grew louder as he approached.

The downed aircraft had shifted. The left wheel was now almost completely submerged in the fast-moving current, and the wings tilted so far that the left wing tip balanced precariously inches from the thundering rapids, while the right wing pointed to the sky. The runoff from the violent storm had swelled the Hoh River, causing it to widen and deepen enough to undermine the wheels.

The water surged by him, making Grant's legs go weak. He stepped back from the edge.

"We need to tie the plane off before we lose it," Rodriguez shouted. He and his two crewmen pulled ropes from their packs. One man stepped off the bank into the icy water and waded slowly out to the partially submerged wheel, holding onto the fuselage and wing to keep from being swept away. He tied his line, and the other man did the same to the right side. Then they anchored the other ends of their ropes to two huge tree trunks nearby. Rodriguez fastened another cord to the tie-down loop on the tail and then to a large rock.

The plane now secure, Grant led the crews to the campground he remembered up the trail, where they could set up their tents on the flat clearing surrounded by trees. Soon the camp stoves were heating water for their meager dinners of dehydrated food and beef jerky.

They sat in a semicircle on logs while Rodriguez used a fire starter stick to get a modest fire going, the wood too wet from the recent storm to burn otherwise. The man who waded into the river sat shivering trying to warm up. It reminded Grant of how cold he had been a few miles from there, when Kate had crawled into the sleeping bag to warm him up—a memory he cherished. Soon everyone had disappeared into their tents and zipped their sleeping bags for the night.

Grant had trouble going to sleep. The river thundered in his ears as images of the last few days flashed before him. Charlie's face as he struggled to breathe. Alice barely able to speak when he lifted her into the plane. The final minutes of Frank's life. He shook his head to clear the memories.

So much heartache. And through it all, there was Kate. He missed her, angry outbursts and all. Being with her had made him feel alive in ways he hadn't experienced before, even with Megan.

He dozed on and off. During the night, the rain returned and beat on his tent. In seconds, it seemed, water seeped in and pooled around him, soaking his pad and the sleeping bag. He started sliding. What the hell?

The stakes had pulled loose, and the current was sweeping him into the raging river.

Oh my God.

The zipper on his bag was stuck. Come on! He frantically felt for the zipper on the tent. It wouldn't budge either.

He was going to drown.

He thrashed wildly to break free. Then he screamed. He screamed and screamed until he woke himself from the nightmare.

His heart raced. Panting for air, he felt around the tent floor beside the sleeping bag. Dry. He unzipped the tent and felt the ground. Dry there too.

"You okay?" someone shouted from their tent.

"Yeah, sorry. I had a bad dream."

The water, the blackness, had seemed so real.

He slid back down into his sleeping bag. Oh man. What was that about?

Charlie, Alice, Frank, and Tom came to mind again. So many deaths. A week ago, all four of them had been alive. They had friends, families, bright futures ahead of them.

And Megan—her life also tragically cut short.

He didn't know what the nightmare was trying to tell him, but he knew one thing for certain. Death could come in an instant. And without warning. So he needed to stop wasting his time on a career, on people, on a life that had no meaning.

31

Hoh Rain Forest Visitor Center
Olympic National Park

Thursday, June 18

The next morning lying in the tent she had borrowed from Michael, Kate felt adrift on her own following the intense few days she had spent with Grant.

It was unlikely they'd ever see each other again. Probably for the best. Her history was fraught with relationship disasters.

But Grant was different. He had been there for her from the start, even putting up with her temper. Instead of taking off for home as many people would have, he didn't hesitate to stay and help the responders. Yes, in just a matter of days, she had come to depend on him, on his quiet strength and good nature—and courage.

While folding the tent, she marveled at the crystal-clear sunrise, the kind that only occurs after the rain has washed all the dust from the air. She gathered her things and headed for the showers in the campground and later passed Walter's helicopter in the parking lot on her way to the visitor center. Using her laptop in the workroom, she listed the tasks she needed to accomplish back on the glacier—including shoring up the tunnel enough to safely study the mammoth.

With all the back-and-forth about whether they would even be allowed to study the mammoth, she'd forgotten about the tunnel. She'd have to break the news to Walter. Lillian would probably squawk because the work setting, as she put it, might fall on their heads—how would that affect their biosafety protocol?

Before she could figure out what to say, in walked Walter and Lillian. She smiled inwardly when she saw them in their pristine, new mountaineer outfits: hiking boots, baggy brown pants, and down vests. They looked like models for an outdoor-magazine ad. She half expected to see the price tags hanging off them.

They had picked up breakfast for the three of them at a diner on the way back to the National Park. Kate closed her laptop and helped arrange the containers of bagels and cream cheese, hard-boiled eggs, and fresh strawberries. Eating on paper plates with plastic utensils, Walter and Lillian sat across from each other, Kate at the head of the table.

Walter opened his three-ring binder. "I received the carbon-14 date on your mammoth this morning from the University of Arizona," he said. "It's approximately twelve thousand years old, which means it could have had contact with early humans."

"How so?" Kate spread cream cheese on her bagel.

"The mastodon rib found in Sequim, not far from here, contained a spear point and tested at thirteen thousand years old. So your mammoth population could have had at least a thousand-year coexistence with humans. We know that mastodons and mammoths sometimes shared the same habitat."

"Good news, Walter."

Lillian shook her head. "Don't get too excited. I still want to inspect your biosafety equipment and procedures before I authorize your study."

Kate ignored her comment but felt uneasy. News of the collapsing ice would cause more trouble. "Walter, we need to discuss the condition of the tunnel."

He looked up from his food. "What's the problem?"

Stalling, she carried her paper plate and plastic cup to the wastebasket in the corner of the workroom and sat again. "I'll be able to show you the mammoth, but no more. The tunnel has begun to deteriorate with the high temperatures we've had. Part of the ceiling collapsed, so Frank had to chisel a hole allowing us to get to the carcass. We barely squeezed in there. As things stand, excavation is impossible."

"Yeah, that's a problem," he said, his bushy eyebrows drawn together in a frown. "But we'll figure it out—these things are rarely simple. I've been through worse. We had all kinds of issues during our excavation in Siberia, and the Russian government wasn't particularly helpful." He popped a strawberry in his mouth. "Any ideas?"

"I know some people at the Colorado School of Mines who might be able to help. Dr. English at the Center for Underground Tunneling and Construction knows all the techniques and materials."

Lillian opened her laptop and brought up her calendar. "I have a limited window available to observe your safety procedures and conduct analyses on mammoth tissues. Whatever you come up with can't take more than a week. Otherwise, I'm going to recommend burning the carcass."

Kate walked toward Ben's empty office and turned before closing the door. "Lillian, you're not helping. I'm going to make some calls. Then we can discuss how to proceed."

Through the office window, she saw the two of them going at it, waving their arms and pounding on the table, their muffled voices raised.

By luck Kate reached Dr. English between teaching a class and attending a faculty meeting. She gave him a detailed description of the tunnel, its history and present condition, but said she wasn't at liberty yet to describe the object at the end of the tunnel. After asking half a dozen questions, Dr. English gave Kate the answer she was hoping to hear—he recommended a method that met all her criteria, except one. It would probably cost more money than she had.

Kate poked her head out and nodded to Walter to join her. He closed the door and sat across the desk from her.

"Okay, here's the deal," she said. "It can be done within a week—if we get the money. Do you know where we can come up with thirty thousand dollars?"

Walter whistled. "No, Kate, not right off, I don't."

"What about the Denver Museum?"

"They have the money, but I believe it's already committed. To tell you the truth, I'm covering the cost of the helicopter charter out of my own pocket. It's going to cost several thousand dollars, and I'm glad to make that contribution—your mammoth is worth it to me."

She dropped her head in her hands. "You've made a huge commitment getting here. But it sounds like we're screwed."

"Don't give up so quickly. Let me think." Walter stood, then sat again. "There is one possibility, but it's a long shot. I could call the museum director and explain our situation."

Kate held up her hand. "But the minute we reveal the existence of the mammoth, we've lost control. We can't release the news yet."

"I know, but let me try."

Walter turned the phone around on the desk and punched in the number. "Hi, Beth, this is Walter Slater. Can I speak to the director, please?" Pause. "Steve, this is Walter. I'm with Dr. Landry in the Olympic National Park, and we could use the museum's help. We've made an exceptional find of an intact carcass, and we need thirty thousand dollars for the extraction . . . I can't disclose that yet . . . Hold on." He covered the mouthpiece. "He's not willing to pay without knowing what he's buying."

"I'm not surprised. You've brought the museum great notoriety. Tell him you've never seen such a perfect specimen."

"But Kate, I haven't seen it."

"Tell him anyway. Trust me."

He put his finger in his collar and pulled it loose. "Steve, can you take a chance on this? I've never seen such a perfect specimen." Walter looked at Kate and shook his head. "I understand. Can you hold again for a minute?" He covered the mouthpiece. "Kate, he won't buy it. We have to tell him or the answer is no."

"Okay, I give up. But please ask him to keep it out of the press."

Walter spoke into the phone, "Steve, we've found a mammoth frozen in the ice of the Blue Glacier on Mount Olympus . . . Yes, flesh intact." A long silence. "You will consider it?" He gave Kate a thumbs-up. "When can we expect an answer? . . . Okay, thanks. I'll give Beth the number."

After he hung up, Walter let out a sigh. "Now we wait. He said a few minutes."

"Oh, Walter, I hope he says yes."

While they waited, Kate filled in some of the details on her conversation with Dr. English about the tunnel construction.

When the phone rang, Walter grabbed the handset. "Steve . . . Yes . . . You will? That's wonderful news. You won't be sorry. I'll email Beth the wiring instructions. But please keep this confidential until Dr. Landry and I make our statement to the press when it's extracted."

Walter hung up and breathed out. "Kate, I put my job on the line for you. I hope you're right about this mammoth, or I'll be out of work."

"I know you took a chance." She walked around the desk and gave him a hug. "Thank you."

They rejoined Lillian in the workroom and reviewed the plan. "Dr. English thought a trained crew of two could do the job in a week if we assisted."

Lillian closed her laptop and pushed her chair back. "My two staff members fly up tomorrow to disinfect the station and set up a portable pathology lab to assess the threat from the carcass. We can then evaluate your biosafety protocols for working in the tunnel—I'm still concerned they might be inadequate or break down."

"Walter and I will review our plans with you before each step." For the first time, she let herself believe they could actually accomplish this—despite Lillian. "Now I'll tell Dr. English to hire the crew we'll need and assemble the supplies for transport. I found a company in Oregon that charters Chinook helicopters. I'll go give them a call too."

After she returned, Walter rose and picked up his new duffel of outdoor gear. "I want my two staff members from the museum to come out tomorrow as well." He looked at Lillian. "We can have my helicopter pilot fly both of our staffs from the SeaTac Airport in the morning."

The three of them headed out to the lobby to board the helicopter for their flight to the Blue Glacier.

"Good morning," Ben said from behind the counter. "Michael told me the three of you were meeting, so I didn't interrupt. Kate, can you come back to my office for a minute?"

"You two go on," Kate said to Walter and Lillian. "I'll catch up."

She went with the ranger to his office and stood in the doorway while he sat behind the desk.

"Kate, I have two messages I hate to deliver. Please close the door and have a seat."

Her heart raced. Had they found Tom? Had something happened to Grant?

"First, I just learned the National Park Service strategic planning committee released a list of man-made structures slated to be demolished next year. One is a dam. The other is the Blue Glacier Research Station. This is part of the national priority to restore parks to their natural wilderness state."

"What?" She folded her arms and leaned on the desk. "I can't believe they'd do that. That station was built by the University of Washington in the 1950s—for basic research. We need it more than ever now to study our mammoth's clues to the Ice Age."

"I know, but the site was leased from the Park Service. Several historic buildings have already been torn down in Rocky Mountain National Park. I'm afraid they won't spare your small station."

"Damn. I know it's not your call, Ben, but I'll see if the university can fight this. So what's the other news?"

Taking a deep breath, he looked down at his hands and then up at her. "Olympic Mountain Rescue found the body of your pilot, Tom Saunders."

"No," she whispered, her eyes filling with tears.

"The mortuary team carried his body down the trail on a stretcher this morning. They arrived a few minutes ago and brought him to their portable morgue unit. He died, as near as they can tell before autopsy, from the same pulmonary distress as your students."

The tears spilled down her cheeks. For eight years, Tom had been a trusted friend as well as her lifeline to the outside world during her summers on the glacier. "We were afraid he might have been infected, but I'd hoped . . ." Her voice broke. "Thanks . . . for telling me." She stood to leave.

"You going to be okay?"

The concern on his face nearly undid her. "I really don't know. Losing my students and Tom and now the station . . ."

"Kate, let the authorities take it from here. You and Grant did a herculean job getting through this and preventing an epidemic. You've turned over the study of the mammoth to the leading expert. Now you need to take care of yourself."

"Thanks, but I have to see this through. You've been so supportive." She hurried out the door. Keeping her head down, she wiped her eyes as she ran to the helicopter where Lillian and Walter were waiting, already buckled in behind the pilot.

32

Hoh River Trail
Olympic National Park

Thursday, June 18

When Grant woke up, twisted in his sleeping bag, he reached down to make sure the bottom of his tent wasn't wet, his vivid nightmare still fresh in his mind. He noticed the rumble of the nearby river and then the faint smell of coffee. Singh, Rodriguez, and their teams had started the stoves and prepared a breakfast of beef jerky and instant oatmeal. Everyone huddled around the small campfire to ward off the morning chill.

Holding his plastic mug between both hands, Rodriguez said, "I'd rather study the plane as is," he said. "But it's too dangerous so close to the river. We'll have to move it first."

As he shouted instructions, all eight of them, including Singh, the mortuary team, and Grant, dragged the plane from the river's edge. Singh had cleared the operation provided everyone wore gloves and limited their contact with the plane's exterior surfaces. It took a half hour of pulling ropes and pushing struts to get the wheels to roll across the rough gravel up to a secure spot on the shore.

Once the plane had been repositioned, Singh, especially imposing in his hazmat suit, guided the three similarly dressed members of his team as they used a strong disinfectant on anything the pilot might have touched and spent extra time disinfecting the passenger seat and baggage area where the two students had been seated. When they proceeded to the students' bodies and removed the tarps, Grant looked away—he couldn't bear to see Alice and Charlie that way.

After the bodies had been placed in bags, Singh guided his team to strap them to stretchers, and then they sprayed the areas surrounding the spots where the bodies had lain with disinfectant. Singh assured Grant the damage to the underlying vegetation would be limited and short-lived.

Rodriguez asked Grant to join him on a log near the plane where they could discuss the NTSB report and confirm the description of the plane as he and Kate had found it.

"I don't remember a lot of details," Grant said. "We had just discovered the bodies, so I wasn't thinking that much about the plane. It was foggy, and we were tired as well."

"Our report will likely include three findings," he said. "First, there was a mechanical failure leading to the forced landing. The loose ski caved in the side of the fuselage and caused the elevator hinge to lock when it hit the tail, forcing the pilot to land immediately. Second, we've concluded the pilot made the right call, saving himself and the plane. He would have had to flare to land upright on this short gravel bar with limited elevator control—an amazing feat of skill. Third, we think the deaths of the passengers were indirectly linked to the forced landing—had they reached Port Angeles and gotten to a hospital, it's possible they would have lived."

Grant shook his head. "So none of this would have happened if Tom's plane hadn't lost a ski. Any idea what caused that?"

"We'll never know for sure. Most likely something tore it loose on takeoff. Flying onto a glacier is risky business."

Rodriguez started rolling up his tent in the campground. "The only feasible way to remove the plane is to tear it down and pack the parts out on foot. The heavy pieces, like the engine, will go by the pack mules the Park Service uses. A team of mechanics can disassemble the parts and prepare the engine for transport later this week."

Singh and the mortuary team said their good-byes, and Grant stood on the trail watching them until he could no longer see the backs of their suits flash white between the tree trunks and ferns. He imagined the shocked reactions of anyone seeing them as they walked through the parking lot in their hazmat gear carrying two bodies.

He had accomplished what he'd been asked to do—lead the crews to the students and downed plane and provide his report. There was little more assistance he could offer.

Since waking from his troubled sleep, his discomfort had only grown. How could he abandon Kate to deal with all of this, including the two feuding professionals? She hadn't asked for his help, but that didn't matter.

By mid-morning when the first responders had completed their work, and the NTSB team prepared to head off after the mortuary crew, Grant had made up his mind.

Standing slightly taller than usual, he shook hands firmly and said good-bye to Rodriguez and his crew. "Please don't radio Kate I'm coming. I want it to be a surprise." He strode away heading upriver, driven by a new conviction, but without a clue about what lay ahead.

33

Hoh Rain Forest Visitor Center
Olympic National Park

Thursday, June 18

Sitting in the front seat next to the pilot, Kate had an unobstructed view forward and down as the helicopter flew easterly following the Hoh River. Above Five Mile Island, she saw the wing of Tom's plane on the gravel bar as they passed quickly overhead, and she thought she spotted people standing nearby. Grant was probably one of them. Her eyes welled up as she pictured him with Alice and Charlie, whose young faces would remain forever in her memory. Poor Charlie would never have his chipped tooth fixed.

When they reached Glacier Creek, the tributary coming down from the Blue Glacier, the helicopter turned south and climbed steeply to stay ahead of the terrain, rising nearly six thousand feet to their destination. As they followed the creek's narrow band of white water, the trees on either side became shorter but were still majestic, eventually replaced by the rich green heather of Glacier Meadows. The foliage gave way to the blue ice of the Lower Glacier and then the pure white of the Snow Dome.

There was the silver-painted roof of the research station—a bitter-sweet sight. Relieved it had survived the storm, Kate would soon have to confront Frank's body inside. She shuddered. It should've been her lying in that bunk. She had no close family. Hell, she didn't even have many friends. Poor Annie and Sammy.

She pointed out a flat landing area, close to where the ski plane typically unloaded supplies. No more planes landing here—at least not until another fearless bush pilot with a ski plane could be found. She closed her eyes, recalling Tom's smiling face as he jumped out of his red-and-white plane. Oh, how she would miss him.

After they climbed out onto the snow and took in the scenery, Lillian said, "I've lived in Washington my entire life, but this is a whole other world I never knew existed. It's breathtaking."

"I'd love the chance to leave the museum for a place like this." Walter walked in a circle as he took in the scenery.

While the helicopter pilot helped the two of them unload their bags, stacks of disposable personal protective equipment, and the food supplies they'd brought, Kate went down to the station to fetch both fiberglass sleds. It felt familiar, yet strange, to be back on the glacier after so much had happened. Without her students to care for and supervise, the surroundings seemed a beautiful place without a purpose.

But she *did* have a purpose—documenting the mammoth and getting funding for new groups of students to come. If Grant were here, he'd say the same thing. And he'd have made it easier to confront Frank's body when the time came.

Back on the Snow Dome, they stacked their cargo on the two sleds, and Kate pulled one while Walter pulled the other over the dense snow down to the rock outcrop in front of the station. On their way, the helicopter flew over their heads down the valley and on to the Seattle airport to meet the four assistants the following day.

After they transferred everything from the sled to the rocks at the front door, they gathered to prepare for going inside. Kate had briefed Lillian and Walter on how Frank looked when they left. But five days had passed since then. She thought they would have to deal with the awful stench of decay even there outside the station, but thankfully she couldn't smell anything.

"The body will have begun to decompose," Lillian said. "Now's the time to put on our protective equipment." She modeled the process as all three put on layers of white gown-like garments that tied in the back, covers over their hiking boots, double layers of gloves, a hood covering their heads, and safety glasses, followed by the bulky respirator.

"I hate having to do this," Walter said, "even though I know it's necessary."

When the three were finally gowned, Lillian walked around inspecting them. Kate opened the outer door and walked through the entry workroom—still no smell. Partway across the main room of the station, she stopped.

"He's gone!" she yelled.

"What do you mean?" Walter hurried to her side.

"That's Grant's bunk. That's where we left him, and he's not there."

Lillian joined them. "Could someone else have been here?"

"No, I highly doubt it. The weather was too bad." She made a quick inspection of the living quarters and entry room—everything was as she'd left it.

"Kate, are you absolutely sure he was dead?" Lillian asked. "Sometimes a patient's bodily functions will slow to the point that it requires a trained physician to make the final call."

"You don't suppose he was still alive?"

"It's possible. Did you check his neck for a pulse?

"No, his wrist."

"A radial pulse isn't a reliable indicator of cardiac arrest—the carotid artery in his neck would probably have told you he was still alive."

"Damn—we didn't know."

"Don't be hard on yourself. Even the experts can get it wrong."

"Kate," Walter said, "I'll have my pilot fly over the glacier and search for him when he returns in the morning."

Lillian reached out and gently grasped her arm. "But don't get your hopes up. He was very sick when you left."

It must have been awful for Frank to wake up only to realize he was alone.

Kate couldn't stand being in there another second and strode to the door, pausing with her gloved hand on the knob. "I need to get some air."

"Take your time." Lillian lifted a bottle of bleach. "Walter and I will begin to wipe things down. But we'll need to sleep outside until my staff arrives with supplies to thoroughly disinfect the bunks."

Kate made it only as far as the entry room and rushed back. "He walked away for sure," she said.

"How do you know?" Walter asked.

"His ice ax, boots, and parka are gone."

Lillian opened her laptop and typed some notes. "That's probably a good sign. Since Frank was close to death but recovered, the virus may prove to be self-limiting and survivable in some cases."

Kate continued outside and walked the fifty yards to the rock outcrop with the unobstructed view to the ocean. She sat looking at the rows of mountains and valleys as they faded into silhouettes in the distance, ending in the line where the Pacific met the sky.

If the slightest chance remained to find Frank alive, she wouldn't give up hope. But where could he be? She hated the thought they'd left him for dead. If only Grant hadn't talked her into hiking out in the middle of the night, then maybe—wait, that wasn't fair. It wasn't his fault. They weren't medical doctors. Besides, the virus could have hit them at any time.

They did what they thought was right. She needed to move past it and tackle the challenges ahead—stabilize the tunnel, extract the mammoth, and publish with Walter. She would dedicate this work to the memory of Charlie and Alice—and to Frank too if it turned out he hadn't made it after all.

34

Hoh River Trail
Olympic National Park

Thursday, June 18

Soon Grant found himself alone except for the gigantic spruce and cedars of the rain forest. He'd known caution, even risk aversion, most of his life. But now his lungs swelled and heart beat with an energy like never before, even though he was out of his element.

Each stride up the trail further convinced him his life had more meaning than it ever had. He'd never run from his fears again. It mattered little that he wasn't sure what he could contribute once back on the glacier—he wanted to be there for Kate.

Grant experienced the Olympic Mountains in a whole new way. The conditions that morning were nothing like those during the storm. The bright sunlight streamed through breaks in the trees and lit up a lush green carpet of grass, moss, and ferns. Now that the puddles and rivulets from the storm had drained away, he could easily detect and follow the trail, so elusive in the dense fog.

The sound from the thundering river penetrated the forest as he meandered in and out of the trees. Humming softly to himself, he turned left around another large spruce—and froze.

About twenty yards ahead of him, a huge black bear sat in the middle of the path, his mouth full of leaves. Their eyes met, and the bear let loose a low growl as he rose onto his hind legs.

Oh shit.

Grant broke out in a cold sweat, and his heart hammered in his chest. What the hell could he do? If the bear charged, he couldn't out-run it. And he couldn't climb a tree—bears are good climbers. Think, man. What were the rules? Make yourself look big and stare the bear in the eye—or was it crouch down and look away? Or was that for surviving mountain lions? Hell, he couldn't remember.

The last thing he wanted was to threaten the bear, so he backed up slowly while the animal watched him, and then Grant took off running into the woods. After crashing through the undergrowth for about fifty yards, he paused and cocked his head to listen, his breathing ragged. He crept ahead through the brush, worried that the cracking branches under his boots would alert the animal and prayed that the booming river masked his noise.

He pushed through ferns, past shrubs and trees, for about a hundred yards and then turned upstream in the direction he had been heading on the path. Stopping again to listen, he heard only the sound of the river.

Wait. Something was thrashing through the bushes. A low growl punctuated the sound. He squatted down behind the trunk of one of the huge fallen trees. The crashing approached and then stopped. He waited, afraid to breathe.

Convinced the bear was no more than a few feet away, he dared not look to see. Instead, he crawled to a branch lying on the ground nearby. He could at least try to club the bear if he attacked. But that was ridiculous. Grant didn't stand a chance.

What did the DMORT guy say about owls portending death?

Leaning back against the log, he started to get light-headed. He closed his eyes and took some deep breaths to calm down.

He was no mountain man—what had possessed him to hike alone? So much for not running from his fears. What a huge mistake. If he survived, should he head back? Then he thought of Kate. He wanted to see her no matter what.

Grant peered around the end of the log. No bear in sight. He got up on his knees and looked around, then stood, his legs trembling. Once back on the trail, he resumed his pace, but now scanning constantly for large furry creatures, his stomach in knots.

The trail rose steeply. His leg muscles screamed, and his body wobbled from fatigue. The two bottles of water he had packed were nearly empty, and his mouth felt parched. Lousy planning. The sun had almost dropped behind the peaks to the west as he pushed on, determined to reach Kate before dark.

Once he found a rhythm again, his thoughts drifted back to his work. For the second time in his professional career, he questioned the value of what he'd been doing. The first time had occurred just a few months earlier, when he decided to leave behind his laboratory in Santa Cruz for a risky job on the glacier. Now he realized recording the work of others, as a hands-off, passive observer, didn't bring the fulfillment he'd hoped either. He wanted to stand for something himself—to fight for a worthwhile cause.

Even though things had ended abruptly on the glacier with the tragic deaths and a hellacious storm, he felt drawn to Kate's quest to make people aware of the effects of global warming. The vision of glaciers disappearing in his lifetime had transformed him—a tragic loss most people never would experience firsthand.

When he reached Glacier Meadows, the path circled around and through the thick undergrowth. But he no longer needed the GPS to stay on course—the white snow signaled his destination.

The glacier had actually become a beacon for a new chapter in his life. He would never forget that emotional, almost visceral connection to the breathtaking beauty he felt on his first night. To think this scene would disappear in his lifetime made him appreciate what Kate was trying to do. He wanted to be with her and support her cause. She was a caring, strong, dedicated woman.

But what would his new role be if he stopped being an observer? He had studied leadership for years. Why not become a leader? He could continue facilitating the team at the station as he had at the visitor center. That was leadership, even though Kate was the designated head of the project.

In the days ahead, he could be active in a variety of ways—writing books, conducting research, giving presentations—all helping tackle climate change. Right now, it wasn't clear to him what interventions he might make to address the challenges facing humanity in making the monumental transition from fossil fuels. But he could start by working with Kate and, at the same time, learn more about the science of global warming.

Change wasn't easy for people—he knew that personally and saw it in his work. It was easy to ignore problems unless they were pounding on your front door. But doing nothing was no longer an option for him, and he wanted others to see that as well.

35

Blue Glacier
Olympic National Park

Thursday, June 18

"You two ready to get some fresh air and see our mammoth?" Kate asked.

By the time she returned to the station, Walter and Lillian had disinfected everything in the station and filled three biohazard waste bags with all the bedding and sleeping bags. The three of them could now remove their protective gear. Lillian's assistants would use a stronger disinfectant on the bunks the next day after they arrived.

Slater clapped his hands. "Yes! Can't wait to see it."

Lillian showed no emotion. "I'd like to collect some tissue samples, but only after we all suit up again."

Kate pulled her ice ax off its hook in the entry next to a coiled rope. "Before we go, you'll need to learn how to self-arrest. We have to traverse a steep, icy slope to get to the tunnel. So grab the axes you brought from Forks."

Outside on the practice slope, Kate put the two older professionals through the same rigorous training she'd given Grant and her students. Unlike Grant, they were awkward and managed somehow to end up in a tangled heap at the bottom of the hill.

Kate would have laughed out loud except the consequences of not learning to self-arrest could cost them their lives—Grant would attest to that. She insisted they climb the hill and practice again and again until they could do it. By that point, they had to drag themselves to the station, where they collapsed, exhausted, by the front door.

During their lunch of cold-cut sandwiches outside on the rocks, her two charges came back to life. Kate told them she would take them across the ice face one at a time. "Otherwise, if both of you slip, I won't be able to hold your combined weight on the rope."

After showing them how to attach spiked crampons to their new hiking boots, the three walked the quarter mile single file from the station to where the side of the hill became steep. Kate tied the rope to Lillian's climbing harness and continued on to the tunnel entrance.

Lillian looked at her across the fifty yards of treacherous, near-vertical slope. "I can't do this," she called out in a shaky voice.

"Yes you can, Lillian," Kate said. "Focus on the path in front of you."

She remained frozen, holding the rope firmly in front of her with a gloved hand. "I've never done anything like this in my life."

"Walter, you're going to have to tie on the rope instead."

"Wait. I have to collect samples and be certain the biosafety protocol is followed."

"You'll just have to come across then." Sometimes Kate had to resort to tough love in situations like this.

Lillian moved toward the tunnel, two inches at a time, her slender body rigid. When she took Kate's extended hand and lunged to the opening, she said, "You never told me I'd be risking my life like this."

"Would it have made any difference if I had?"

She gave a crooked half-smile. "Probably not."

Walter, more sure-footed despite his ample girth, traversed the slope slowly but steadily, grabbing Kate's hand at the entrance. They put on their protective suits, strapped headlamps on their foreheads over the white hoods, and adjusted their safety glasses and respirators.

"Walter," Kate said, "I never dreamed I'd be doing glaciology dressed like this either." She started down the tunnel and led the way, followed by Walter and then Lillian.

It had been several days since Kate last saw the tunnel, so she watched for signs of instability. The deep rumble of ice grinding over rock was detectable, but no worse than before. The smooth ice surface showed none of the pockmarks they'd seen last September, and meltwater had yet to fall from the ceiling.

Reassured, she moved ahead to the narrow opening Frank had chiseled out of the slab, and then turned sideways to avoid blinding Slater with her headlamp. "Walter, give me a boost here." He leaned over and weaved his gloved fingers. "Help Lillian the same way after me, okay?"

Once Kate crawled into the hole in the ice with her arms stretched in front, the walls started closing in. The bulky hazmat suit made it impossible to move, and she couldn't see a thing through the fogged-up safety glasses. She couldn't breathe either. In her desperation, she managed to dislodge the face mask enough to gasp for air. To hell with the respirator. Besides, she had survived the virus so far.

"You doing okay in there?"

Kate could hardly make out Walter's muffled voice from behind. "Give me a minute," she said.

After gulping some air, Kate managed to wiggle the rest of the way through and dropped down to the base of the tunnel on the far side. She replaced her respirator and turned to help pull Lillian through.

Slater slowly approached the two of them with his arms extended. Would his waist fit through the opening? After some struggle, he made it to the other side. They continued single file to the end of the tunnel where the mammoth's trunk protruded from the ice—more exposed than Kate remembered. Tufts of reddish-brown fur had surfaced on both sides of the trunk.

"Incredibly well preserved." Walter leaned in closer.

Lillian squeezed past him. "Before you touch anything, I must get uncontaminated samples." She scraped the skin at the end of the trunk with a scalpel and placed the shavings in a plastic vial. Then she moved on to collect tissue from the side of the mouth and even the edge of the tongue where a portion protruded from the ice.

In their eagerness to see the twelve-thousand-year-old extinct creature, Walter and Lillian crushed Kate into the ice, and she had to squeeze past them.

Walter took hold of Lillian's arm. "That's enough. You have your sample. If you take any more, you'll damage the scientific integrity of the specimen."

"Walter, stop interfering. I know what I need to do."

"You're desecrating this incredible creature."

"If you don't let me finish collecting samples, I won't be able to identify the pathogen, and I'll have no choice but to order the mammoth destroyed."

"That's enough, you two," Kate said. "You'll have lots of time to study the mammoth after we stabilize the tunnel. Let's leave it for now."

As soon as she had managed to get the dueling doctors' out-of-shape bodies back to the station, she escaped, returning to the rock outcrop overlooking the Olympic Mountains and the Pacific Ocean beyond.

One more remark from Lillian about how Walter wouldn't have to worry about his precious career since everyone would be dead from a pandemic anyway, she would smack her—which, of course, would completely destroy any chance of keeping Lillian from putting a match to the carcass.

Kate found solace, once again, in this peaceful spot, the last rays of the sun disappearing where the placid water meets the sky. As she stood, ready to return to the station, she spotted a small, dark figure on the top of the Snow Dome. Hard to tell for sure in the twilight. Her heart skipped a beat. Could it be Frank?

Transfixed, she sat motionless as the figure grew larger. Why would someone be hiking alone on the glacier so late? It had to be Frank. Would he be furious they had abandoned him for dead? It would be so good to see him.

She wanted to run toward the hiker, but her feet wouldn't move. As the man grew closer, the last rays of sun shot out from behind and shone on his fluorescent green parka.

"Oh my God," she said out loud. "It's Grant."

Kate jumped up, every muscle in her body quivering—she didn't think they would ever see each other again. After clambering off the rock outcrop and climbing past the research station, she sprinted as fast as she could toward him.

36

Blue Glacier
Olympic National Park

Thursday, June 18

Grant bounded down the side of the Snow Dome, his backpack bouncing. What a blessed relief—Kate seemed as excited as he was. They reached each other on the slope where she had given him such tough self-arrest training. Without saying a word, they hugged each other.

"I had to be here with you," he said softly into her ear.

"I'm so glad you came."

"I started missing you the minute I left."

"Let's go somewhere to talk."

She took his hand and they climbed the rock outcrop leading to the station. Passing the building, they found a smooth spot and sat close, their thighs touching.

"What prompted you to hike up here alone? It's so dangerous."

"Well, I did run into a bear, but obviously it turned out okay."

"A bear! Are you serious?"

"I made it here in one piece. That's what matters." He shrugged. "Kate, I've done a lot of thinking. I just couldn't walk out on you."

"To be honest, I could have used your help today."

He paused, eager to tell her about refocusing his career, but he needed more time to organize his thoughts. "I felt sick when I saw Alice and Charlie's bodies in the daylight. They were so energized and inspiring, though I didn't know them long. I keep asking myself what more I could have done to save them."

"We did everything we could. We couldn't have known Tom's plane would go down."

"Yes, I know that intellectually, but it helps to hear you say it." He fell silent for a moment. "There's something else I want to tell you." He described his history with Megan and her tragic death. "I didn't have the guts to go with her that day, and it has eaten at me ever since." He choked up and looked away.

"That surprises me," she said softly. "I don't see you that way at all. You've taken such risks here. I would never have guessed you to be afraid of anything." She reached over and took his hand in both of hers. "I'm glad you told me. It's tough . . . we all have demons." She turned to the mountain peaks across the valley as the first sliver of the full moon peeked from behind. "I went through something similar—though not recently."

"Tell me."

"When I was seven, my mom was diagnosed with breast cancer. She died on my eighth birthday." She paused, staring down at her hands.

"My God, that must have been devastating."

Kate went on to tell him about how her dad changed and how he expected her to take care of her younger brothers. "I was just a kid. I didn't know what to do. And I missed my mom so much—I still do." Her voice broke, and she dug in her pocket for a tissue. "I've cried more in the last three days than in the last twenty years."

"That's all right. It's good to get it out."

"I resented my dad for putting me in that position. I would burst into a rage at the littlest thing. He and I still don't get along. We're practically strangers."

"Now I see why you reacted to me the way you did when I challenged you."

"Your remarks were nothing compared to Dad's, but yes, you ticked me off pretty good." She smiled weakly.

"I'm sorry." He put his arm around her. "Thanks for telling me. I consider it a gift."

He wasn't sure how to ask the question that had been on his mind and braced himself for the answer. "What was it like to see Frank?"

"Believe it or not, he wasn't there."

"What?" He jumped to his feet. "You think someone took his body?"

"No, I mean he's missing. God, I hate to tell you this. He didn't die—at least when we thought he had. When we left, he was still alive."

He slowly sat down. "Jesus, how's that possible? We couldn't feel a pulse."

"Lillian says we needed to check the pulse in his neck. Even then, it's often hard to be certain when death occurs."

"Can we do anything?"

"We've alerted Olympic Mountain Rescue to look on the Hoh River Trail. Walter's helicopter will begin searching in the morning. I'm hopeful, but not optimistic. He nearly died."

He shook his head. "I can't believe this. You think he walked away?"

"I don't know. He might have tried to hike down the Hoh River Trail once he saw everyone was gone."

"I hate to think of him out there alone and sick." How could they have been so wrong? He and Kate should have checked on Frank again before they left.

"Is there anything I can do to help now?" he asked. "How's it going with Walter and Lillian? Are they still giving each other a hard time?"

"They're arguing more than ever. I've barely managed to keep them from killing each other. I'm worried that Lillian's patience—what little she has—is running out, and she'll have the mammoth destroyed. Maybe you can help me arbitrate—you're so good at it. I can figure out ice and snow and teach students, but I don't do well with warring adults."

"I'll do what I can." He smiled inwardly—she needed him after all. "Meanwhile, what about the tunnel?"

"I started planning the logistics to begin work on the expansion and reinforcement. You were already gone when I arranged for it, but I can fill you in."

"When does that start?"

"The crew and supplies arrive the day after tomorrow by helicopter. Construction starts the next day." She gave him a brief rundown of her conversation with Dr. English at the School of Mines.

They continued talking as the full moon came up over the mountain range to the east. The Snow Dome glowed cool white, so bright they could have hiked anywhere on Mount Olympus without a flashlight.

"Everyone has to sleep outside tonight," she said. "Tomorrow we'll be inside, after the techs finish disinfecting the bunks."

She snuggled her head on his shoulder. "We can't do a lot while Lillian clears space for her lab equipment, and Walter plans to study the mammoth now that he's seen it. Let's hike back toward the Cirque tomorrow and look for Frank."

His heart fluttered having her so close. "That's a good plan. Right now, I'm really beat."

"We better let Walter and Lillian know you're part of the team again. But I hate going back inside with all the bickering going on."

"Let me worry about them. You just focus on the tunnel."

She squeezed his hand. "I'm so glad you're here."

37

Blue Glacier
Olympic National Park

Friday, June 19

Kate rushed through the entry door and was relieved to find Grant sitting at the desk. "Hey, what are you doing up so early? I woke with the sunrise and saw your empty sleeping bag. I was afraid you'd left. Walter and Lillian are still asleep."

"I'm not going anywhere. You're stuck with me." He smiled and reached up to turn off the battery-powered lantern he'd been using.

"What are you working on?" She sat in the other desk chair and rolled it next to him.

He covered the pad in front of him. "It's something special I want to show you. Just not yet. It's not finished."

"That sounds intriguing. How'd you sleep?"

"Not too bad, but I thought I heard an animal walking around during the night. I didn't want to go to the privy in the dark. Might've been a bear. Did you hear it?"

"No, didn't hear a thing. I slept like a rock—on a rock." She laughed at her own joke. "It's strange, but I feel lighter after telling you about my family."

"You look happier—more relaxed."

"Maybe, but I keep thinking about Frank. I'd love to tell Annie he's okay."

"Let's grab some breakfast and look for him."

Walter walked in from outside, wearing long underwear and holding his back. "Those rocks are hard, even with an air mattress. Can't wait for a real mattress tonight."

Lillian came through the door fully dressed, having slept in jeans and a sweatshirt. Her long dark hair, normally so neat, hung in strands around her face. "Reminds me of my nights as a resident—little sleep on a hard bed."

Grant asked the two of them if they had heard what sounded like a large animal—neither had.

After checking the time, Kate called the Olympic Mountain Rescue with a hand-held radio, their only source of communication with the outside world. No one had found any evidence of Frank along the Hoh River. She felt sure his missing gear suggested he tried hiking down the glacier to civilization. The crew promised to keep searching.

Ben joined the conversation on the radio from the visitor center. "There've been some developments at this end," he said, his voice booming from the speaker so loudly Kate had to lower the volume. "You remember the TV reporter who was asking questions in the lobby when you were here?"

"Yes . . ." This wasn't going to be good.

"She managed to find out about the deaths of the students and the pilot. Not only that, somebody told her they are connected with the discovery of a mammoth on the glacier."

Kate groaned. "Damn it." Grant put his hand on her shoulder.

"You wouldn't believe all the craziness," Ben said. "Reporters from the international press and cable news have been here. Have you copied so far?"

"Yep. Sounds bad. Go on."

"I've directed all questions about the virus to the Centers for Disease Control. We've assured the press we're on top of the situation. Could you ask Dr. Lee if there is still a possibility the illness could spread?"

Kate held the button on the transceiver while Lillian spoke. "Yes, this is Dr. Lee. As representative of Washington State Public Health Department, I can only say at this point that we have no confirmation of other infected individuals." Lillian gave the other three a steady look, warning them not to elaborate.

"What about Frank?" Ben said. "I know we're searching for him. Could he infect others?"

Lillian snatched the transceiver from Kate's hand. "This is Dr. Lee. I share your concern, but let's not announce this publicly until Frank has been located. We don't want to start a panic, and we're still hoping he's alive."

Silence, followed by static.

Kate took the transceiver back from Lillian. "Ben, are you there?"

"Yes. There's more. To avoid a free-for-all up there on the glacier, the FAA has instituted a TFR, a temporary flight restriction. This reinforces the prohibition of low-level flights and unauthorized landings in a national park. Random reporters should be kept out. Have you copied all this so far?"

"We hear you loud and clear, Ben. Anything else?"

"Yes, a movie director from the National Geographic Society wants to document the mammoth and film its removal from the glacier. I thought that publicity might enhance the public value of your discovery."

"Roger that. Let me talk it over with Dr. Slater before I give you our final decision. Blue Glacier out."

As soon as she set the radio down, Kate turned to face the others. "So much for confidentiality. What about inviting National Geographic to make a documentary?"

Walter nodded vigorously. "Yes, this discovery needs to be recorded and shared with the scientific community and the world at large."

"Their reporting is reliable and scientifically valid," Grant said. "Like it or not, we have to deal with the media. National Geographic sounds like the best choice."

Lillian shook her head. "Absolutely not. I won't allow it."

Kate narrowed her eyes. "What's the problem, Lillian? We're all taking precautions. You could ensure the film crew isn't exposed."

Lillian stepped back from the rest of them. "My job here is to prevent an outbreak that could potentially kill thousands, even millions."

Walter held his hands up, signaling a time-out. "We're aware of that—"

"Don't time-out *me*. Let me finish." Lillian stared angrily at Walter. "First, the lab equipment to analyze my tissue samples won't arrive until this afternoon. We must determine what it will take to kill the virus before anyone studies the mammoth unprotected. Second, it is critical to find Frank to be sure he doesn't infect others. Until we accomplish those two things, I consider this area an uncontained hot zone for a pandemic outbreak. As I've said before, any violation of these conditions, and I'll personally see that the mammoth is turned to a pile of ash. So the answer to having the film crew is a definite no."

Grant stepped between Lillian and Kate and put his hands out. "Hold on. Before we give Ben a final answer, let's think a minute. Lillian, if we meet your two conditions before removing the mammoth, might it then be safe to invite the film crew?"

"Yes, I suppose. If we eliminate the threat, but that's a big if at this point."

"This is what I suggest," Kate said. "Let's tell Ben to notify National Geographic that they have the rights to the documentary but can't come to the glacier until we're ready. They don't have to know the reason for the delay." She knew Grant would help facilitate.

"So, Lillian," Water said, holding his steaming mug, "do you expect us to sit here and wait while you and your technicians do the analysis? Two of my people are joining us this afternoon on the same flight as your techs."

"And don't forget," Kate said, "the helicopter will be unloading the two construction workers and their equipment tomorrow to begin reinforcing the tunnel."

Lillian held up her hand. "I want to be clear. I'm not saying that work can't be done in the tunnel. It must be done wearing personal protective equipment, of course. My staff and the workers you mentioned, Walter and Kate, can do their work with proper protection. We can't open this up to the world—that's what I'm saying."

Kate grabbed Grant's arm and guided him outside where they could talk. "We have some time before the helicopter returns with the technicians and lab equipment Let's go now to look for Frank."

Walter and Lillian would just have to battle it out by themselves.

Kate roped up with Grant, and they started the hike up to the top of the Snow Dome, maintaining a hundred-foot separation between them to allow for a self-arrest should one of them step through the snow into an unseen crevasse. This danger, although ever-present, increased over time as the snow melted.

The separation made conversation difficult, and Kate thought again about the last two weeks. She'd lost so much, and she faced the threat of more loss to come. No funding, no research station—and no mammoth if they couldn't meet Lillian's conditions. Should she follow Ben's advice and pack it in? Maybe her father had been right—maybe it was a waste of taxpayer money to traipse all over glaciers. Her legs felt like lead—she would have stopped right there had it not been for the rope connecting her to Grant.

She clenched her fists. No! She wouldn't give up. That's not what she was all about. Besides, she had a lot of support. Grant obviously had strong enough feelings for her to risk his life returning to the glacier. Ben showed concern for her and her work. And Walter, good old Walter—he was totally committed to their joint project. Even Lillian's dedication came across in her intense efforts to keep them safe, despite their complaints.

There had to be a way to get more funding, and she'd find it. Then she would recruit another team of students up here. Maybe they would have to set up tents, maybe they couldn't do the same kind of research, but she would teach them about this beautiful, challenging, and special land at the top of these mountains. So much remained to be learned. Looking at the rugged wilderness around her, she was struck again by its magnificence, and tears streamed down her face.

They stopped at the rock outcrop where they had a view of the entire Snow Dome and the Lower Glacier. Grant, standing close to Kate but facing a different direction, lowered his binoculars. "I don't see anything that looks like Frank, moving or still."

"Me either." Her voice broke.

"Hey, you okay?" He put his arm around her.

"On the way here, I started to question my whole life's work, that's all." She paused. "I'm starting to see that science is about much more than collecting data and writing papers. It's truly a shared experience. You, Walter, Lillian, Ben—have all been part of this. So were Charlie, Alice, Frank, and Tom."

"Science is about us as much as it's about what we're studying. Maybe your future research could be dedicated to the memory of Alice, Charlie, and Tom."

They fell silent.

Grant stood before her and took her hands in his. "I had similar thoughts about my own work after my run-in with the bear yesterday."

"I'd like to hear."

"I've decided from now on to work in applied settings, preferably outdoors," he said. "And participate actively—not be a passive observer in a university lab. Kate, I'd like to join you and your new team to help get the word out about the impacts of global warming and what's happening up here. To show you how taken I am with this place, here's what I drew this morning."

Grant reached in his coat pocket, pulled out a sheet of paper and handed it to Kate.

"What's this? A map? Wow—Mount Olympus, Blue Glacier, Hoh River Trail. What prompted you to draw this?"

"If I'm going to be working up here next year, I don't want to get lost." He laughed. "Seriously, I want to make a difference, and I think I can do that here. Your strong commitment is what convinced me."

"That's sweet, Grant. I'm delighted you want to come back but—" She stopped and looked into the distance.

"What's the matter?"

"God, I'd love to have you here again. But it might be impossible." She told him about the National Science Foundation pulling their funding and the Park Service decision to demolish the station. "I want to build a case for funding and preserving our station based on the mammoth and its link to the glacier and climate change. I'll speak before Congress if I have to."

"I'm confident you can do it."

"But we first have to deal with the virus and finding Frank. I believe Lillian is serious. There's still a strong possibility she'll destroy the mammoth."

"So we have to keep searching."

As they hiked down the Snow Dome, Kate led the way above the ice fall to where they could scan the Lower Blue for any sign of Frank and to ensure the tower and instruments remained where he had anchored them. The strain gauge was okay, but what was that on the edge of the crevasse?

"I see something," she yelled to Grant. She ran over. It was Frank's blue cap, the one he always wore. She stared at the footprints and skid marks in the snow leading to the edge, then leaned over, peering cautiously into the blue-black void.

Grant walked the length of the rope and came alongside her.

"Frank must have slipped," she said. "I can't see him, but he could have fallen out of sight."

"It doesn't look good."

"First we leave him for dead and then he goes for help—so sick he can barely walk, I'm sure—and dies at the bottom of a crevasse. It's all our fault." The peaks across the valley grew blurry through her tears.

Grabbing Grant's jacket sleeve, she leaned into his shoulder and cried. She cried for the students and their families and for her own family and the little girl she once was, feeling the tears would never stop.

38

Blue Glacier
Olympic National Park

Friday, June 19

Kate and Grant sat in the snow near the crevasse, holding hands and staring silently at the mountain ridges across the valley. Comforted by his presence, she calmed down, then stood and steeled herself to carry back the bad news.

As they walked across the Snow Dome, the rhythmic beat of a helicopter filled the air. The promised staff members had arrived.

By the time she and Grant reached the station, the helicopter had departed, and four brightly colored tents were lined up on the snow below the station. To Kate, used to being alone with her small team, this felt like a crowd.

Inside, they had to squeeze around the suitcases, boxes of laboratory gear, and food supplies stacked in the entry. She counted eight people, including herself and Grant, attempting to move around in the cramped living quarters. "I'm Dr. Kate Landry," she said, extending her hand to the nearest of the four newcomers, a young, petite woman with short black hair arranging bottles of chemicals on the desk.

"I'm Marie," she said, looking up. "I'm here to assist Dr. Lee."

"Do I detect an accent?" Grant asked from behind Kate.

"Yes, I'm from the Philippines—I came to the US for nursing school and decided to stay and work in public health."

The young man standing behind Marie reached out and shook Kate's hand, then stretched to reach Grant's. "I'm Tyler. I'll be operating the lab equipment in those boxes you passed as you came in—the latest technology for identifying pathogens."

"That's a lot of hardware." Kate pointed her thumb toward the entry behind her. "I'd like to get a demonstration when it's all set up."

Walter walked over from the kitchen side of the room to introduce his two assistants. They looked slightly older than the health-department techs—maybe mid-thirties. The man, Nikolai, had a large build like Frank's with the stereotypic appearance of a field paleontologist: full beard, khaki pants, and shirt. Kate couldn't help but laugh. "You look like Indiana Jones."

He grinned. "I'll take that as a compliment."

"I met Nikolai studying frozen mammoths in Siberia," Walter said. "And this is my assistant, Erin." He motioned to a tall woman with a deep tan. "We've been doing field work together for what—ten years?"

"Yep, since my undergraduate days." Erin's rugged clothes and scuffed climbing boots told Kate she could handle herself in the mountains.

Kate cleared her throat and smiled at the room full of newcomers. "On behalf of the Blue Glacier Project, welcome to paradise." She reached out with her left arm toward Marie and Tyler. "Your mission will help us get to the bottom of the tragic deaths of my students." Then she gestured toward Nikolai and Erin. "I'm counting on you to open a new chapter in our understanding of woolly mammoths and why they became extinct."

Marie stepped forward. "We're sorry for your loss, Dr. Landry." The others nodded in agreement.

"Thank you. I'm afraid I have more bad news . . . Frank was our missing graduate student. Grant and I found his hat next to a large crevasse, and we believe he slipped . . . and fell to his death." Her bottom lip quivered, and she took a deep breath to gather herself.

"Oh no," Walter said.

Lillian touched her shoulder. "We'd hoped for a better outcome."

"Thank you, Lillian." Kate was surprised to hear such softness in the doctor's voice."

The technicians voiced a low murmur: "So sorry."

"That brings me to the harsh reality we face." Lillian addressed Walter's technicians in the kitchen area. "Although the fall into a crevasse ultimately killed Frank, he nearly died from a virus coming from the mammoth. I'm afraid if we can't rid the carcass of that virus, you may have come all this way for nothing. The risk of the illness spreading is too great."

Walter stepped closer to Lillian. "That's uncalled for. I've already briefed my staff on your position regarding the mammoth."

Kate didn't have the energy for this. She turned to face Grant, her back to the others. "Help," she mouthed.

Smiling, he stepped forward. "Dr. Lee, I know that you, with the help of Marie and Tyler, will do everything humanly possible to make the mammoth specimen safe to study."

Walter gave Lillian a dirty look. "I've already explained the need for all of us to wear personal protective equipment when working in the tunnel. So let's focus on what we're here to do."

Lillian kept her dark eyes on Walter. "I just want everyone to be clear about the situation."

She always had to have the last word.

Shaking his head, Walter turned to his techs. "Let's go outside so Dr. Lee's team can finish decontaminating the bunks. I want to sleep on a mattress tonight." He herded his assistants toward the door.

Grant whispered to Kate, "Want some help training these three on self-arrests?" He nodded toward Walter and the museum techs. "Given the crowd, most of my time will be spent outside the next few days."

Her eyes locked on Grant's. "My thoughts exactly." She raised her voice. "Hold on, Walter," she called out. "Everybody grab an ice ax."

Kate picked up her own ax and headed toward the door. She knew Frank no longer posed a risk of spreading the virus. But what if Lillian's team couldn't disinfect the specimen, and it couldn't be studied as thoroughly as it deserved? She wouldn't let her students' deaths be for nothing. She headed out into the blinding sun to the practice slope on the Snow Dome, Grant at her side and the others trailing behind.

When Kate reentered the station at noon, she unpacked the satellite phone Walter's pilot had delivered and called her voicemail at the University of Washington. Two messages were waiting for her: the first gave Kate a summary of the arrangements Dr. English had made, and the second requested her to call the crew at the Chinook helicopter's airport in Oregon for input on last-minute purchases.

When she called, a male voice answered. "This is Greg. Is this Kate? I was hoping it was you. We've assembled everything we'll need for the tunnel except the lumber for the walkway. Can you measure the distance to the entrance from the level snow?"

"Sure, give me about a half hour."

She recruited Grant to help. They roped up, and Kate walked out to the tunnel entrance while he stood on the level snow. When she looked back at him, the rope was stretched to its full length.

"Let's call it a hundred and sixty feet."

When she gave Greg the measurements, he said, "Now we can buy the walkway lumber. We've loaded everything else on the Chinook. See you in the morning."

Later that afternoon, Kate approached Slater as he stood on the snow west of the station tying the rope to his climbing harness.

"Walter, I'd like to work with you and your assistants as you free the mammoth for transport."

"Sure. I'd welcome your help." He finished fastening his rope and glanced up at her. "That is, if Lillian does her job and doesn't screw up the find of a lifetime."

Kate fidgeted with her gloves. "As you may recall, one of my specialties is applying palynology to glaciology. I've collected and studied pollen and spores buried in ice layers as indicators of the changes in vegetation growing on the hills below."

Walter looked puzzled. "So how might that approach apply here?"

"There's probably pollen residue on and near the fur of the carcass, right?"

"Yes—I see where you're headed."

"Using the frozen pollen, I could build an ecology profile of the plants the mammoth walked through the day it died."

"Brilliant. If we can determine the plants that existed here then, do you realize the implications?" He began pacing awkwardly over the uneven snow surface.

"Confirm that climate change might have been a major stressor on the mammoth population."

"Yes, it would let us test a major theory about extinction," he said. "Your pollen could reveal vegetation incompatible with mammoth habitat—a reasonable hypothesis. Let's see what your pollen tells us."

"All right then," she said. "I'll study the layer of ice in contact with the carcass under my microscope. But I'll need your help collecting the samples."

That night Kate's mind reeled. Lying on her back, she stared at the bunk above and imagined how she could use the palynology angle, broader than her usual glacial geophysics, to link the mammoth to climate change and make her research more appealing to a wider scientific audience—and even to the public. The National Science Foundation might then be persuaded to restore the grant money she needed.

Her eyes finally started to close, when a crunch of footsteps outside on the rocks brought her fully awake. From the heaviness of the steps, it had to be something large. What kind of animal would be prowling around? A bear sniffing out their food? A wolf? Then she remembered the techs camped in tents at the base of the rocks. One of them, probably the big guy, Nikolai, must be up looking for the privy.

Kate returned to thinking about her promising research, overshadowed by guilt and regret that Charlie, Alice, and Frank couldn't share in the rewards.

39

Blue Glacier
Olympic National Park

Saturday, June 27

Kate joined Walter, Erin, and Nikolai in the tunnel, lit bright as day by halogen shop lamps powered by a portable generator. After helping to enlarge the tunnel, the paleontologists could now return to their primary mission.

She thought back to what they had accomplished the week before, beginning when she, Grant, Walter, and his assistants had climbed the side of the Snow Dome to meet the two tunnel construction workers after they landed in a huge Chinook helicopter. All of them helped unload materials while Lillian and her techs remained in the station analyzing samples.

In no time, the crew had built a boardwalk, supported by horizontal beams anchored in the side of the mountain. What a difference—no more risky traverses with ropes and crampons. Then, using chain saws, the crew expanded the tunnel enough to extract the mammoth. When Kate noticed cracks forming where the slab had fallen earlier, the workers used a shotcrete gun to apply cement over a wire mesh, providing an effective, if temporary, reinforcement. The week-long effort ended when the Chinook flew off with the workers and their equipment.

Now, after that hectic activity, everyone bunched together near the trunk of the mammoth. "How's it going?" Kate's voice, although muffled by the respirator, seemed much clearer to her without the construction racket in the background.

"Kate, this is truly an amazing find." Nikolai held a tape measure to place markers for cutting the ice and avoid damaging the mammoth. "I can't wait to see what it tells us once it's in the lab."

As she observed the three paleontologists from a few feet back, their bodies blocked a clear view of the mammoth, but she heard a steady stream of comments.

"The fur is so red. "

"Complete set of teeth."

"The tongue is perfect."

Her heart swelled with a mixture of relief and pride. Her instincts to preserve this specimen for scientific analysis would pay off, if only it could be removed—

"Excuse me, guys." Tyler pushed to get through the huddle. "Dr. Lee needs more samples from the mammoth." He clipped a tuft of red hair from under the chin and collected swabs from along the tongue. "Man, you guys weren't joking—this mammoth is so well preserved. God, I hate to think we might have to destroy it."

"That's not going to happen." Nikolai stepped up and stood in Tyler's face.

Tyler leaned back and put both hands up in truce. "Hey, I'm not the bad guy here. We want to preserve this thing too, and we're doing all we can, I promise."

Walter returned to chipping ice with his hammer and chisel. "We're counting on it."

As the day progressed, Walter's team made significant headway. The battery-powered saw Nikolai used to trim large sections from the top and side of the block of ice screamed so loud in the confined space Kate worried about hearing loss. She wore earplugs and made sure the others did too as she chiseled ice samples from the fur—samples she hoped would contain the pollen of ancient plants.

Erin and Walter used chisels to crack and peal small chips of ice away from the body to expose it without causing damage. As they removed ice from the midsection, they came upon a rough piece of wood, almost black with age, about the diameter of a broom handle and splintered at the end—clearly exiting the side of the carcass.

"Kate, look at this!" Walter shouted.

She moved around from the mammoth's trunk and leaned over to see.

"Your specimen is a paleontologist's dream—I think we've found the sought-after 'smoking spear.'"

"You mean that shaft of wood? What is it?"

"Yes, yes, yes! This looks like a goddamn spear, Kate. We'll still have to confirm this when we X-ray for a spear point, but it appears your mammoth had been hunted just as you suspected. They probably chased it up the side of this eight-thousand-foot mountain.

Erin pointed to the hair on the side of the mammoth's body. "I think that's frozen blood on the carcass—there, below the spear."

Kate touched the wood shaft gently with her gloved hand. "Incredible. How can the carcass be so well preserved? If it was hunted, why wasn't it butchered? Or why didn't the flesh rot?"

"Just a guess." Walter traced his finger around the edge of the wound. "The mammoth likely fell into a crevasse out of reach of its pursuers while being chased. That would explain how its body was preserved so quickly and thoroughly in the ice."

"We have to document this. Where's our camera?" Walter turned as Grant, dressed in a hazmat suit, quietly approached and handed him a camera case.

"Grant, I didn't know you were here." Kate stood up from examining the spear to face him.

"I've been observing. Someone has to document this. You guys are making history."

That night during dinner, all eight scientists crowded around the table made for six. Walter, Nikolai, and Erin sat on one bench facing the other crew—Lillian, Marie, and Tyler. Grant and Kate squeezed into two chairs at one end.

Walter couldn't stop talking. "I'm confident our specimen can help explain what led to the extinction of mammoths."

"Why do you say that?" Grant helped himself to a piece of pan-fried trout—part of the fresh groceries the helicopter brought—and handed the platter to Kate.

"There have been three main theories," Walter said. "Hunters, disease, and climate. I believe that all three probably played a role in the extinction of the population. However, the spear we found today is the only hard, physical evidence we have about this individual mammoth."

He took a bite of fish but stopped his fork midair. "We can only glean clues about the other two factors. The spear suggests hunters may have wounded this animal, but it's unlikely the spear caused its death. The body's too complete and well preserved. Most likely it froze."

"I'm aware of the disease theory," Lillian said, helping herself to mashed potatoes and passing the bowl to Marie. "The evidence we're collecting supports a cross-species transfer of a life-threatening illness from mammoth to humans. It could well have happened in reverse— the mammoth could have been afflicted by a virus that originated from contact with Paleolithic humans."

"As to the climate change theory," Kate said, "my pollen samples may provide critical evidence. It's too soon to tell."

"In other words, folks, this *one* specimen"—Walter held up his index finger—"let's call it the Blue Glacier Mammoth—contains multiple clues to the extinction of large North American fauna. I can't overstate its importance. What an opportunity."

He paused and took a deep breath. "Lillian, what progress have you made so we can proceed with our extraction?"

She dropped her fork onto her plate with a clank. "This work takes time, Walter. We've had to isolate and attempt to culture the virus."

"You haven't answered my question."

"We're working on it," she said, raising her voice. "You'll hear from us when we're ready."

He shook his head. "This has gone on over a week."

Lillian's response began as a tectonic rumble from deep within her like a volcano ready to blow. "Walter, I'm well aware—" Everyone at the table stopped breathing. "There is nothing to report. But if you keep pushing me, I'll have the damn thing destroyed TOMORROW!"

Walter's neck and face flushed bright red, and he squeezed his water glass in both hands with such force Kate was afraid he'd break it. If Lillian said one more thing, he'd for sure jump up and strangle her.

All the assistants sat in silence, studying their plates. Kate turned to Grant and squeezed his hand.

He opened his mouth to intervene but closed it and shrugged. This time, even he couldn't think of anything to say.

40

Blue Glacier
Olympic National Park

Sunday, June 28

Sitting at the table the next morning, Grant reviewed his notes on the interactions he observed yesterday as Walter, Kate, and the technicians worked together in the ice tunnel.

He shifted his gaze to Lillian and her technicians, who continued analyzing mammoth tissue samples, all three of them in white lab coats. Lillian and Tyler worked on their laptops while Marie stood staring at the flat panel screen on a large piece of equipment perched precariously on the desk. In the entry, the paleontology crew, led by Walter and Kate, wrestled with their hazmat suits, getting ready to leave for the tunnel.

"This is strange, Dr. Lee," Marie said. "I've just completed the analysis of all the virus cultures we've had growing in the chicken embryonic media. Every result is negative."

"What? What did you say?" Lillian flew out of her chair. "You found absolutely no virus in *any* of the samples we've cultured all week?"

Tyler jumped up and looked at the screen.

"That's correct, Dr. Lee," Marie said. "I've run immunoassay tests on every sample from the mammoth using our automated analyzer."

Walter's head jerked around, and he rushed back to squeeze next to Lillian, the other three close behind. Grant sprang from his seat to join them.

"What are you saying?" Walter shouted. "The mammoth's not a threat?"

Lillian pushed him away. "Just relax. I haven't had a chance to confirm the data. I've been waiting all week for the results of these tests." She turned to Marie. "Tell me again what you've found," she said, her voice urgent.

The young woman rested her hand on the device. "We ran each test twice to be sure. No virus detected. Let me show you." She pressed a button on a small keypad on the front panel, and colorful bar graphs appeared on the screen. "These display the individual test results. They're all the same—no viruses."

Lillian reached past Marie and pressed the key herself while scrutinizing the screen. "That can't be right." She looked from Marie to the machine and back. "Did you try recalibrating the UV lights?"

"Yes, Dr. Lee." Marie crossed her arms and shifted her weight nervously. "Everything's within specs."

She turned to Tyler. "What about the genetic tests? Surely they show a virus."

"I've just analyzed the test results from the same mature cultures using our Polymerase Chain Reaction technique designed for detecting RNA from virus—"

"Yes, I know, I know, the RC-PCR machine," Lillian interrupted. "The most sensitive tool in our arsenal. If it didn't show a virus signature—"

"Well it didn't. They're all negative," Tyler said.

Shaking her head and muttering, Lillian shoved past the crowd to the stove. She poured a cup of coffee, dumped in a tablespoon of sugar, and rejoined the group. "We need to collect more tissue samples from the mammoth."

Tyler held up his hand. "With all due respect, Dr. Lee, no, we don't. You know we've collected and cultured multiple samples."

Marie pointed to the display panel on the instrument. "Our instruments don't lie. Tyler's data and mine indicate the same thing—the deadly influenza did not come from the carcass."

Tyler nodded. "I have to concur with Marie."

Lillian paced back and forth between the bunks and the desk, her hands behind her back. "That leaves us with a serious public health dilemma, doesn't it?"

"Could the temperature have been too high?" Marie asked. "Or maybe the samples were diluted?"

Lillian stopped and shook her head.

"What about the disinfectant?" Tyler asked. "Could there have been some residue on the equipment?"

She shook her head again.

Walter stood next to her. "We have to come up with other possibilities here. There's too much at stake to destroy such an important paleontological discovery."

"Hush!" Lillian yelled. "Let me think. We can't simply ignore four awful deaths from an infection. Unless we identify the source, the epidemic may reemerge."

"The mammoth's a carrier," Maria explained to Walter. "It's called a 'vector' in public health terms. If we rule out the mammoth, we must find an alternative source."

Erin shouted over Maria at Lillian, "Can't you just clear the mammoth so we can procced?"

Tyler yelled back, "But the mammoth is the only common factor."

"Now our research is being blocked in spite of the data." Nikolai shook his head and bellowed at no one in particular. "THAT'S NOT RIGHT."

The room erupted—the hazmat suits versus the lab coats—neither side listening to the other. Grant wanted to intervene—but how? He put two fingers between his lips and whistled. They all stopped and looked at him. "We need to help Lillian figure this out, folks. She's right—three people have died from this virus, another nearly did, and we don't know why. Let's sit down and brainstorm."

Everyone took the same positions around the table they had the night before. Lillian's thin frame seemed more vulnerable somehow as she sat down on the end of the bench.

"Let's all take a deep breath," Grant said. "We have to analyze this as scientists. Lillian, why don't you lead the discussion?"

"Okay," she said. "We can't confirm the virus came from the mammoth, so let's retrace what we do know. Kate, everyone was healthy when they arrived at the station as far as you know. Is that correct?"

"Yes. Everyone was healthy until after they went into the tunnel."

"I know you already told me this," Lillian said, "but describe again when the first person got sick."

"Charlie got the first symptoms the day they collected samples in the tunnel," Kate said. "But he did his work until later the next day after becoming too sick."

Lillian typed notes on her laptop. "Did Charlie have the respiratory symptoms when he collected specimens from the mammoth?"

"Yes," Kate said. "I wasn't there, but Frank told me. He, Charlie, and Alice spent several hours chiseling ice away from the carcass and taking samples. He said Charlie complained of a sore throat soon after entering the tunnel, and then he coughed and sneezed most of the time they were in there."

Lillian typed steadily as Kate spoke.

"That afternoon," Grant said, "Charlie was coughing so much Frank gave him some Benadryl under Kate's orders."

"The following morning," Kate continued, "he had what I would describe as full-blown flu symptoms—sore throat, deep cough, runny nose, and probably a fever. He insisted, against my recommendation, on traveling to his research location and collecting data with Alice for most of the day. When they returned, he was considerably worse, with a temperature of 103. Alice was getting similar symptoms, so I sent them both to bed."

"Was Frank sick at this point?" Lillian asked.

"No."

"This might help," Grant said, holding up a piece of paper, "I printed this article when we researched pandemics at the visitor center. It says the 1918 pandemic traveled through the population in waves. 'What began as a common influenza virus mutated to a deadly form in subsequent outbreaks.'"

"Hmm . . . That gives me an idea. Hold on." Lillian stood with a blank stare, walked slowly to the far corner of the room, and started pacing again.

No one said a word. The only sound in the room came from the squeaky floorboard she stepped on every few seconds.

What could she possibly be thinking? They had retraced this history several times before.

Lillian stopped abruptly in front of the bunks, her back to them. "Yes, that's it," she said to herself. Returning to the table, she slid into her place on the bench, a firm expression on her face. "I may know the source of the deadly strain of virus."

"So, if Charlie brought the virus," Walter blurted out, "the mammoth had nothing to do with it."

"Wait a minute," Lillian said. "You're getting ahead of me." She turned to Grant. "I believe Charlie may have brought a common strain of influenza. He was infected, but his symptoms didn't emerge until he was in the tunnel."

"So it *was* the flu?" Grant asked.

Walter smirked. "As long as it wasn't the mammoth."

Lillian vaulted to her feet and stared down at Walter. "Would you hush? Let me finish."

"Sorry. I'm sick of this damn hazmat suit."

She sat down in a huff. "Look, we had to take precautions. Four people died. We only just now determined the carcass shows no live virus, right?" She looked around the table.

They all nodded.

"Okay. Viruses mutate so fast because their genetic structure is determined by single-strand RNA rather than the more stable double-strand DNA found in most cells." She lowered her voice and spoke slowly as though she were telling a ghost story. "The carcass contains no live virus, but *fragments* of the deadly virus's RNA may have remained intact."

"You mean partial viruses?" Kate shook her head. "You can't get sick from a partial virus that's thousands of years old. Viruses need special conditions to survive."

"That's true." Lillian waved her finger at Kate. "But it is possible Charlie's lungs became the incubator for a deadly strain of virus *after* he inhaled fragments of RNA preserved in the mammoth carcass. This process of genetic mutation in viruses has been documented—it even has a name. It's called *re-assortment*."

"Good point," Walter said. "It's true that a 1918 influenza victim's corpse contained enough genetic material, when unfrozen, to provide a profile of that deadly virus. But what are the odds of this recombination occurring in a living human virus exposed to an extinct mammoth's viral RNA fragment?"

"The odds are small, I admit," Lillian said. "However, this is my professional opinion. I'll need to confirm it at the lab in Seattle. We'll bring tissue samples back with us and test for the RNA fragments. And we can try to replicate the full RNA sequence of the deadly virus. What we do know for sure, Walter, is the mammoth carcass you have been studying is *not* the source of the deadly virus."

"Lillian, are you stating an official position as an officer of the Washington State Public Health Department?" Grant asked.

"Good question," Walter said.

"It's not official yet, of course." Lillian pulled her hair back over her shoulders. "But the mammoth tissue samples have ruled out what our department calls a "reportable influenza outbreak" since there was no virus identified by the RC-PCR equipment—one of the reporting requirements. Yes, the mammoth is cleared."

"Hallelujah!" Walter smiled broadly. "Kate, our mammoth is safe."

"I would still advise," Lillian said, "that no one be allowed near the carcass with symptoms of the cold or flu. In fact, I insist all researchers working near the mammoth, including now, undergo periodic screenings to ensure they don't have a viral infection."

"What's involved?" Grant asked.

"Not much. We need to take a nasal swab from everyone. Then we'll use the same immunoassay equipment we used on the mammoth specimens. Each test takes only fifteen minutes."

"That doesn't sound too bad," Walter said. "Let's do it."

"But, Lillian," Kate said, "if your theory's correct, why did Charlie die so fast?"

"Remember the flu he brought with him was a common strain." Lillian began speaking more rapidly. "Then, once he breathed in the mammoth RNA, it mutated and spread quickly. Charlie's lungs had no prior contact with this mutated form and were, therefore, incapable of responding as they would to a familiar form. His system quickly became overwhelmed, and his airways filled with fluid, because of his aggressive immune response. Young adults are particularly vulnerable because their systems are so strong."

Kate shook her head. "Poor Charlie."

"If we contact Charlie's family, we might discover that someone close to him also came down with the common flu. Perhaps a roommate or girlfriend."

Grant wasn't convinced. "But how did the deadly form of virus get onto the specimens and containers?"

"That one's easy," Lillian replied. "Charlie's repeated coughs and sneezes contaminated the samples he collected—and most likely led to Alice, Frank, and Tom getting sick."

"If this is true," Walter said, sounding vindicated, "it means the carcass was never the source. Rather, it contributed to the mutation of a living virus."

"That's exactly what I believe based on the evidence." Lillian nodded. "You were just too eager to hear me say that before I could finish my story."

They finally had the green light to proceed with their plans to extract the mammoth—but Grant felt uneasy. "Lillian, what about the deaths? All we have is your hypothesis."

"Yes, that's true. Unfortunately, this isn't the first time the exact source of a new strain of influenza remains unclear while scientists search for the origin. Think swine flu. Think bird flu. Think Ebola. All we can do is be vigilant, take precautions, and continue our research. Once we get back to Seattle, I hope to learn more."

"And what about Kate and me? How did we escape it?"

"Yes, that bothers me," Lillian said.

"Uh-oh," Walter said, fidgeting in his seat. "Is that a problem?"

"We still don't know why Kate and Grant were never infected, in spite of prolonged exposure to the students' coughs and sneezes, whereas Tom got so sick he died after less contact. Something protected the two of you. Did you do or ingest anything that the others didn't?"

"We've been asking ourselves that question for days," Kate said.

Lillian's eyes darted back and forth between Grant and Kate. "While the three students collected samples, what did you two do?"

"We hiked up to Athena's Owl," Grant said. "Then we had lunch, and on the way back . . . oh . . ."

"Tell us," all seven of them said.

He turned to Kate. "You and I ate some watermelon snow."

"I remember," she said, smiling. "You tricked me into tasting it." She looked around the table. "It's a pink algae that grows on the snow at high elevations."

"Algae," Lillian said, tapping her fingers on the table. "That's actually a valid hypothesis. Bring us some, and we can test it with our equipment. In the meantime, Walter, you can extract the mammoth now."

Walter threw both hands in the air. "Wahoo! We've saved our mammoth."

Nikolai and Erin gave each other high fives, followed by more high fives across the table from Marie and Tyler.

Lillian walked around to Grant and shook his hand. "Thank you for bringing that article to my attention. It gave me what I needed to solve the puzzle. It made no sense, a deadly influenza outbreak without a source. But we still need to confirm my hypothesis."

"You put the pieces together," he said. "I just brought one piece."

Lillian shook Kate's hand. "Good luck with your research."

Walter stood up from the bench, his stomach barely scraping past the table top, and walked around to Lillian. "No hard feelings. I know you were doing your job."

"And you were as well. Perhaps a little too eagerly?"

He gave her a weak smile.

"Always the last word," Kate whispered to Grant.

He turned to see her grinning but with tears in her eyes. "You helped save my career." She rose on her toes and planted a kiss squarely on his lips.

He held her tight, his heart soaring.

As soon as the meeting broke up, Grant and Kate retrieved a sample of watermelon snow from a patch just to the west of the station that Alice had noticed and commented on the day she arrived. They left it in a cooler for Lillian and her assistants to analyze.

Later that same day, Grant joined Kate, Walter, and the two paleontology assistants on the rocks in front of the research station to celebrate their good news with some wine in plastic cups. Kate's smile sparkled—her mammoth could bolster her career after all.

Lillian and her two assistants came from the station and approached the group. She had the broadest grin Grant had seen on her face since he met her. Everyone turned her way and stopped talking.

"We've now conducted nasal swab tests for influenza on everyone, and you're all free to work without protective equipment."

Walter held up his wine glass. "That's truly good news—I'll drink to that."

"But there's more. We believe we've confirmed your watermelon snow theory."

"You have?" Kate climbed over the rocks toward Lillian.

"Yes." Marie stood next to Lillian, facing the group. "We tested it against the deadly strain of influenza virus Dr. Fitzgerald found on the tissue samples."

"What happened?" Kate asked.

"All the virus was dead within minutes of exposure."

"We think it might be related to the antioxidant flavonoids," Lillian said, "or possibly antiviral lectins they may contain."

"Remarkable," Walter said. "Grant and Kate owe their lives to their chance eating of algae."

"It's not the first time some random event resulted in a medical breakthrough." Lillian poured wine and handed cups to her assistants. "Maybe we can isolate the active compounds in watermelon snow to create a vaccine to destroy viruses, similar to how antibiotics work against bacterial infections. As a matter of fact, I recommend everyone working with the mammoth take a regular dose of it to protect themselves." She held up her cup. "Here's to watermelon snow."

Grant took Kate's hand in his. Her face, radiant in the late afternoon sunlight, along with the brilliant blue of her eyes, triggered a shiver of excitement down his spine.

"Now all we have to do," she said, "is get our mammoth to its new home in the freezer in Seattle."

41

Blue Glacier
Olympic National Park

Thursday, July 2

Kate lay awake in her bunk at 4 a.m., anticipating the moment when the mammoth would emerge from the mouth of the tunnel later that morning. This would be the first time the creature from the Pleistocene Era had seen the light of day in thousands of years. As much as she needed it to help boost her career, right then she felt the wonder of it all, like a kid on Christmas morning about to unwrap the biggest present of her life.

The rhythmic breathing and snoring in the nearby bunks told her that none of the other scientists shared her excitement—at least not at that hour. She slid quietly out of her sleeping bag to polish an article about the mammoth she and Walter planned to submit to a paleontology journal. Publication meant recognition, future funding for her research, and professional advancement. She could hardly sit still and focus on her laptop. That day was going to be a good day, the best day ever.

Shortly before daybreak, Walter joined her, the ring of hair surrounding his bald head all askew.

"You want to take a field trip?" Kate whispered. "It'll be light soon."

"Sure—where to?"

"The tunnel."

She wanted him to go with her to inspect preparations for extracting the mammoth, and she was too excited to wait for the others to get up and moving. They put on their boots and jackets quietly.

As they hiked down the hill from the station toward the tunnel, Kate walked past the two motorized winches that had been installed on the rocks. One winch would lower the carcass, suspended by ropes, from the mouth of the tunnel to the snow near the entrance. The other would pull the carcass, mounted to a wide sled, up the steep hill to the location where it could be picked up by a Chinook helicopter. Four workers had flown in Walter's helicopter from Port Angeles two days before to install the necessary equipment, ropes, and supports.

"This is a major logistical feat," she said as they neared the boardwalk leading to the tunnel.

"You're so right." He followed as they clomped noisily. "I've never had to arrange anything this complicated before."

As she walked to the entrance, Kate looked up at the heavy ropes and block-and-tackle pulleys tied to six steel rods above her. "It looks secure from here. How far do the rods go into the ice?"

"About ten feet—should be more than enough."

Once inside the tunnel, she tugged on the ropes securing the carcass tightly to the wooden pallet. The pallet had runners of wood for sliding it toward the mouth of the tunnel. The heavy rope that connected the pallet to one of the winches was in place and lying on the ice floor. "Walter, you've done a fantastic job," she said. "I can't think of anything we missed, can you?"

"No, but I'll feel a lot better after the mammoth's safe in the old meat locker we've prepared for it in Seattle."

After lunch, the time had come to transport the frozen, Ice Age mammal. The four workers who installed the winches were now ready to operate the levers, motors, and gears—one man behind each winch and a second to monitor and adjust things as needed. The scientists and technicians stood on the rocks in a semicircle, facing the mouth of the tunnel. The film crew from the National Geographic Society, two men and two women, was already documenting the historic event with their tripods and cameras on the rock outcrop overlooking the operation west of the research station. Kate stood next to Walter and

Lillian on the overlook down the ridge from the film crew, and Grant watched the tunnel entrance through binoculars a few feet below Kate.

Walter lowered his arm—the signal to pull the mammoth from the tunnel. "Begin the operation," he shouted. The engine on the first winch roared to life, jerking taut the heavy rope attached to the wooden pallet supporting the mammoth. Nothing appeared to be happening. Then slowly the mammoth tusks and head appeared at the mouth of the tunnel and a cheer went up.

The second diesel issued a deep-throated rumble as the operator engaged the other winch. They all hushed as the mammoth floated above the icy ravine, having been hoisted up by the ropes above. The pallet moved sideways toward the smooth snow near the research station.

A series of loud cracks like rifle shots echoed across the ravine as first one rope, then the next, broke free from the steel supports above the tunnel. The engine grew louder as the first winch operator tried to compensate by pulling the mammoth sideways faster, but this caused more ropes to snap.

Slowly at first, but steadily gaining speed, the mammoth carcass dropped to the ice below the tunnel. The operator of the first winch and his assistant pulled levers to reel in the mammoth, but the gears slipped and the rope unwound. Still mounted to the wooden pallet, the mammoth slid toward the chute of the West Couloir, dragging the loose rope behind.

"NOOOOO!" everyone shouted, as the pallet careened away.

Kate's jaw dropped. She reached out with both hands into the air, as if to grab the carcass, seeming to move away in slow motion.

As the mammoth slid down the icy ravine, it gained momentum, first bouncing to the right, then to the left, and it must have hit one last hummock of packed snow because it appeared to go airborne before sailing, nose first, out of sight.

No one moved. Kate's stomach contracted—she was about to lose the bacon and eggs she had for breakfast—her dream gone in an instant. She glanced at Walter and Lillian, their faces ashen, and turned to Grant and grabbed both his hands in hers, his open mouth and look of shock reflecting how she felt.

"Kate," Walter said, "Someone up there is calling you." He pointed to the figure of a man standing on the other side of the ravine, above the steel anchors where the ropes had snapped. The man held what looked like a hand ax in one hand. She strained to hear what he was saying.

"I'm . . . so sorry . . . Kate. That wasn't . . . I tried . . . protect . . . for you."

A prickling sensation ran down her spine. "Oh my God, Grant. Is that Frank? But it can't be. We found his hat. He died in the crevasse."

Grant looked through the binoculars and shouted, "It is Frank! That son of a bitch sabotaged your mammoth."

Her shock from losing the mammoth went to intense anger at Frank, then to relief. "Frank's alive!" She threw her arms around Grant.

One of the cameramen standing on the rock outcrop above the scientists pointed to the west and cried, "It's still there! The mammoth didn't go off the cliff."

Kate scrambled the twenty yards up the rocky ridge to where the videographer stood to see the carcass for herself. "He's right, Walter," she called down. "I can see the top of the mammoth's back. Looks like it's wedged somehow."

The scientists jumped and whooped and hugged each other.

"Can we get to it?" Walter yelled.

"It's in a bad spot. The ice slopes to a drop-off. But we'll find a way." Then Kate shouted to Grant, "Go get Frank. I'm mad as hell at him, but damn, it's good to see him alive. I'm going to try to rescue the mammoth."

Grant grabbed Tyler and Nikolai. "Come with me," he said, and the three headed up the side of the Snow Dome. When Frank saw them climbing toward him, he turned and ran up the slope in the direction of the rocky summit of Mount Olympus.

Kate clambered back down the rocks. "Walter, I'm going to save our mammoth, but I'll need help. It'll be dangerous. Are you up for this?"

He didn't blink. "Tell me what to do."

"Ask Erin if she's willing to go with us. We need crampons and ropes. Hurry, though. I can't tell how long the carcass will stay wedged in the ice."

42

Blue Glacier
Olympic National Park

Thursday, July 2

As Nikolai and Tyler followed Grant up the steep side of the Snow Dome above the tunnel, Grant could make out the stains on Frank's old sweatshirt and hear his heavy breathing. Frank had to be weak—no way could he have caught up with him before. But how could he still be alive? What had gotten into him? Had the illness made him insane? That must have been Frank prowling around the station in the middle of the night—it wasn't a bear, but a man they'd left for dead.

After chasing Frank a couple of hundred yards, Grant was close enough to throw himself at his back. They dropped onto the snow, and Frank flipped them both over. Grant clamped his arms around Frank's broad shoulders and held on. They rolled once, twice. Grant's hands started slipping at the same time Tyler caught up and dove across Frank's legs and Nikolai grabbed Frank's flailing arms.

"What the hell do you think you're doing?" Grant yelled as he lay across Frank's chest.

"Let go," Frank shouted. "I was trying to save Kate's mammoth."

"What? By sending it off a cliff? Hold still, dammit."

Frank squirmed but could barely move his arms and legs. Then he lay still. Grant didn't get up and told the technicians to hold on.

"You're that Dr. NASA, right? You and your astronaut friends were trying to steal the mammoth. I've been watching you."

"Astronauts? What astronauts?"

"Don't yell, dammit. My head hurts as it is. I saw you and your buddies going to the tunnel in your space suits."

"This is priceless." Grant glanced up at Nikolai and Tyler. "Those weren't space suits, you idiot. They were hazmat suits. We thought the mammoth was infecting people."

"So that's what caused it!" Frank rolled his head from side to side. "I was sick as a dog. And you and Kate left. Where did you go? No radio. No idea where you'd gone."

Grant knelt next to Frank as Nikolai and Tyler stood by in case he tried to run.

Frank struggled to sit. "I tried to keep the mammoth in the tunnel so we could study it. I made the clutch on the winch slip. Weakened the ropes. But I screwed up. Now it's gone."

"You screwed up all right. I don't understand you."

"Stop shouting." He put his hands over his ears. "My head is killing me."

"We'll get you help. You're still sick. Come to the station."

"No way. I saw how you took Kate hostage. She never would have told strangers about the mammoth. That's why I had to protect it. Besides, they warned me about you."

"Who warned you?"

"I don't know. I never met them. The wise ones who live in the rocks on Panic Peak. They talked to me at night. They told me what you were up to—how to save the mammoth. But I've been so damned tired. I told them I couldn't do it. They said I had to."

"Oh, Frank, you're not doing well."

"No shit," Tyler said. "Can we bring him back down?"

"Let's go back." Grant stood and pulled on Frank's arm.

"Hell no, man!" He pulled his arm back. "I won't be a hostage like Kate."

"Frank, listen to me. We'll take you to Kate. You'll see she's not a hostage. Think about Annie and your son. They need you at home."

"Oh God. Annie." He began to cry.

"Come on, Frank, let's go."

Grant and Nikolai helped Frank to his feet, and he stumbled down the hill with three pairs of hands alternately shoving, supporting, and restraining him.

As they neared the station, the group of winch operators, videographers, and scientists were talking with one another, recounting the disaster they had witnessed. A hush fell as they watched Frank being escorted past them.

Kate, preparing to rescue the mammoth, rushed over to him. "I'm so happy to see you." When she reached up to hug him, he stood passively, looking down, his arms at his side.

"I messed up big time, Kate. I'm really sorry."

"I don't understand what happened, but we can see the mammoth, and I'm going to try to retrieve it. What matters most is you're alive."

"I'll go with you to get the mammoth."

"No, you stay here with Grant." Lillian walked over. "This is Dr. Lillian Lee. She's a medical doctor—she'll help you."

"Kate, I was trying to help you keep your mammoth, and everything went wrong." He closed his eyes. "I have such a horrible headache."

"I know you meant to help. Now go inside."

He let himself be led to the door.

Grant and Lillian steered Frank to a chair by the desk while Nikolai and Tyler stood guard in the pantry near the only entrance in case he tried to run. Grant and Lillian sat on the bench facing him.

At first no one spoke while Frank squirmed, his face scrunched in pain.

"I can give you a mild sedative to help you feel better," Lillian said. "You look uncomfortable." She rummaged in her medical bag and pulled out a vial and syringe. "Keep him talking," she said to Grant, while giving Frank the shot in his upper arm.

"Frank, I'm sorry we left you," Grant said. "We thought you were dead. We couldn't feel your pulse, and your face turned blue. Kate and I were worried we'd get sick too. We didn't know how much time we had."

He looked up at him through tired eyes but didn't speak.

"I'm truly sorry." Grant smiled. "But I'm glad you're alive. It's a miracle. What happened?"

"It was sunset when I came to. I must have been out a long time. So weak and all congested—couldn't breathe. I crawled to the privy and started the generator. Then lit the stove, had some soup. Collapsed until sundown the next day."

"It's amazing you survived. You're one strong man."

"I started to feel a little better, but then I got this awful headache. I couldn't make it all the way down the mountain on foot. And I knew Kate would come back sooner or later."

"Why didn't you just wait for her in the station?"

"I needed to get out of here, away from the nasty germs. When I was strong enough to walk, I took some food and supplies and pitched a tent on the back side of Panic Peak." He reached out his arm and gestured behind him.

"We've disinfected this place, so you don't have to worry about germs," Lillian said. "Go on with your story."

"The day I left, Kate and some people came in a helicopter. I figured they must have held her against her will. She would never have revealed the mammoth to strangers—and then they prepared to take it away. But I couldn't do much. I was still worn out."

"Was that you I heard walking around the station at night?"

"Probably. I needed tools from the shed to stop them. Then I got the idea of planting my hat at the edge of the crevasse so you'd think I had fallen in. I couldn't let you know I had survived."

"The trick worked. We found your hat. It broke Kate's heart, thinking you'd fallen to your death."

"It couldn't be helped. You'd have found me otherwise."

"Frank, the virus didn't come from the mammoth. The illness you, Charlie, Alice, and Tom got—"

"Wait. Tom got sick too?"

Grant glanced at Lillian and then looked back at Frank. "Tom died from the same illness you had."

"I can't believe it—Tom's dead?"

"It's worse than that." Grant took a deep breath and told him about Tom's plane and about Charlie and Alice. "They're all dead."

"Oh no." Frank covered his face with his hands and leaned forward. His body heaved with sobs.

Grant gave him a few minutes to absorb the news. "Listen, Frank. Dr. Lee found the source of the deadly illness. It turns out Charlie brought the flu. The mammoth contributed but didn't cause the illness. I'll explain more when you're feeling better."

Frank sat up, his eyes red and swollen. "That's hard to believe. You figured that out?"

"Yes she did," Grant said, "and Kate wants to give you the credit you deserve for finding the mammoth. She's even including you in her article. It's a good thing you survived, buddy, because you've got an excellent career in front of you."

Frank shook his head. "I've ruined everything. I had no idea. I'll probably go to jail for what I've done."

"That won't happen. Kate will make sure there are no charges against you."

Lillian put her hand on Frank's shoulder. "Are you feeling better? You seem more comfortable."

"My head still feels like it's about to explode."

"That's a symptom of the flu. So are the voices you've been hearing. Now you need to get some rest." Grant and Lillian guided Frank to Grant's lower bunk.

"If you're okay," Lillian said, "I need to talk with Grant a minute. We'll send in Tyler and Nikolai to be with you."

Standing outside on the rocks, Lillian said, "I believe Frank is suffering from what has been called IAE, or influenza associated encephalitis, an inflammation and swelling of the brain. The headaches, delusions, and hallucinations Frank described all point to that."

"It sounds serious."

"It can be, especially when accompanied by coma, which he may have suffered, leading you and Kate to believe he was dead. But since he's recovered this much, most patients make a full recovery in a matter of weeks."

"We'll let Kate know after she retrieves the mammoth," Grant looked in the direction of the West Couloir. "With all her determination, I hope she's being careful. Can you watch Frank while I monitor the rescue operation from the rocks?"

"No problem."

As he looked down the couloir with his binoculars, Kate was heading toward what appeared to be a drop-off into thin air.

43

Blue Glacier
Olympic National Park

Thursday, July 2

Roped together and wearing crampons, Kate, Walter, and Erin stepped carefully down the West Couloir, a narrow ravine shaped like a funnel and tilted at a forty-five-degree angle. Although wide at the top, where the tunnel had been chipped into the ice of the south wall, the couloir narrowed as it dropped west and ended in a near vertical cliff of rock and ice. A few boulders protruded through the edges of otherwise solid ice.

About the time Kate neared the end of the funnel and the two-thousand-foot drop-off to the White Glacier, the insanity of their precarious position hit her. Because they were roped together on the slick surface, if one of them fell, they could all go sailing off the end. This mission would challenge an experienced mountaineer, let alone two novices. Her determination to save the mammoth overcame any fear for her own safety, but she worried about the others.

Forcing herself to speak calmly, she said, "Be careful, you guys. Let's see what we're up against. I'll make the risky moves."

She stepped cautiously down to the lip of the couloir and peered over the edge. About twenty feet below, the carcass lay on its side, the wooden pallet wedged in a crack in the rock outcrop—and beyond the mammoth was a sheer drop to the White Glacier.

When she climbed back up the ten yards of ice to Walter and Erin, she said, "It's not going anywhere as long as the ropes hold. But how the hell can we drag this thing up the hill?" Nothing seemed even remotely feasible.

"What about the Chinook?" Walter asked. "What if it lifted the mammoth off this rock instead of the Snow Dome? Maybe it can pull the pallet free somehow."

"Might work. But somebody has to fasten the hoist cable from the helicopter to the mammoth. None of us knows how." She pulled a handheld transceiver from her pocket. "Grant, we need your help."

A moment later, Grant's voice crackled through the device. "Go ahead. I can see you through the binoculars."

"Call Ben on the Park Service radio. He knows the Chinook helicopter crew is waiting for instructions at the Port Angeles airport. Ask him to call to see if they could lift the mammoth from the side of the mountain."

"Okay. Hold on."

Minutes went by while Kate and her team gazed warily over the edge, their crampons gouged into the ice.

"The longer we stand here, the more nervous I get," Erin said, her face tight. "I can see myself slipping and falling off."

"It's hard to wait," Kate said. "You two sit over here." She motioned to one of the boulders protruding through the ice to the side of the drop-off.

Her legs trembled with fear too, but she didn't let on. "Walter, you doing all right?"

"Oh sure." He smiled weakly. "I retrieve mammoths off mountaintops all the time."

Grant's voice, mixed with static, buzzed through the speaker. "They're willing to give it a try. They suggested lowering one of their crew on a cable to attach the mammoth to their hoist. Is that doable?"

Walter nodded.

Kate looked up the couloir to Grant standing on a rock outcrop in the distance. "Yes, tell them to come."

"There's a catch, though. They need someone else down there to assist the crew member in securing the cable."

"I can do that," Kate blurted out. "Piece of cake." Christ, what was she thinking?

Walter leaned close and whispered in her ear, "Are you sure?"

She nodded and said into the radio, "When will they get here?"

"In thirty minutes. They're ready—just waiting to hear from us."

Not knowing what she'd be up against, Kate started to move. She untied from the climbing rope attaching her to the others and pulled a nylon cord from her backpack. A prominent rock served as an anchor for her line, which she ran from the carabiner on the climbing harness at her waist up over her left shoulder and around her back. She would use her right hand across her body as a brake.

Carefully walking backward down the face, she fed the cord gradually through her hand. Once she got to the ledge, Kate fastened the end of the rope to her climbing harness. "Walter, could you provide a belay in case I slip?"

"Sure, hold on." He bent over the edge. "I'll sit on the ice and brace my feet against one of these boulders," he called down. "Then I'll run your rope behind my back and hold it across my chest like I saw you do."

"You got it." Kate gave Walter a thumbs-up, and soon the line went tight over the ledge above her. "On belay?"

"Belay on," he shouted.

While she waited on the narrow ledge for the helicopter, Kate felt a connection to the beast. The red-brown fur looked particularly rich in the daylight. Fortunately, the air was cool enough to prevent much melting, although she detected a musty smell. The tusks almost gleamed white, they were so perfect. She knew this was her only chance for such an intimate experience. Once the mammoth was placed in the freezer for study, it would never be outside in the sun and open air again.

Maybe from the effort she'd poured into preserving it or the threat of falling from the precarious ledge, Kate didn't know, but she started talking to her mammoth. "It won't be long. You'll be safe. I'll take care of you. We'll get through this together."

She heard the rhythmic thumping of the twin rotor blades of the approaching Chinook before she could see it. Then the helicopter floated into view and hovered—a monster suspended overhead making a deafening sound and spewing exhaust. She wrapped her arms around a column of rock to keep the gale force downdraft from blowing her off the ledge.

A tall man in a flight suit and helmet descended slowly from the helicopter on the end of a metal cable. Upon reaching the ledge, he handed her the straps and fasteners he would need to secure the carcass. Then he moved quickly and gracefully over the rocks and ice, wrapping two thick woven nylon straps around the body and a third around the neck. He motioned for her to hand him the heavy metal ring he used to bind the three straps together above the mammoth's back.

She yelled over the helicopter's roar, "Have you retrieved many frozen mammoths in your career? Sure looks that way."

He smiled through his visor and gave her a thumbs-up. "After they pull me up," he yelled, "they'll lower this cable to you. Before you touch it, let the cable fall to the rocks to ground any dangerous static electricity. See this clip on the end?" He held up what looked like a large metal hook with a safety cover.

She nodded.

"You'll attach it to the ring on the mammoth's back. That's all you have to do. We'll take care of the rest. Any questions?"

Kate shook her head. "Thanks for your help."

"Good luck." He signaled with his hand to the hoist operator in the helicopter to lift him up.

Once the man was inside, the operator lowered the cable again. Kate followed his instructions, but when she tried to attach the clip, she couldn't reach the ring—it was about a foot too high. The man who had attached the ring was over six feet tall.

The helicopter hovered—it was dangerous to wait too long. She jumped up off the ledge to reach the ring and still fell about six inches short.

Looking around frantically for something to climb on, she realized that the ends of the boards used to construct the wooden pallet made a sort of ladder. She held on to the clip attached to the cable in one hand and used her other to climb the edge of the wooden pallet to the mammoth's legs. Sliding on her stomach, she moved across the red-brown fur to the mammoth's back.

She had to stretch both arms to reach the ring. SNAP. The clip held, hooked securely to the ring on the straps surrounding the mammoth.

By now her body was so far over the back of the curved frozen carcass that she started to slide, nose first, off the side and into the two-thousand-foot void. Oh no! She scrambled to grab at the fur with both hands, but her center of gravity carried her steadily forward, slowly at first, and then faster.

"Walter, I'm falling!" she screamed. The slack ran out of the rope attached to her climbing harness, and she stopped, lying head down with her legs stretched over the mammoth's side.

She managed to maneuver sideways over the mammoth's head and drop her legs down to the ledge. Her heart pounded fiercely. She had come so close to giving her life for this beast.

Kate waved her arm to tell the helicopter that everything was ready and sidestepped on the narrow ledge as far away as she could. The cable went tight. The carcass jerked against its ropes. Nothing happened—the wooden pallet didn't budge. As the helicopter continued to hover, the hoist groaned and the cable stretched, but the mammoth remained stuck—the wooden pallet was wedged. If it didn't slide free, the cable could snap. Or, God forbid, the helicopter might crash. Something had to be done—fast.

Walter yelled down to her over the roar, "Cut the ropes."

At first, Kate couldn't believe what she thought she heard. Did he want her to sacrifice the mammoth?

"Cut the ropes," Walter repeated.

Then she realized what he meant—free the mammoth from the stuck pallet. She took out her pocketknife and started sawing at the heavy ropes. As the ropes were cut, one by one, the weight of the carcass began to shift into the nylon straps and move away from the ledge.

Finally, as she cut the last rope, the mammoth swung far from the ledge, suspended by the three straps the man had wrapped around it. Then it swung back toward her like a huge, five-ton pendulum.

She struggled to get out of the way, but the ledge was too small, and it was two thousand feet of air between her and the White Glacier below. The mammoth she was trying to save was about to crush her as its tremendous mass swung directly toward her, closer, faster. At the last second, with no other option, she jumped off the ledge.

The climbing harness sliced into her thighs, and the nylon climbing rope stretched as she dropped below the ledge and bounced like a spider on its web. The huge frozen carcass slammed into the rocks directly above her. Rock and ice debris showered onto her head and shoulders, stinging her scalp. Panicking, she choked on the dust. The helicopter veered up and away with its strange load, heading north out of the mountains.

Kate's knees shook so badly she almost slipped twice climbing back to the ledge. Surely her heart would explode in her chest. Once on the ledge, she looked up and saw Walter's round face and ring of hair bending over the edge of the cliff, and relief flooded through her.

"Kate! You okay?" he shouted.

"Better than okay. The mammoth's on its way to the research lab." She planted her feet and began to climb up the wall she had repelled down while Walter kept her on belay. About ten feet off the ledge, the adrenaline wore off, and her wobbly left foot slipped out of an icy crevice. Again, she dangled by the rope attached to her climbing harness over the two-thousand-foot drop-off.

"Damn it, I'm climbing like a novice." She replanted her feet on the ice wall and climbed up to join the two waiting for her at the bottom of the couloir, both greeting her with high fives.

Walter put his arm around her. "What you just did was the stuff of legend. I'll personally make sure the world's paleontologists sing your praises for years to come."

As the three moved carefully up the icy slope, it began to sink in for Kate. "Wow. What a close call."

When they climbed out of the icy chute of the couloir and onto the rocks, Kate's legs felt like rubber, and she found a place to sit. But she couldn't stop smiling.

Grant walked up and pulled her off the rock into a long embrace. She leaned back, still in his arms. "How's Frank?"

"Shaken up. He's trying to understand everything, and he's pretty confused and weak. He took all the deaths really hard, and feels terrible about damaging the winch and ropes. Lillian said he has a rare side effect of the flu that affects the brain, which explains his bizarre behavior. He was probably in a coma when we left him."

"Poor guy. I want to see him and let him know we saved the mammoth. Forgiving him is a lot easier now the mammoth is safe. I can't wait to tell Annie the good news."

44

Blue Glacier
Olympic National Park

Thursday, July 2

Kate and Grant sat watching the last rays of the setting sun on the outcrop west of the station. After the adrenaline jolts of the last few days, she welcomed the time alone together. The winch operators, the National Geographic film crew, and Lillian and her technicians, along with Walter, Nikolai, and Erin from the Denver Museum, had all flown off the glacier that afternoon in several helicopter trips.

A deep quiet settled over her on their peaceful rock overlook. "I can't believe the mammoth is already safe in a freezer in Seattle. So many times, I was afraid we wouldn't be able to pull it off."

"We almost didn't." Grant tented his knees and hugged them with both arms. "You did a brave thing—but stupid. We could easily have lost you *and* the mammoth."

"I know." She leaned against him. "What do they say—all's well that ends well?"

Another block of ice tumbled down the icefall on the other side of the Snow Dome, the loud roar filling the air.

"What did the sheriff say before they took Frank away in the helicopter?" she asked.

"No charges were filed. He was flown to a hospital in Seattle for observation. They'll keep him there until he recovers from the encephalitis, and then most likely, he'll be released to his family with some outpatient follow-up."

"He's a good guy. When I get back to Seattle, I'll look in on him and Annie. He tried to save the mammoth for us—his intentions were good. But he didn't know what he was doing. Who would, after nearly dying and being abandoned with a brain infection?"

"It's hard to believe he survived—he's unbelievably strong."

She stared at the reflection of the last rays of sunlight off the Pacific. "You know, I never could have gotten through the last few weeks without everyone's support, and I want to pay that back. For starters, I'm letting Walter take the lead on publicity for the mammoth—it's his field after all. I offered to go with him to share our story at conferences. And you and I can visit NASA together if they want to understand the team building I've done. I would be glad to help you fulfill your grant obligation."

"I'd really appreciate that."

"I told my boss, John, that I'd meet with Charlie's and Alice's parents when I get home. It'll be tough, but I owe them that. And you won't believe this. Lillian and I are getting together for lunch in Seattle—that's the least I could do considering all the grief I gave her."

Grant put his arm around her and looked into her eyes. "I've admired your passion and knowledge since I first met you, and I respect your willingness to open up to others—it isn't always easy."

"Thanks. That means a lot." She squeezed his hand. "I've decided to try to reconnect with my dad. I'm going to call him and arrange a visit to the ranch—my first time in years."

"That should help you both."

"I've kept him at a distance. It wasn't all his fault."

"I have a confession myself." Grant picked up a small rock and pitched it at a boulder protruding from the snow a few feet away. "I came here to prove something—that I wouldn't play it safe and run away when others were drowning, literally or figuratively. You've shown me what that looks like, what it feels like, to hold my ground and be there for someone else."

The band of clouds above the horizon transformed from red to orange and yellow. Then the last sliver of sun disappeared below the ocean on the far horizon.

She jumped up. "Did you see that?"

"What?"

"The flash of green. I've wanted to see it for years!"

"What are you talking about?"

"The rainbow spectrum: red, orange, yellow, green, blue, indigo, violet. As many times as I've watched these sunsets, I've never seen past yellow. The theory says we should see green. I saw it for the first time just now."

Grant stood with his arm around Kate's shoulder as they both faced west. "That must be good luck for us."

"For us," she said, raising her right fist.

Grant pulled her into a hug. "I'm going to miss this place, Kate."

"Me too. After we shut things down tomorrow, I'll be going back to city life in Seattle."

"I've decided to resign from my position in Santa Cruz." Grant rested his chin on the top of her head. "And sell my house in the woods too."

"What'll you do then?" she asked. "What are you going to live on?"

"I don't know right now. I just know I'm willing to take the risk. That's a big step for me—terrifying but exciting. What are you going to do about your research?"

Kate turned to face him. "With all the chaos today, I didn't get a chance to tell you—Dr. Rollins called on the satellite phone—the National Science Foundation restored funding for my research because they liked the palynology work I've brought to glacier studies. So, yes, I'll be back."

"That's wonderful news! And what about my—"

"And also Ben radioed that the Park Service removed the Blue Glacier Research Station from its list of structures to be razed. They want to use it to explore how the mammoth could have ended up in a National Park."

"Kate—my question. Can I join you here next summer?"

She studied his face. "Grant, whatever happens—whatever you decide to do—I want you in my life." She brushed her lips lightly against his.

"That means so much to me." Cradling her face in both hands, he gave her a long, heartfelt kiss.

A little breathless, she reached into the inside pocket of her parka and pulled out a piece of paper and handed it to him. "I guess you're going to need this now."

He held it up to catch the last glimmer of daylight. "My map. I'll never forget."

They sat back down on the rocks holding each other, saying little as twilight faded to crisp, clean darkness. She never wanted it to end, although their time together in this majestic place was nearly over—for now.

The moon rose behind them, its luminescent reflection causing the Snow Dome to glow as if lighted from within. The dark, rocky summit of Mount Olympus stood above them like a sentinel. The city lights of Victoria twinkled in the distance. The wind, gentle but cool, soon would force them inside, but for as long as possible, they would relish their last moments, wrapped in each other's arms on top of their world of ice and snow.

Acknowledgments

How can one possibly acknowledge all those who made a contribution in some small or large way to my first novel, which represents my life's primary creative work to this point? My wife, Nancy, encouraged me to take whatever time I needed during the two and a half years to write, rewrite, and learn the tools of fiction and social media required to produce a book in this age. She also proofed the manuscript meticulously, was a sounding board for ideas, and told me almost daily how much she admired my creativity and stamina. I couldn't ask for a better writing partner.

My editor, Laurel Kallenbach, took my initial novella, written unknowingly in nineteenth-century omniscient point of view, and helped me bring it into the twenty-first century with alternating third-person perspectives. She taught me that my characters shouldn't be so nice to each other and that I needed to "chase my protagonists up a tree and throw rocks at them." I never would have guessed.

How fortunate that my publisher, Sandra Jonas, could see the potential in what I had written. Between her many questions and suggestions and her content editor Trish Wilkinson's frequent "show don't tell" reminders, the story was fleshed out into a novel I couldn't have created alone. Trish encouraged me to infuse the story with tension—so much so that I worried the reader would be exhausted. Instead, I discovered it worked brilliantly. Sandra's commitment to the process of patiently shepherding my rough "final draft" into a polished piece took additional rewrites and countless email exchanges over the past year.

I must acknowledge the support I received from friends and family who read the manuscript and gave me feedback along the way: Teri

Eastburn, Susan Eberhard, Kathryn Eilerts, Scott and Jennie Eilerts, Bill Gail, Rudy Malesich, Gary Maykut, Xenofon Moniodis, Israel Nelson, Tom Parrish, Yaga Richter, Jon Riedel, Stan Schroeder, Joe Tanner, Bob and Robyn Turrill, and Daryl Weaver. Stan Schroeder and his son, Matthew, deserve special recognition for accompanying me on a four-day backpacking trip up the Hoh River Trail in the Olympic National Park as part of my research for the story. Together we lived some of what my characters experienced.

Allison Shanks, my stepdaughter, applied her skills as a graphic artist to create the map of Mount Olympus and the Hoh River Trail that appears in the book. She also designed the table-top banner for showcasing the book at conferences and book signings and developed the initial concept of the cover.

Jim and Tricia Fitzpatrick designed and implemented my author website, reflecting the drama of Mount Olympus. The Boulder Writers Alliance provided both guidance and support while I worked to become a writer of fiction.

Our two cats (don't laugh), ET and Daphne, were great companions at five every morning when I could be most creative. They would sleep nearby while I dictated the first draft using the speech-to-text software on my laptop.

I'm convinced I could not have completed this novel without lessons I learned from my mentor, Dr. Frank B. W. Hawkinshire V, while studying for my PhD in applied social psychology at New York University. He taught me that an idea, no matter how brilliant, doesn't exist unless it is written down. I learned from him how important it is to "stand for something," so I wrote *Watermelon Snow* with the conviction that it is worthwhile to take a stand against global warming. He also gave me the discipline to write for hours and across years to complete my dissertation, serving me well as a novelist.

Finally, I must credit my father, William Liggett Sr., who was an English teacher before he became a physician, with teaching me to value books and express myself through writing. Observing my mother, Dora, a consummate artist and teacher, instilled in me the excitement of creativity and the hard work needed to master a craft.

About the Author

Bill Liggett writes fiction that blends behavioral and earth sciences in the new literary genre "cli-fi," or climate fiction. His goal is to paint a hopeful future, based on solutions to global warming.

He holds a BS in geology and an MA in education, both from Stanford University, and a PhD in applied social psychology from New York University. Among the many positions he has held over the years, he taught in high school and college, conducted behavioral science studies for IBM, and consulted with health care and educational organizations.

Wherever he lives, Bill loves being outdoors. Home for him has included the West Coast, East Coast, Alaska, and now Colorado, the state of his childhood. He and his wife, Nancy, live in Boulder, where they enjoy the cultural and academic opportunities of a university community. Between them, they have five children and six grandchildren.

For more information, visit his website: www.williamliggett.com.

72919101R00144

Made in the USA
Columbia, SC
29 June 2017